Thoroughbred Legacy

DARCI'S PRIDE

Jenna Mills

Published by Silhouette Books

America's Publisher of Contemporary Romance

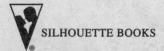

SILHOUETTE BOOKS

ISBN-13: 978-0-373-19934-1
ISBN-10: 0-373-19934-1

DARCI'S PRIDE

Special thanks and acknowledgment are given to Jenna Mills
for her contribution to the Thoroughbred Legacy series.

Visit Silhouette Special Edition and Thoroughbred Legacy
at www.eHarlequin.com.

Printed in U.S.A.

JENNA MILLS

Bestselling author Jenna Mills has been creating stories for as long as she's been able to string words together. A daughter of the South, she grew up immersed in legend and lore, the abiding love of family and, of course, romance. Today, these are the elements that shape her stories.

A member of Romance Writers of America, Dallas Area Romance Authors and North Louisiana Storytellers, Jenna has earned critical acclaim for her stories of deep emotion, steamy romance and page-turning suspense, including the 2007 Gayle Wilson Award of Excellence. *Darci's Pride* is Jenna's seventeenth book for Harlequin/Silhouette.

When not writing, Jenna spends her time with her husband and young daughter in a house full of cats, dogs, plants and books! You can visit Jenna at her Web site, www.jennamills.com.

There are many kinds of love: that between man and woman, parent and child, man and the land, man and animal. *Darci's Pride,* a story that explores each of these facets, is dedicated to Team Barbaro, in particular the dedicated staff at the University of Pennsylvania's New Bolton Center and all the FOBs (Friends of Barbaro) who give so tirelessly of themselves to make sure Barbaro's legacy lives on.

Acknowledgments

A special thank-you to Melissa James for all things Australia, Linda Castillo and Ken Casper for all things equine, and to Stacy Boyd and Marsha Zinberg for inviting me into the exciting world of THOROUGHBRED LEGACY!

Chapter One

He stood beneath the gnarled branches of an old gum tree. The late-summer sun baked the normally lush land of Australia's Upper Hunter Valley, but the heat did not seem to touch him. He stood with uncanny ease despite his size, concealing the intense focus that simmered beneath the surface.

A mere passerby would never know someone wanted him dead.

"Came in the mail, just like the first one."

With a foot perched on the bottom rail of a freshly painted white fence, Tyler Preston looked from the newsprint his trainer had just handed him to the gorgeous Thoroughbred in the pasture. Lightning Chaser grazed quietly, as he always did, but Tyler knew the horse too well to fall for the illusion. He'd helped deliver the colt one damp spring night three years before. He'd been there when the big mare went into distress. He'd gone down on his knees and helped her through her delivery. He'd been the first to see the foal.

The first one to...*know*.

Even then, in the first minutes following birth, Lightning Chaser had been tall, with the kind of presence a gangly newborn rarely possessed. There in the brightly lit barn, he'd lifted his head and shown off his blaze, and Tyler had rocked back on his haunches and...known.

This was *the* horse.

It was a big dream, an even bigger responsibility to heap on one so young, but big dreams and big responsibilities were something Tyler knew well. He'd been given the dream by his father. He'd blown the responsibility all by himself.

It was up to him to restore Lochlain Racing to the respectability he'd trashed through one careless mistake.

And Lightning Chaser was the horse to do it.

The big bay colt stood benignly in the shadow of that lone tree, ears perked, tail swishing rhythmically. In three years they'd come far. As a two-year-old, Lightning had burned up the track, garnering seven wins to only two losses. He'd come on strong at the prestigious Queensland Stakes, pulling away from the pack and engaging the favorite in a thrilling dash for the finish.

More Than All That had crossed first.

Tyler had been disappointed, but had set his sights on the upcoming Outback Classic—until his trainer had walked into his office the following morning. More Than All That had been disqualified. Steroids had been detected in his blood. Lightning Chaser, who'd run a close second, was named the official winner.

The racing community reeled. Allegations of fraud in the sport, quiet since the mysterious death of another racehorse, resurfaced. Everyone had their own opinion about who'd doped Sam Whittleson's horse—and why.

Tyler's name had been on just about every short list.

An ocean away, in America, another branch of the Preston family had been going through an equally nasty scandal.

That's why his cousin Andrew, one of the Kentucky Prestons, had decided to run for presidency of the International Thoroughbred Racing Federation. To restore dignity to the Preston name—and integrity to the sport of kings.

With a twist to his gut, Tyler glanced down at the bold words scrawled atop the picture of Lightning Chaser. "Unmarked envelope?"

Daniel Whittleson nodded. "Just like the one my father received."

The two had known each other since they were boys, when Daniel's father had worked as a trainer at Lochlain. Sam had gone on to travel the world, eventually returning to Australia, where he'd fulfilled his dream of opening his own stables.

Daniel had stayed in America, working for Tyler's uncle until eight months before, when he'd finally come home after a dispute over water rights had landed his father in the hospital.

"How's he holding up?" Tyler asked.

"Still drinking more than I would like." A quietly serious man, Daniel looked off in the distance, where beyond the drought-parched hills, his father's property lay. "I'm not sure he's ever going to get over losing the Queensland."

It had been awkward. Daniel, Sam Whittleson's own son, had returned to Australia to take over the training of Lightning Chaser. The racing community had had a field day with Daniel's so-called desertion of his father. And though his friend seemed impervious to the criticism, Tyler knew it burned.

"No one really believes he drugged his own horse," Tyler said. Sam would have had to have been crazy to do so. Not only was he guaranteed getting caught, but More Than All That had been a favorite. The horse could have won easily without the aid of an illegal substance.

But that was a chance someone hadn't been willing to take.

"I know that," Daniel said, squinting against the glare of the sun. Over three weeks had passed since the last rain, and that had only been a few drops. "And rationally he does, too. But…"

The words trailed off. Both men knew. Much like the impact of the drought on the land, the damage had been done. Sam's name had been smeared. His stables were tainted.

It was a situation Tyler knew well.

"He'll rebound," he predicted. That's what his own father had promised him six years ago. They'd stood just inside Lochlain's newly completed state-of-the-art barn. But instead of colts and fillies shuffling in their stalls, there'd been only the smell of hay and tack, and the sound of silence. In the parking area beyond the paddock, the banker had been sliding from his dust-covered sedan.

The word foreclosure had stuck in Tyler's gut.

One mistake, that's all it had taken. One lapse in judgment. One touch—

Tara.

His mouth flattened. Letting out a rough breath, he focused on Lightning Chaser, standing tall and proud in the hot breeze. But he saw her anyway, as she'd been that very first time, that very first night—the straight, sunshine-blond hair and sparkling blue eyes, the wide, teasing mouth. Smiling, laughing. Lying.

The memory seared.

Shoving it aside, Tyler lowered the brim of his bush hat and turned toward Daniel. "It just takes time."

And distance.

"I talked him into going on safari," Daniel said. "Bought the tickets and took him to Sydney last night. His plane left a couple of hours ago, at ten, I think."

"Well, there you go. That should be—" Tyler stopped, Daniel's words registering. "A couple of hours?" Glancing at the watch his father had given him on his eighteenth birthday, a watch that had been in the Preston family for generations, he swore softly.

He'd completely lost track of time.

"Late?" Daniel asked.

"Andrew's campaign manager." She'd cooked up some big gala fund-raiser at Lochlain for the night after the upcoming Outback Classic. With that date closing in on them, she'd insisted they needed to meet in person to finalize details. Tyler didn't much care about invitations or napkins, but he did care about his cousin. And horse racing. And if the fund-raiser could help Andrew garner Aussie support, then Tyler would do his part. His cousin had been staying at Lochlain since arriving in Australia, using the stud as his base of operations.

The last thing they needed was the Australian candidate, media mogul Jackson "Jacko" Bullock, winning.

"We were supposed to meet at one." It was now one-thirty.

"I'll finish up with Lightning," Daniel offered.

"Thanks, mate," Tyler said, glancing toward Midnight Magic, the sleek black horse Daniel had raced out to the back pasture. Taking the reins, he slipped his foot into the stirrup and swung his leg over the horse's back.

"Wish me luck," he muttered, then with a gentle nudge to the horse's sides, put the animal into a lope toward the main complex.

A few white clouds drifted across the western horizon, but Tyler knew they would not bring rain. His pop had taught him that, how to tell which clouds brought rain and which only teased, just as David Preston had taught his son how to run a stud farm. The son of an Irish horseman, David had tried to pass on all that his own father had taught him, but Tyler had needed little teaching. He'd been riding before he'd started running.

It was in the blood, David had decided. His eldest son had received the Preston horse gene. His younger, Shane, had not.

With the blistering sun beating down on him, Tyler urged Midnight Magic toward one of the three barns on the far side of the paddock. A fourth was under construction. The mares and new foals had claim to the largest structure. His two- and three-year-olds occupied the middle building. The third, original structure, was used primarily for Lochlain's boarding business.

The buzz of activity intensified as he approached. Most of the training was done for the day, had taken place during the cooler hours before sunrise. But there was still work to be done, and like clockwork, young Heidi Hastings stood in the shade of several gum trees, feeding an apple to her little filly, Anthem. Her father didn't understand her fixation with the animal she'd sweet-talked him into buying, but Tyler suspected Heidi's frequent presence at Lochlain had as much to do with a certain groom hovering nearby as it did her interest in horses.

"Afternoon," he called as his three border collies bounded

up to greet him. Carbine and Windbag were pushing ten, but they still thought they were as young as the pup, Tulloch.

Heidi glanced up with a smile so bloody sweet, Tyler winced. Her father was a good man, but Tyler didn't know how any man could raise a kid alone, much less a young girl racing toward womanhood.

"I think something's wrong," she said, with worry both in her eyes and her voice. "She doesn't want her apple."

Tyler's chest tightened. Bloody hell—after the girl's mother abandoned them, Dylan Hastings had his hands more than full. "Just the heat," Tyler said. The animals didn't like it any more than the humans did. They needed rain—badly. But with rain would come lightning, and with the land as parched as a sponge in dry rot, lightning could mean disaster.

Just the week before, some bloke had tossed a cigarette out the car window, and before the sun had set, more than a hundred acres of bush had been scorched. Two national parks had been lost.

"Try this," he added, pulling a couple of peppermints from his back pocket. He tossed them to her and winked. "Anthem just needs a treat is all."

Heidi's smile turned lopsided. "Thanks, I should have thought of that myself."

"You will," he promised in the best fatherly voice he could find. "Just give it—"

A blur of motion from the office complex snagged his attention. He squinted against the glare, bringing his office manager, Peggy, into view. She hurried toward him—something she rarely did. In her midfifties, she was an air-conditioning kind of woman.

"—time," he finished, pulling Midnight Magic to a stop. He swung his leg over the horse and handed the reins to one

of the young grooms—Zach, Heidi's so-called "friend."
"Cool him off," he instructed, already striding toward Peggy.

"Mr. Preston," she called as she always did, refusing to
call him Tyler, as he'd asked her to a million or so times.
She was a stickler for formality, a master at organization,
and somehow kept the administrative side of the business
running smoothly. "Your one o'clock is here."

Tyler glanced toward the parking area, where a shiny
white convertible sat in the closest space. Looked as though
he'd have to talk napkins after all.

"On my way," he said, veering toward the office building's shaded entrance. The first stones had been laid six
years before, but the facility had only been completed the
previous winter.

"But aren't you—"

With Windbag trotting at his heels, Tyler stopped and
pivoted, felt his mouth curve at the look of horror on
Peggy's face. She was old enough to be his mother—
barely—but she almost never questioned him. And never,
ever corrected him.

"Yes?" he prodded, trying not to laugh.

She bit down on her lip. "Nothing. I just thought…
well, she's a pretty thing. I thought maybe you'd want to
clean up first."

Now he did laugh. Loudly. *A pretty thing.* It figured. His
mother, his new sister-in-law, his office manager…even
Daniel's American wife. It seemed the women of Lochlain
and the surrounding area had a bloody intense case of
matchmaking fever.

"Freshen up?" Without cracking a smile, he glanced
down at the damp white cotton pressed against his skin, his
dusty jeans and mud-caked boots, then shot the dog a grin.
"What? She thinks I might run the party planner off?"

Peggy had the good grace to flush. "Of course not... I just thought..."

"Right-oh," he said, adjusting the bush hat that had seen rain and heat and far better days. He knew what Peggy thought...what they all thought. Thirty-four years old was well and past time for the Preston heir to settle down.

"No worries," he deadpanned with a quick rub of the old dog's head. "I'm sure Miss—" He slipped off his sunglasses, but couldn't come up with Andrew's campaign manager's name. "I'm late enough as it is. I'm sure she'd rather get this over with than wait for me to shower."

Peggy sighed. "You make it sound like torture."

She knew him well. He wasn't a party kind of guy. He didn't do galas and benefits. He didn't do tuxedos or cologne. He only knew a Shiraz from a Chardonnay because his mother, daughter of a local vintner, had drilled it into her boys.

With his best trust-me smile, Tyler sent the dog off to play and strode toward the office.

Air-conditioning blasted him the second he walked inside. The scent of vanilla and sandalwood came next, courtesy of the cluster of candles Peggy kept on her desk. Just because she worked at a stable didn't mean she had to smell hay and manure all day, she insisted.

It was a modest building by comparison to the nearby Fairchild Acres, but with four offices, a file room, a video room and adjacent meeting room, plus a small lunchroom, the facility suited him. He'd left the decor to Peggy, who'd chosen the same dark woods and rustic furniture found in the main house a couple of hundred meters away.

With the thud of his boots against the hardwood floor drowning out the soft, new age music Peggy said created ambience, Tyler covered the distance to his office and pushed through the partially open door. He had less than twenty minutes to give her. Andrew had departed Sydney a little before noon. He'd return to the stud soon. They had business to discuss. Andrew needed to know about the recent threats. Any talk of the party—

She had her back to him, but the gruff words Tyler had been about to offer stuck in his throat anyway. She stood there so unnaturally still, her posture boarding-school perfect, pale blond hair fastened behind her head in some sleek, elegant twist. A tidy cream suit hugged her willowy frame much too tightly considering the heat that baked the valley. She had to be burning...

The scent slammed into him on a soft wave of air-conditioning, the unmistakable whisper of baby powder and roses—and everything inside of Tyler tightened.

Familiarity came hard and fast, followed by a sharp twist of denial. There was nothing unique about baby powder and roses. He knew that. It was a common scent, pleasant even. Soft.

There'd been nothing soft about her.

Tara Moore had been like an explosion of danger and mystery and temptation, as far removed from the cool sip of Chardonnay standing across from him as cyclone season was from drought. But he stood there anyway, unmoving, barely breathing...and watched her.

As he'd done so many other times, in so many other places, when he'd damn near choked on something as benign as roses. And powder.

Andrew's campaign manager had a picture in her hand. It was one of the early ones, its black-and-white image faded by time and sun. He knew that from where she stood, toward the left of the crowd of photographs and yellowed newspaper articles, blue ribbons and trophies, certificates. Those photos were from Lochlain's adolescence, when his father had worked sunup to long after sundown to carve out a place for himself in Australia. To prove that he was every bit as worthy as the older brother he'd left behind in America.

Those pictures were from when Tyler and his brother, Shane, had been adolescents, as well. When Tyler had raced out of bed before first light, while Shane had often lingered at the house.

Those pictures—the one she held in her fine-boned hand—were of the time when a big beautiful foal had first come to Lochlain, and Tyler had named him Lightning's Match, telling his father that only lightning could beat the big bay colt with the proud stance and white blaze.

It had been the beginning of a legacy, a legacy Tyler had worked to build and fortify for more than twenty-five years.

A legacy whose near destruction Tyler thought of every time he smelled baby powder and roses.

Slowly Andrew's campaign manager turned, and something inside Tyler just…stopped.

Chapter Two

Those eyes. Goddamn, he knew those eyes, wide and blue and so full of temptation they should have been illegal. But there was no temptation in them now, only a cool, distant refinement that sliced like a chilled knife.

"Tyler," she said, and her voice was different, too, no longer laughing and daring, infectious, but strong and graceful, as bloody elegant as the rest of her. "It's been a long time."

What have they done to you? That was the first question that fired through him. *What had her father done to her? What had England done? Oxford?*

Where the hell was...Tara?

But just as quickly those questions fractured into the only truth that mattered.

The seventeen-year-old with the ultrastraight, ultra-blond hair and low-rise jeans, with the trio of hoop earrings and the galloping filly tattooed at the base of her back…no longer existed.

Bloody hell, she'd never existed at all.

She'd simply been an illusion.

A lie.

Through the quiet, Peggy's Celtic music gained tempo, a flute and a drum merging into a staccato rhythm. He'd been about to swipe off his hat. He'd been about to stroll into the room as big as Australia, covered in dust and full of excuses, and charm his way out of discussing the merits of hors d'oeuvres until Andrew arrived.

But now he lounged in the doorway, and watched.

And something entirely different streamed through him.

"Tara." That was the name she'd given him, the name he'd whispered as she'd twisted beneath him and he'd twined his fingers with hers as his thoughts had drifted to the future.

It was a damn odd time to smile, but his lips curved anyway, slowly, with deceptive languor. "Oops," he said with all the remorse of a nine-year-old caught with his hand in his grandma's cookie jar. "My bad."

Her eyes—impossibly, ridiculously blue—darkened. She stepped toward him, photo still in hand, but before she could so much as breathe, he rolled right on.

"It's Darci, isn't it, sunshine?" The endearment, first drawled that long-ago night when she'd sauntered up to him with mischief gleaming in her eyes, sliced deep. "Darci Parnell." Daughter of Weston Parnell, currently serving as Australia's ambassador to Britain. At the time, six years before, he'd been serving his second term as president of the International Thoroughbred Racing Federation—the role Tyler's cousin Andrew now sought to claim.

Back then, when Darci had claimed to be twenty-three-year-old Tara Moore, Weston Parnell had been one of the most influential men in the Australian racing community.

Hell, in the entire country.

Darci had been seventeen. Seven-bloody-hell-teen.

Tyler had been twenty-eight.

Preston Heir Robs The Cradle

He still had that newspaper, not framed and displayed like the ones chronicling Lightning's Match and the growth of Lochlain, but tucked inside the bottom left drawer of his desk next to a foreclosure notice, as a reminder of just how steep a price carelessness could demand.

"I know this must come as a surprise," she said in that thick, cultured voice, the one that curled through him, even now. "But I thought it best—"

"You thought it best." He pushed from the wall and strolled closer, enjoying the way she tried to back up, but had nowhere to go. Except into the Preston-fortified bookcase. "You have a habit of that now, don't you, sunshine?"

Color touched her cheeks, not enough to be called a blush, but a flush, much like the night he'd looked down at her through the flickering light of a candle, and seen a soft glow to her cheeks.

And her chest.

Now her chin came up. "I knew you wouldn't be happy—"

"But why let something insignificant like that stop you, right?"

"I believe in Andrew," she said, and for the first time, fire flared in her eyes, not the recklessness of before, but something harder and deeper, wounded almost.

Tyler just barely bit back the growl that formed in his throat.

There was nothing wounded about Darci Parnell.

"He wants to make a difference," she said. "He's the only one who can. If Jacko gets elected—"

"Jacko is your father's friend," Tyler reminded her, but the obvious did not need to be pointed out. They both knew of the relationship between Weston and Jackson Bullock. With several newspapers and television stations fortifying his portfolio, Jackson had been more than happy to help his mate squash the bug who'd dared to put his hands on Weston's precious little girl.

The memory—the truth of it all—flashed in Darci's eyes. "And he's done enough, wouldn't you say?" Her voice was quieter now, almost sad. "It's time for fresh blood and new ideas, and that's what Andrew represents. But he's got an uphill battle in Jacko's backyard. That's why this party at Lochlain is so important. That's why I didn't use my name in our correspondence—"

Why she hadn't called, hadn't let him hear her voice. Even with the change, even with all that elegance and breeding, he would have known.

Tyler didn't need a mirror to know that the truth of it all burned in the dark green of his eyes. "Some things never change, do they, *sunshine?* You still color the truth to fit all nice and tidy into your pretty little world."

She winced. "Think what you will of me," she said, and her voice was stronger now. "But I'm standing here, aren't I?"

Yes, she was. She was standing in a sliver of sunlight, right in front of the family bookcase as if she had every right to be there. He took the last three steps that separated them and did what he'd been telling himself not to do. He lifted a hand toward the side of her face, and touched.

He wasn't sure what he expected…wanted. For her to turn away, twist away. Lift a hand to his wrist and yank it from her face. Tell him to go to hell.

For her to step into him, lift her own hand to his face, push up toward him, tell him that she was sorry…

She lifted her eyes to his, but made no move to step away, no move to break contact. The new age music had faded to a low, soft chant, leaving only the sound of their breaths and the burn of the heat.

"You've done well," she said quietly, and he felt himself stiffen as if she'd used her hands on him, rather than just her voice. "That's all I ever wanted for you."

The words fell into silence for a long, slow heartbeat until the soft music shifted to a new song, this one with a shrill feminine wail.

He jerked back, broke every sliver of contact, but bloody hell, even as he let indifference fall around him, he couldn't help but wonder if any of Tara still existed beneath that trim-fitting suit, where he'd once run his mouth down the curve of her back to the little filly—

"Peggy will get what you need," he said roughly, as a mobile phone started to ring. Not his. He hated the things, rarely carried one, certainly not one that played Irish rock music as a ring tone. He turned, refusing to look at her one second longer. To let himself wonder.

He strode toward the partially open door as the phone rang again, and again, the old braided rug muting the sound of his boots. It had been one of his father's first purchases after moving to Australia. He'd hung on to it all this time, a reminder of what it was like to start with nothing. True, he'd had his name and a sizable trust fund, but back then David Preston had not had the one thing that had mattered to him.

"*Ty.*"

The quiet voice slipped across the office and the years. Time moved forward. Tyler knew that. To get where he was going, a man had to keep his eye on the destination.

But he also knew the value of looking back. Of remembering—of never letting himself forget where he'd been.

It was the only way to make sure he never went there again.

Slowly he stopped, and slowly he turned. And this time he was prepared. He was prepared for the sight of her standing there, the sight of Darci Parnell in her chic little suit, holding the picture of him in her hands, the picture he'd caught her looking at when he'd first walked into his office, of him sitting atop Lightning's Match, when the gum trees his father had planted had been too young to give off shade. He'd been wearing a bush hat even back then, and against the glare of the summer sun, he'd squinted at the camera.

"I'm sorry about the mess with Sam," she said, looking up from the photo to the man. She hadn't answered her phone. "I know you didn't do anything wrong."

But someone didn't. Someone thought he'd drugged Sam Whittleson's horse. And someone wanted to make him pay.

"Lightning Chaser is an amazing horse," she added. "I'm looking forward to the Classic."

One side of his mouth lifted. With More Than All That sidelined, the field was wide open, and rumors were running rampant that a filly who rarely ran with the boys might give the race a try. A filly owned by none other than the former owner of Warrego Downs...Weston Parnell.

A filly named Darci's Pride.

Somehow, Tyler thought it fit.

"Well then," he said, "that makes two of us, sunshine."

Her smile was brief, fleeting, politely formal.

"I'm looking forward to seeing what Darci's Pride is made of," he added with a wicked surge of adrenaline. "See if she's all that she's made out to be."

Darci's chin came up. "She is."

He shouldn't have winked. Tyler knew that. But damn it all to hell, he did.

Habit, he told himself. It was just a bloody habit. "I prefer to be my own judge."

Her smile widened, reminding him for one cruel moment of that girl he'd seen—

He broke the thought, the memory. "I'll send Peggy in," he said, and then he was gone, didn't trust himself to linger, to look, for one second longer. It was well and fine to glance back…but only a glance.

She watched him go. She stood there in his large, Spartan office, not trusting herself to move, barely trusting herself to breathe, and watched Tyler Preston walk out the door.

Again.

She should have been prepared.

The last time, she'd been naked, clutching only a sheet. But somehow, through the years and the miles, the distance she'd injected between them, she'd forgotten. She'd forgotten what it was like to be in the same room as Tyler Preston, to feel the gleam in those dark green eyes, to see how his mouth could curve into those naughty, wicked smiles, smiles that had the simultaneous power to seduce and destroy. She'd forgotten how his voice, that low, irreverent Aussie drawl, could swim through her and touch places she hadn't been touched in six long years.

She'd forgotten, because she'd had to.

She'd forgotten, because remembering would have made walking away, moving forward, impossible.

And if there was one thing Darci was determined to do, it was move forward. There'd been no future for her in Australia all those years ago, a seventeen-year-old whose face had been splashed on the cover of every tabloid. Everywhere she'd gone, people had looked at her. They'd stared—and they'd known. She was the girl who'd seduced the man, the jailbait who'd gone to bed with the cowboy.

The harlot who'd smeared the reputation of one of Australia's favorite sons.

The shame had followed her everywhere, until finally she'd stepped onto the big jet that hot March afternoon, and never looked back. England, Oxford, had been a world away, and with the miles and the years, she'd moved forward.

But then she'd run into Andrew Preston at a party in London, and all those hard broken edges she'd pushed deep had shoved their way forward, and she'd known. Finally, after six years, she'd realized how to fix things. How to make things better, to give Tyler back all that she'd taken from him.

That's what she wanted. To give Tyler back the respectability her recklessness had cost him, to prove to him and her father and everyone who still saw her as frivolous that she was no longer that reckless, irresponsible child. That she was competent, could be trusted. That she was no longer that motherless girl spinning so desperately, horribly out of control. Then she would be free of the past. Then she would walk away, walk forward. Finally, at last, get on with her life.

She'd planned and she'd analyzed, just as she'd learned to do at Oxford. She'd struck up a conversation with

Andrew and the two had quickly realized how much they had in common. It had been easy between them. He hadn't recognized her name, hadn't recognized her as the girl who'd almost destroyed his cousin.

The invitation to join his campaign had been natural, easy. He needed help in Australia. She was Australian. Her father had served two terms as president of the ITRF. Despite her six-year exile, she knew people. She had friends, influence. She could help Andrew as no one else could. She could help him gain Australian support, despite the popularity of Jacko Bullock.

The opportunity had been all but gift wrapped, the kind of chance she'd been craving since earning her degree in commerce and political science.

She'd wanted to say yes, absolutely, to shout it from the rooftop of her London flat. But she'd realized she couldn't, not until she'd told Andrew the truth about her and his cousin. She'd learned the consequences of lies, even seemingly harmless little white ones. So she'd talked to Andrew and held her breath, and after a long, unsteady heartbeat, he'd smiled warmly and held out his hand, told her the past was the past.

But then Tyler strode into his office, tall and dusty, damp from his land, in need of a shave and with that battered hat pulled down low on his head, and something inside her, all that determination and resolve maybe, the nice little speech she'd rehearsed, had simply shattered.

The years had been kind to him. Amazing, actually. He was still lanky, but no longer in the way of the brash cowboy half the country had been in love with. He was a man now, with all the confidence and awareness that came with the years. Even the gleam in his eyes was different, still bloody irreverent, but more focused now.

Dangerous.

And in the moment she'd first seen him standing there, she'd realized how wrong she'd been. How badly she'd misjudged the situation. All that she'd forgotten, all she'd refused to remember, had surged back, tightening around her like a shiny new vise.

One glance at the picture in her hands, of Tyler so long ago, and the ache in her chest deepened. He'd been young then, innocent in the way only a child could be. But even then, when he could have been no more than eight or nine, the grit had been in his eyes, the dreams and the determination to make them come true. And the hat…

She smiled at the sight of it sitting crookedly on his head, much like a similar hat he'd worn when she'd first seen him all those years ago. She'd been bored, flipping channels on her television, when she'd landed on a local access cable station, and seen him. She hadn't known the horseman's name, had only seen the naughty gleam in his eyes, heard the irreverent drawl, and from that moment forward, she'd been hooked. She'd made it her mission—

Her mission. It always had a way of getting her in trouble.

She set the picture back on the shelf and fished around in the leather satchel that doubled as a briefcase, locating her mobile phone. She pushed the button to see the missed call, braced herself even before her father's name appeared.

He'd been trying to reach her for several days.

Sighing, she jabbed a few buttons and brought the phone to her ear: "Sweetheart, I do wish you would answer your phone. I have decided to fly into Sydney a few days in advance of the Summit."

Darci closed her eyes and let out a slow breath. It was one thing to avoid her father with an ocean between them, something entirely different when he was only two hours south.

"We can have lunch," he said in his booming formal voice, the one he always used. The only one, Darci had learned, he knew how to use, even when she'd been a young girl who'd needed something so...different. "I will be at the Observatory, as usual. Barbara will set something up."

She wanted to resent him for that, and maybe once, she had. Most fathers didn't need an assistant to arrange time with their children.

But Weston Parnell was hardly most fathers, and he never had been, even before, when her mother had been there to soften him.

"I need you to think about what we discussed last week," he said, as he had in every message he'd left her over the past four days, since she'd boarded the plane at Heathrow. He'd actually insisted on driving her there, but in the end, she realized he'd only driven her there to try and talk her out of leaving. "Now is *not* the time to get involved with the Prestons."

They were an upstanding family, but he made them sound like pariahs, something dangerous to be viewed with mild curiosity, but only from a safe distance.

"Not even Andrew. I am hearing things—"

She stiffened. That was new.

"I know you think you have something to prove, Darci-Anne, but aligning yourself with that family at this point in time is not the way."

The chill down her spine was immediate. It almost sounded as though her father was warning her.

Through the window, she saw Tyler squatting next to two black-and-white dogs in the shade of one of the old gum trees, his attention on a young girl with a high pony-tail. They were laughing.

"Please be careful," her father concluded. "Please think about all that I have advised you."

His words fell silent then, leaving only the haunting thrum of the music piped through the office.

"Miss Parnell?"

Hiding her unease, Darci turned toward the tidy woman with the surprisingly long gray braid standing in the doorway.

"If you'll follow me," the woman who'd introduced herself as Peggy said. "Mr. Preston requested that we use the conference room."

The quick blade of disappointment shouldn't have surprised her—she didn't belong in Tyler Preston's office any more than she belonged in his life.

"I take it you've increased security?"

Staring out the window, Tyler threw back the last of his Scotch. Night had long since fallen. Deep in the shire, over thirty kilometers from Pepper Flats, the nearest town, darkness swallowed the land. But he could still see her, damn it. Still see Darci walking with his cousin to her shiny little sports car. Andrew had pressed a hand against the small of her back. He'd opened the door for her. Before she'd disappeared inside, she'd turned toward him and slipped off her sunglasses, beamed a smile up at him. He'd smiled back at her, warmly.

Intimately.

"Around the clock," he said, turning from the memory and toward the man. Darci had gone, but Andrew had stayed. "Called a private security firm this afternoon. They'll have someone here in the morning." Maybe it was an extreme step, but Tyler wasn't taking chances. "Until then, the grooms are taking turns staying awake, just in case."

Leaning forward in one of two leather wing chairs,

Andrew frowned. The two had grown up a world apart, but with the same height and short dark hair, they could easily pass as brothers.

The Irish blood of their paternal grandfather ran strong like that.

"If I didn't know better, I'd think someone was targeting the family," he said.

Tyler pushed from the window and strode toward the small table where the whiskey bottle sat. He rarely had more than one glass, but tonight he was pressing for his third. "Not the family," he said, offering the bottle to his cousin.

Andrew tossed back the rest of his glass and extended it toward Tyler.

"It's bigger than that," Tyler said, pouring. "Corruption is everywhere, and the Internet is only making it easier. The syndicate sees money to be made."

And they didn't give a damn who fell in the process.

Andrew's gaze turned speculative. "Darci thinks…"

His cousin kept talking, but his words barely registered. *Darci says. Darci thinks. Darci believes.* It had been that way all evening. No matter where the conversation turned, it always twisted back to Darci Parnell.

And even a deaf man could have heard the admiration in Andrew's voice.

"I'm so damned lucky to have her," he said, and Tyler refused to let his fingers tighten against the glass. "She's really giving me her all."

Tyler bit back the hard sound that wanted to break from his throat. "She's a go-getter," he drawled. "Always known how to get exactly what she wants."

Andrew stiffened, swore softly. "Christ, will you listen to me? I'm sorry, man. I wasn't thinking. She told me about you two." He stood, spread out his hands. "If having her around is a problem—"

"No problem at all," Tyler assured. "You won't find anyone who can do for you what she can."

Somehow he didn't choke on the words, and the image they immediately evoked, of Darci smiling as she pushed up on her toes and curved her arms around Tyler's neck…

Andrew didn't look convinced. "I'm not here to—"

Tyler lifted his hand. "It's all good, mate. Darci is good, the fund-raiser is good…your campaign is good."

The blue in Andrew's eyes darkened, but he said nothing. They looked like brothers, but they weren't. They were cousins. An ocean had separated them most of their lives. They knew how to talk horses and campaigns, but that's where it stopped.

Hell, even Shane didn't bring up Darci Parnell.

But long after Tyler had gone upstairs, long after the big stone house had gone quiet, the scent of rose and powder overrode that of leather and sandalwood.

He should have slept. Sunrise would come whether he wanted it to or not, and with it a full day of training and finalizing security for LC. But sleep eluded him. He tried reading. He tried some of Peggy's new age music. He tried another drink.

But the restlessness kept right on surging.

Shortly after one o'clock he turned out the lamp and resigned himself to counting wallabies.

He'd reached fifteen before the bullhorn broke the silence.

He was on his feet before the red glow coming from his window registered. For one sickening second everything slowed, blurred—the shouting, the glow that turned into flames, the acrid intrusion of smoke.

The frantic scream of horses.

But just as quickly adrenaline punched through the haze and he was yanking on his jeans and his boots, grabbing a shirt as he lunged for the door.

Chapter Three

This was when he woke.

This was when he always, always pulled himself awake.

When he ran toward the fire. When the orgy of flames streaked against the night sky and the smoke poured from the windows, when the alarm kept droning against the normally quiet night, when the horses cried. That's when he made the nightmare end, when any horseman would sit up drenched in sweat, heart slamming and breathing hard, shoving aside the residue of the nightmare. *Before.* Before they ran into the barn. Before they smelled the stench of burning—

Tyler didn't wake up. Because he wasn't asleep. And the strobe light pulsing against the night sky from the barn complex was not a drill.

"Jesus, God," Andrew shouted from two steps behind, but Tyler kept right on running. They'd prepared for this, trained for this.

But it was instinct that took over, instinct that drove him straight for the flames shooting from Barn B—and the fifty-eight two- and three-year-olds trapped inside.

His staff was already there, grooms and trainers and exercise riders fighting the fire and wrestling the terrified horses out one at a time. If one horse spooked—

"The far pasture!" Tyler barked as he passed head groom Charlie Moore. "Make sure someone stays with them!"

Grim-eyed, Charlie nodded, and ran.

Both men knew what would happen if the horses were not contained. They would try to return to the barn, their home. Where they felt safe.

It had happened before.

"Where's Daniel?" he shouted above the pulse of the bullhorn.

"Inside!" Mac, another groom, answered. "He called 000, then went in!"

Tyler didn't hesitate. The bush fire brigade was on the way, but there was no time to wait. Sucking in a sharp breath, he grabbed a flame-retardant blanket and ran into the darkness, veering left while Andrew went right. Flames greedily consumed the center section, where they kept the tack.

Trying not to inhale, he ran down the corridor until he found an occupied stall. Halters and lead ropes hung outside each, illuminated by glow-in-the-dark tape. Coughing, he lunged in and reached for the horse.

"Hey there, mate. No worries now," he rasped, pretending everything was fine, that there was nothing to worry about. "How about a little nighttime walk?"

Whinnying, the colt shuffled deeper into the illusion of safety offered by his stall.

From the ceiling, flames curled downward. "Easy

now," Tyler choked out, and this time he used more force, draping the horse in the blanket and urging him from the stall.

The burning in his lungs demanded that he run, but Tyler kept his movements contained, measured. If the horse sensed his alarm—

On a fresh burst of adrenaline, he staggered into the night, tried to breathe. But it was smoke that he dragged into his lungs.

"I got him," one of the young trainers said, falling into the assembly line evacuation plan they'd designed, but never thought to use. Only Tyler and Daniel and a few others were designated to be in the barn. That would keep the process as orderly as possible. Everyone had a place, a role. Rescue horses. Secure them. Fight the fire. If someone turned up missing—

Simultaneously Andrew and Daniel staggered from the cloud of smoke, each wrestling an antsy horse.

"Ty!" came an urgent voice, and then his brother, Shane, was there, running toward him. "I came as fast as I—"

"The pasture!" Tyler called. "Make sure none of the horses—"

A loud groan killed his words, followed by a long, tearing crack, then a crash somewhere inside the barn…and the panicked scream of a horse.

"No!" Charlie roared, but before Tyler found the groom, a thrashing Appaloosa broke from the direction of the pasture toward the barn. Charlie bolted after him. "Someone get him!"

Tyler started toward the horse, but Shane took off first, grabbing the horse's lead as he reared up against the flames.

"Got him!" Shane cried, fighting to bring the panicked animal under control.

Tyler pivoted back to the barn where another trainer dragged two more horses into the marginally clearer air.

In the distance, the blare of the fire engines merged with the bullhorn. From the main road, the lights of several cars and trucks could be seen racing toward the ranch.

They'd never make it in time.

Running back inside, Tyler again veered left. That was his corridor of responsibility. Daniel had the right. When they ran their drills, he and Daniel blindfolded themselves to simulate the smoke and the darkness. But the absurdity of that ground through Tyler. There was no simulating the heat scorching through his clothes, or the acrid smoke choking off his breath. His body fought to breathe, but he pushed himself forward, toward the back of the barn where Lightning Chaser—

The fire roared, a living creature consuming the barn at a vicious pace. Coughing, Tyler dragged his damp shirt over his mouth and struggled to breathe…run.

But with another groan, the section of barn in front of him collapsed.

Tyler twisted into the side of a stall and out of the path of a burning beam.

"H-help!"

The cry barely registered over the hunger of the fire.

"S-some…one he-elp!"

Smoke stole visibility. Eyes burning, Tyler staggered into the stall and used his hands to find the side. There he could climb. On pure determination he made his way into the next stall and jumped to the hay below.

Hay. As a precaution, they stored it in another building, but there was enough in each barn to feed a fire into an all-out inferno.

"H-elp!"

The voice was weaker now, but Tyler fought his way toward the far side of the corridor. "Who's th-there?" he choked.

The sound that greeted him was not human, but equine. A big black shadow moved against the glow of the fire, gyrating frantically. "Easy." Tyler coughed, reaching for the lead. "Easy now, boy."

The horse reared away.

"Thank God," rasped the voice he'd heard before, and through the suffocating darkness a hand closed weakly around Tyler's ankle.

"Christ almighty," he swore, dropping to his feet where he found the man. "What the hell—"

"B-broke away," Reynard, one of Lochlain's most recent hires, choked out. "Tried to get back to his stall."

And knocked his rescuer down in the process. Reynard was lucky he hadn't been trampled to death. "Come on," Tyler said, easing the older man to his feet. "We gotta get you—"

"Preston!" With the new voice came the hard rush of water and Tyler knew the brigade had arrived. The flames devouring the beam that had blocked the corridor hissed against water as three uniformed firefighters surged toward them.

"Here!" Tyler shouted, handing off Reynard. Pivoting, he ran for the spooked Thoroughbred, finding a saddle blanket to cover the animal's eyes.

"Got him," called one of the men, reaching for the lead. Tyler released the horse, turned back to the far end of the barn.

"Preston! You gotta get out of here!" the firefighter called. "The whole place is about to come down!"

But Tyler was already lunging toward Lightning Chaser's stall. He had to be sure. He had to check.

Staggering, he veered into the stall and, eyes burning, saw

through the sickening red glow. The horse that had grazed so quietly just that afternoon, the champion Thoroughbred who'd run a breathtaking last leg of the Queensland Stakes. He fought against the back corner of the stall he equated with safety, literally trying to climb the wall.

The shadowy sight hit Tyler like a punch to the gut.

"Easy, mate," he tried to drawl, speaking to the animal as a parent would speak to a child. But his voice was a choked rasp. Fumbling for a blanket, he grabbed the halter and lead and moved forward. "Howzabouta l-little midnight—" His throat burned. His lungs screamed.

His vision blurred.

He'd been in too long. He knew that. He'd done the research, consulted with the fire brigade. They'd run the drills. He knew how long he had, how long he could be inside before the smoke overcame him and he became useless.

But he pushed forward anyway. From his first days of training, Lightning Chaser had given Tyler his all. Just like his grandsire had, all those years ago. A Thoroughbred down to his hooves, the horse never said no. He never protested. He trained and he performed.

And now he was in trouble.

Tyler could no more abandon him than he could have left his father or brother.

Staggering, he reached for his horse even as one of the firefighters reached for him. Then something was thrust against his face and he was choking again, harder, not from the smoke but the rush of oxygen. He gulped greedily, taking what he needed to ease Lightning Chaser from his stall.

The animal's guttural cry sickened him. He put his hands to the colt's back and tried to reassure him, get him to quiet. Quickly he affixed the lead then ripped off his overshirt and pulled it over the animal's eyes. Then, in tandem with the firefighter, they led Lightning from his stall and down the corridor.

Through the darkness Daniel appeared. And Andrew. His trainer took the horse. His cousin took him. Coughing, they burst from the building and into the night.

It was all Tyler could do not to go to his knees.

But this was his barn, his stable. These were his men. And they looked to him for leadership. Direction.

Assurance.

He could not go to his knees in front of them.

Hands then, lots of them. Reaching for Tyler. Pulling him farther from the inferno. Shouts.

An oxygen mixture pressed to his face.

He sucked it in as greedily as before, trying to orient himself. Around him, everything blurred, slowed. The strobe light still flashed in obscene synchronicity with the lights on the fire engines. The bullhorn still pulsed rhythmically. He could see his men, all of them doing what they'd been trained to do. And Christ, he could see the other barn then, Barn A, the original structure—the one used for boarding.

Up in flames.

All those horses…some of them weren't young, weren't in the same top-notch condition as the Thoroughbreds. Some of them were older, slower.

One was blind.

Anthem…

"Here," someone said, and he blinked to see a young man with soot-smeared cheeks thrust a glass of water into his hands. A towel then, damp, cool, against his face. He blinked and tried to bring the kid into focus, could make out little more than a scrawny frame and an old, torn bush hat.

"Thanks," he said, or tried to say, but wasn't sure the words made it past the rawness of his throat.

"D-Daniel—" But before he could locate his trainer, Peggy was there, with her long gray hair loose around her face, wearing what Tyler would swear was only a nightgown. She lifted her hands as if to inspect him.

"Don't you ever do that again!" she scolded, and then she started to cry. Peggy. Stalwart, unflappable Peggy, started to cry. "Going into that inferno like that!"

"Easy now," he choked, but every time he opened his mouth, air rushed the back of his throat, and he coughed abrasively.

"Don't talk," she said as one of the paramedics—Pete Rutherford, he thought—kneeled in front of him and started to check him over.

"I have everything under control," she announced, tears over, and magically, with the same efficiency she did everything, she produced the laminated checklist they'd designed for emergencies. "I've called your parents," she said as old Windbag materialized at his feet, panting frantically. "And Russ." She glanced toward the shadows milling nervously in the far pasture. "He's already here."

Russ Chaplain was their head veterinarian.

"Have we..." Tyler coughed as Peggy shot him a look of reprimand. "The horses," he got out with a hand to the dog's back. "Have we lost—"

"Too soon to tell." That was Daniel. With the whites of his eyes glowing against a face covered in ash and maybe a smear of blood, he crouched in front of Tyler. Andrew and Shane flanked him. Daniel started to speak, but when he coughed instead, Shane took over.

"As best as we can tell, all barns are empty," Tyler's brother said, and relief rushed in like oxygen. "We've evacuated Barn C as a precaution." Shane was not a horseman, never had been. He'd chosen the family's other business, a vineyard elsewhere in the Valley. But in that moment, with the hat pulled low over his head and the ferocity in his eyes, he looked as though he lived and breathed the land every bit as much as Tyler did. "The horses are in the pasture. They're secure. We're trying to count them, but…"

The words trailed off, didn't need to be said.

Not all animals were accounted for.

"Light…ning?" He could still see the animal frantically pawing the back of his stall.

God, even over the shouting and the sirens, the fire and the water, he could still hear him….

His brother and Daniel exchanged a tense look. "Russ is with him," Shane said. "He took in a lot of smoke."

Tyler's eyes burned. Lightning Chaser was a fighter, Tyler knew that. If any horse could survive—

Survive. That was the best they could hope for. For Lightning Chaser to survive.

But already Tyler knew his champion Thoroughbred, the big strong bay colt who loved nothing more than to run, would never race again.

"The brigade is wetting down the surrounding area as a precaution," Shane explained, but the words barely registered. Tyler stared dry-eyed at the gnarled flames devouring two of his barns, and felt the sickness churn in his gut. Just that afternoon—

He could still see young Heidi sitting in the shade of a now scorched gum tree, with an apple in her hand.

Acutely aware of his brother and cousin, he straightened his shoulders and stood, noticed the young groom standing with the other two dogs. The kid was covered in smoke, had rips in his baggy, long-sleeved plaid shirt and something that looked like blood on the side of his face. But his eyes…it was his eyes that got Tyler, the horrified, haunted glow of shock.

No one would walk away from this unscathed.

"Preston," said a quiet, intense voice over the wail of the fire engines. Tyler turned, saw Detective Sergeant Dylan Hastings of the Pepper Flats station striding toward him, not in his normal attire of jeans and a button-down, but the protective gear of a volunteer firefighter. And in that instant the voice clicked and Tyler realized who had followed him to Lightning Chaser's stall and pressed the breathing apparatus to his face. "Pete here tells me you're going to be okay."

Tyler stuck out his hand. "Thanks to…" he started, but another spasm stole his words. He cleared his throat, tried again. "Thanks to you, mate."

Hastings's eyes were hard, flat. "Just doing my job."

That's all he ever said. Tyler had been teaching young Heidi the ins and outs of riding for almost a year, but her father still treated Tyler with a formality typically reserved for strangers.

Heidi.

He glanced toward the remains of Barn A. A smaller building, the fire there had already been put out. "A-Anthem?"

Hastings shook his head. "Don't know yet," he said grimly, as Tyler again noticed the groom in the bush hat hovering nearby. "I'm needed back over there, but before morning we'll need a full accounting of what happened here tonight."

A rough sound broke from Tyler's throat. He turned toward the inferno that had once housed his Thoroughbreds, his entire stable of two- and three-year-olds, surrounded now by the fire brigade. Hoses shot water against flames that didn't seem to give a bloody damn.

"The note," Tyler muttered, and Dylan's eyes met his. The two had talked earlier in the day, when Tyler had called to report the threat against Lightning Chaser. "God Almighty."

Dawn brought an otherworldly glow to the eastern horizon.

"We're lucky," David Preston insisted. He had been the one who had first walked the rolling hills of the northern Hunter Valley that had become Lochlain, who'd struck out from America almost forty years before, who'd used his inheritance to found the dynasty denied to him in America.

He and Tyler's mother had arrived from Sydney just as the main fire had been brought under control, less than two hours after Peggy had called them. The horror of what he'd found burned in his hooded, dark green eyes.

"That's what we have to focus on," he insisted, standing with his two sons outside the corral where the horses milled. They were quieter now that the strobe light had been turned off and the bullhorn had fallen silent.

Quieter after the fire went dark, and the remains of the stables had fallen.

"We can rebuild," David said in the same strong, stoic voice Tyler remembered from his childhood, when Tyler had found his father kneeling in the soft hazy light of sunrise, next to a mare and a foal who'd both been lost in childbirth.

It was the same voice David had used six years before, when Tyler had gotten caught with his pants down, literally, and almost lost Lochlain.

Tyler looked at him now, at his father, strong and robust even in his late fifties, at the lines carved into his weathered, rancher's face, the tight lines of his mouth and the devastation he couldn't quite hide, and quietly vowed to make sure David Preston never had to see Lochlain in ruin again.

"You're alive," father said to son, and Tyler felt his chest tighten. He should say something. He knew that. But that would mean letting go of the tight rope he'd been holding since staggering from the barn with Lightning Chaser. And once he let go…

"No one was seriously hurt," David went on. Cuts and bruises, a groom with a broken wrist, another—the new handyman Reynard, who'd fought to control the panicked horse after a beam had fallen—diagnosed with fractured ribs. "That's what we have to focus on."

But the same could not be said of the horses. Three had yet to be found. Two had been put down shortly before sunrise, one due to a shattered right front femur, the second to intense smoke inhalation. The others…

"Lightning will recover," David Preston said, tapping into his son's thoughts just as he always did.

"You saved his life," Shane added, but the trace of hero worship in his younger brother's voice, something Tyler had not heard since they were kids, scraped.

He glanced from the smoldering remains, where the fire brigade still battled hot spots, toward the horses on the other side of the soot-smeared white fence: the big bays and chestnuts; the shiny black two-year-old who'd run his first race only the week before; the Appaloosa who started each race like a streak; and the little filly who'd never even gotten a chance to show her stuff. Her maiden race was still two weeks away.

"They're goddamn bloody innocent," he finally said, and even now, hours after he'd emerged for the last time from the burning barn and sucked in fresh oxygen, each word seared against his throat. "They didn't deserve this."

But his father misunderstood. "Son," David said, and with the quiet word, put a hand to Tyler's shoulder. "Don't."

Tyler's throat tightened. He turned to meet his father's gaze, felt something hot and salty sting his.

"This is not your fault," David insisted. "You did everything right here. You don't store hay in the horse barns. Smoking isn't allowed. The wiring is new…hell, Peggy says it passed inspection just two months ago. There's no bloody way—"

Tyler's eyes must have flashed. He felt the streak of fury, saw the confused look that passed between his father and his brother.

"Someone did this," Tyler said, pulling the crumpled note from his pocket and pressing it into his father's hands. "Someone *wanted* to hurt him." Hurt Lightning Chaser. To punish him. Punish them all. "Because of the Queensland," he gritted out. Because More Than All That had been disqualified, and Lightning had taken home the purse.

Shane moved beside his father, and together they stared down at the thick words scrawled against the picture of Lightning Chaser in full, magnificent stride.

It was a long moment before they looked up. "You think it was arson," David said.

The words were hard, incredulous, and Tyler felt his jaw tighten in response. He glanced back toward the horses, automatically searching for young Heidi's horse, Anthem. He'd yet to account for the filly. "I know it was."

"I'm on my way now. My plane leaves Louisville first thing in the morning."

Phone in hand, Tyler strode across the muddied paddock toward the small brick building that housed Lochlain's medical facilities. They were equipped for routine maintenance and injuries—not triage. But each horse needed to be evaluated before individual arrangements could be made. Neighbors from throughout the shire had been arriving in a steady stream since long before the blaze had been put out. They had their trailers. At their stud farms, they had barns. They wanted to help. Fairchild Acres was the only stud that hadn't sent assistance, and yet even Louisa's head trainer had phoned to express his horror.

Tyler was quite sure Louisa had not authorized the call. She made no secret of her disdain for the Prestons, whom she still considered nothing more than newcomers.

"There's really no need, mate," Tyler told his former trainer, Marcus Vasquez. "Your hands, they're full with Lucas Racing." Marcus had relocated to America the year before and was working to establish his own stable.

Half a world away, Tyler wasn't sure how Marcus had already found out about the fire.

"I was there when Lightning was born," he reminded. "We were both there that first morning he—" His voice thickened, bringing with it the faintest trace of his Spanish heritage. "I was there," he finished abruptly, and in truth that said it all. He'd been a hell of a lot more than just Lightning Chaser's trainer. "And I need to be there now."

Tyler understood.

He ended the call and kept walking, turned off his phone. There'd been enough calls. Enough questions.

Too bloody few answers.

"The insurance investigator rang," Peggy said, as he passed. "She'll be here within the hour."

He nodded, kept walking. He'd met Beverly Morgan a time or two in the past. She was fair, but she took no prisoners. She would have her own set of questions.

And she would not appreciate his lack of answers.

Over four hours had passed since the fire had been put out, but the heat kept boiling. Tyler's watch said it wasn't yet ten, but the morning sun scorched like midafternoon. With every breath, the stench of smoke burned, and everywhere he looked he saw the lingering smear of smoke.

Even when he closed his eyes.

God, *especially* when he closed his eyes.

He'd yet to go inside. His mother had tried to get him to shower and clean up, to eat something. To have some tea. She meant well, he knew that. She wanted to help. But she hadn't understood that he couldn't. If he put so much as one bite of food in his mouth—

His stomach roiled at the thought.

Tyler rounded the corner and slipped in the back door. From the front of the brightly lit facility he heard Russ's voice in a serious conversation with one of the three additional veterinarians who'd arrived with the sunrise.

But it was the soft voice from the stall to the right that stopped him. Low, sad…oddly reassuring.

He moved closer and looked, saw the boy. Scrawny, covered in soot with a bloodstain on his torn shirtsleeve, he stood next to Lightning Chaser with a hand on the colt's neck. Stroking. Slowly. Gently. And his words, they were too quiet to hear, but the cadence almost sounded like…a lullaby.

And in that moment the juxtaposition hit Tyler, hit him in a way that nothing else had. The kid had been there all night. He'd been arm to arm with the men. He'd been the one to shove a glass of cold water into Tyler's hands, and now he was bloody singing to his horse. Lightning Chaser stood there quietly with his head bowed, but his ears perked, almost relaxed despite the equipment monitoring his vitals.

The last time Tyler had seen him he'd been fleeing the fire with Tyler's shirt covering his eyes.

Tyler stood there now, in the back room of the medical

clinic, alone for the first time since he'd crawled between his sheets and forced himself to count wallabies over ten hours before. And everything started to rush. The brightly lit room whirled around him, bringing with it the bullhorn and the shouting, the cries of the horses. It all rushed around him like some sick, twisted soundtrack that refused to die.

Then the boy shifted, and the hair slipped from beneath the tattered bush hat.

Blond.

Long.

Like goddamn sunshine.

Chapter Four

She sensed him before she heard him. She stood there in the brightly lit back room with her hand on Lightning Chaser's velvety neck, not trusting herself to move. She hadn't wanted him to find her like this.

She hadn't wanted him to find her at all.

From the relative quiet of Whittleson Stud, where her father's former trainer Sam Whittleson had invited her to stay despite his absence, she'd heard the bullhorn, and the horrible rush of cold had been immediate.

In horse country, the sound of a bullhorn breaking the night could only mean one thing.

She'd run to the window and seen the strobe gyrating against the darkness to the east in the direction of Lochlain.

Everything else was a blur. She'd thrown on clothes and run to her car, sped toward the awful red glow. That's what people did. That's what everyone in the shire did. When there was trouble, everyone came. Everyone helped.

That's what she told herself. She was there because it was the right thing to do, because horses were in trouble and every able body was needed.

But the second she'd seen Tyler emerging from the smoke, tall and commanding, that air of authority enveloping him despite the horror drenching his eyes, she'd known the truth.

She'd come for Tyler.

She stood there now with her back to him, not allowing herself to move. Because if she moved she would turn, and if she turned and saw him, the urge to go to him and put her arms around him…

She should have gone home. She should have slipped out with the sunrise, once the fire was under control and she knew Tyler was okay.

But Tyler was not okay, and Darci wasn't sure he ever would be again. Lochlain was his life, the horses, every one of them, his children. Once, he'd almost lost it all. That had been the price all those years ago, the fallout from a stupid schoolgirl desire she'd been unable to control.

This time, she knew…this time would be different. It had to be. She'd left Australia a girl, but she'd returned a young woman. She had goals. She was deliberate, methodical. And she wasn't about to fall into the same trap she'd fallen into before. She had a career to build, a future to claim.

But she couldn't just stand there like a coward, either, not when she could feel him behind her, watching.

Not when she knew that her hair had given her away.

Slowly, she turned. And slowly, she saw. He stood not five meters behind her, in a shaft of sunlight cutting in from a high window. It exposed him—the smoke smeared against his face and the battered Akubra hat he always wore, the grime on his clothes and the rips in the once-white undershirt. They exposed the minor burns and dried blood on the arm that hung oddly at his side—blood she knew his mother had tried to wipe away.

But it was his eyes that got her. Normally they gleamed like raw emeralds. Normally the deep dark green glimmered with intensity and enthusiasm, with energy, excitement. Awareness.

Now they were grim, flat...and so damn agonized she almost forgot every promise she'd made to herself, every goal. Every dream. Because in that one moment, there was only Tyler Preston...and the low, hard thrum of her heart.

"You're hurt," she said inanely, and like a fool, she started toward him. Toward Tyler.

Once, all those years ago, when she'd caught his eye and sashayed over, when she'd worn low-rise jeans and a flirty tank top, he'd lounged against the wall with a drink in his hand, and watched. His eyes had gleamed.

Now he turned, and walked away.

Darci stopped midstride and watched him make his way toward the front of the clinic, where the team of veterinarians examined the horses as quickly as possible. She'd heard them for the past thirty minutes, since she'd slipped in to check on Lightning. Over and over and over, the prognosis was the same: severe smoke inhalation. The horses would live...most of them.

But Lochlain's finest would never race again.

Her throat worked. She fought against it, fought against the hot sting of moisture in her eyes. But then she turned and saw Lightning Chaser watching her through those gentle, melted-chocolate eyes, and she couldn't fight it anymore. The tears came.

"Sweet boy," she murmured, stepping into him and wrapping her arms around his neck, nuzzling her face against his mane. "You didn't deserve this."

None of them had.

For a long while, she just stood there, holding and stroking Tyler's horse, whispering, singing the lullaby her mother had once sung to her. The words came easily, but with the years the sound of Anne's voice had faded from the last corners of memory.

"You're going to be okay, big guy," she promised Lightning Chaser. Then, with one last kiss to the side of his face, she turned and went in search of Andrew.

"You need to let someone look at that, Ty."

He looked away from the X-ray of Anthem's lungs toward Russ, who was studying him as intently as he'd been watching each horse he examined.

She was gone, he knew. He'd heard her leave. Only a few minutes before he'd heard her singing again.

Before that, he'd heard her crying.

He'd almost turned. Like a needy little boy he'd almost turned and gone to her, yanked her into his arms and buried his face in her hair, breathed her in. Held on.

"It's fine," he barked now, frowning when he realized he'd been unconsciously cradling his left arm. "Just a little sore."

Russ crossed the sterile room and put his hands to Tyler's forearm. "Here, let me—"

Tyler swore the second Russ shifted his arm.

Grim-eyed, Russ released the arm and stepped back. "I'm betting it's broken," he said, but Tyler didn't think so. If his arm were broken, he would know it, feel—

Feel it. Feel *something.*

"You can't wrestle fifteen-hundred-kilogram animals

and expect not to get hurt," Russ lectured. Despite the ten years he had on Tyler, they'd practically grown up together. It was only recently that Russ's aging father had turned his equine practice over to his son. "Get it checked for me, okay?" he said as the phone on the wall started to ring. He grabbed it, muttered a few words before handing it to Tyler. "It's Peggy."

Tyler took the receiver, but it was not his office manager's voice that greeted him. It was a Yank.

"I just heard," his cousin Robbie said. "Andrew filled me in. How's Lightning Chaser?"

Tyler glanced toward one of the stalls in the back room, where the three-year-old now stood alone. "Stable."

"Well, thank God for that," Robbie said. The youngest of Tyler's three male cousins, Robbie had always been the easiest to talk to. Whereas the older Kentucky Prestons had a taste for the business side of racing, for Robbie, it had always been about the horses. "Look, if there's anything I can do, I'm there. Just let me know."

Turning toward the window, Tyler looked beyond the pile of rubble that had, twenty-four hours before, been a state-of-the-art barn, and assessed the horses. Their ranks were thinning. Close to thirty had already gone home with neighbors. They would live there until Lochlain could rebuild.

"I appreciate that," Tyler said. He did. "But I don't really know—"

"Anything," Robbie said. "I've got room here at Quest. I know it's a long trip, but I can take in as many horses as you need. They can stay here, I can train them until you're back up and running…"

Robbie kept talking, but the words ran together. Tyler looked from the horses to the paddock, where Andrew and Daniel led two colts and a filly toward a waiting trailer. All his life there'd been the Kentucky Prestons, and the Australian Prestons. Tyler's father had never spoken an ill word of his brother, Thomas, but the undercurrent had been there. The competitiveness. That's why David Preston had left America. That's why David had founded Lochlain. He'd needed an entire ocean to get out from his brother's shadow and create his own legacy.

The families had gotten together occasionally, for weddings, funerals, but there'd always been a line. A divide. His blue-blooded Kentucky cousins had grown up with everything. Their position in the racing community had been established before they'd even been born. In Australia, Tyler's father had started with little more than dirt and dreams.

But here, now, as he watched Andrew, hot and sweaty and laboring beneath the blistering sun, with his shirt-sleeves rolled up and soot still covering his face, with Robbie on the phone from half a world away, offering to help in any way possible, the invisible bonds of family wrapped around Tyler, and he realized just how strong the Preston blood ran.

Over the past year they'd all been targeted. Scandal had rocked them, every single one of them. His American cousins had been stripped of both the Kentucky Derby and Preakness titles and their racing privileges. They'd come bloody close to losing everything. But they'd endured. They'd banded together and cleared the family name. They'd emerged stronger, more unified than ever.

And now they were here.

Tyler wound down the call with Robbie and started outside, stopped when he saw Darci approach Andrew. Still dressed like a scraggly ranch hand, but with her blond hair tangled around her face and the puppy Tulloch at her

heel, she hurried up to Andrew with a glass in her hand…
and offered it to him.

It was hardly an intimate act. Darci was Andrew's employee. Andrew was hot, tired. She was just bringing him
something to drink.

But something dark and hard twisted through Tyler.

Frowning, he ignored the burn and turned back to
Anthem's X-ray.

She found him at the far paddock. He stood with his
back to her, staring at some point on the horizon. She'd
seen him off and on for the past few hours talking with the
fire brigade and Detective Sergeant Hastings, walking the
smoldering remains of his barns with his father and shaking
hands with several neighbours, who'd come to offer shelter
to Lochlain's horses.

Now, for the first time all afternoon, he stood alone.
There was an unnatural stillness to him, as if some kind of
invisible barrier separated him from the rest of the world.
Darci knew better than to go to him, knew she should just
go home. He'd walked away from her earlier. There was
no place for her in this day.

But with the lemon cordial she'd gotten from Tyler's
mother in hand, she quietly covered the hard, dusty ground
separating her from Tyler.

She knew he sensed her presence. She could tell by the
way his body changed. It was subtle, but he stiffened, went
a little more rigid.

"Tyler," she said as the hot wind blew against her face. Her
body ached from head to toe. She'd been up all night. She
should be tired. But the rush of adrenaline refused to let go.

He didn't turn, didn't say a word. Just kept standing there
looking out on the parched rolling hills of Lochlain. They'd

been spared. If the wind had picked up during the night, the fire could have spread from the barn complex to the bush.

Somehow, she didn't think that was the right thing to say.

"Here," she said, extending the glass even though he'd yet to look at her. "I thought you might be thirsty."

He did turn then. He turned with a near violence that stunned her, and stared down at her from beneath the brim of his bush hat as if she'd just shoved a knife into his gut.

His eyes…they'd been flat before.

Now they gleamed. It wasn't the roguish sexual gleam from all those years before, but a hard, predatory gleam that sent her heart into a cruel rhythm.

She wanted to step closer. Instinct warned her to step back. Instead, with the sun baking against her skin, she forced her mouth to curve into the same kind of tight, aching smile she'd given her father in those dark months after her mother had died.

"Lemon cordial," she said, lifting her hand. "You've got to be parched."

He looked from the sweaty glass to her face, and something inside her twisted. And in that moment, all those years, all the lies and truths, the consequences, fell away, and there was just her and Tyler.

"I know you're exhausted," she said quietly. She'd tried to forget about him. She'd *wanted* to forget about him. But sometimes, alone at night in her father's stuffy London town house, memories would stir. Sometimes it was the accent that would jar her, sometimes the name Preston. Several months before, it had been the man himself. She'd been about to switch the channel when coverage of the Queensland Stakes had come on, and she'd seen him. He'd been part of a profile on his brilliant three-year-old, Lightning Chaser, and the reemergence of Lochlain Racing.

She'd sat there, frozen. Aching.

When she'd run into his cousin Andrew a few months later, it had seemed that fate had gift wrapped the chance she'd never thought to receive: the ability to make things right for Tyler.

"Maybe you should head on inside," she said.

He looked beyond her toward the barn, where a member of the fire brigade led a muscular yellow Lab through the remains. The dog's name was Millie, and she had a talent for sniffing out accelerants.

"Your arm," she said, and without thinking she reached for him. "Have you had it looked at?" Her hand brushed his left wrist. "I noticed you're favoring it—"

He didn't jerk away as she'd expected, instead just stood a breath away and bloody near pierced her with the gleam in his eyes. "You brought me a lemon cordial."

The sting was quick and brutal, and with it her throat tightened. But then his voice registered—not harsh or mocking as it had been the day before, but raw and hoarse and…gentle, almost.

"Do you have any idea—" He moved so fast she had no time to prepare. No time to step back. He crushed the distance between them and brought a hand to her face, stroked the hair back from her cheek. "What were you thinking? What in God's name were you thinking coming out here in the middle of the night?"

That was easy. She didn't stop to edit or plan, didn't stop to consider implications. The truth, something she'd kept too much of from him six years before, simply came out.

"I heard the bullhorn," she said, rocked by the feel of his roughened fingers against her skin. "And I saw the strobe." And she'd wanted to throw up. "I knew it was Lochlain and I couldn't…" The words, the awful possibilities, jammed in her throat. "I had to be here," she said. "I had to come."

"You could have been hurt," he said, sliding his hand down to her arm, where cuts and bruises crisscrossed her flesh. "You could have—"

"So could you have," she shot back. "The way you kept running back into that barn—" The memory chilled her. That last time, when he'd eventually come out with Lightning Chaser, he'd been in too long. She'd grabbed the firefighters as soon as they'd arrived, had begged them to go in after him....

"I had to," he said. "They trusted me."

And to him, she knew that said it all.

"I could hear them..." His words trickled off into the buzz of activity coming from the barn, but above the wind and the voices she could hear them, too. Hear the horses. Their panicked cries would haunt her for a long time.

"You got them out," she said, and now she was touching him, a hand on each of his upper arms, pushing up on her toes as if not a day, a lie, stood between them. "You did everything humanly possible."

The lines of his face tightened. "So did you."

The words were so quiet she wasn't sure whether she'd heard them or imagined them.

"You should go now," he said, and the disappointment cut to the quick.

He stepped back but did not release her, kept his hands on her body as he openly inspected her, his gaze sliding from her face to the damp, smoke-stained shirt and jeans clinging to her body. "Take a shower," he said. "Get some rest."

She felt her back go a little straighter. "There'll come a time for resting, Tyler, but it's not now." Lifting her chin, she again extended the glass. "Now here, drink."

His eyes sparked, reminding her for a brief heartbeat of the brash young man she'd first seen on television one Sunday afternoon, telling anyone who cared to listen the proper way to saddle a horse.

"I know what you think of me," she said, swiping a tangled strand of sooty hair from her face. "But I'm not that spoiled girl you remember from six years ago."

He took the lemonade and brought it to his mouth, drank it in one long sip. But his eyes never left hers. "You have no idea what I remember."

From a starkly cloudless sky, the sun seared even hotter. "Then tell me."

Chapter Five

The words, soft, challenging, slipped through Tyler, burning where seconds before, the lemon cordial had cooled. He looked at her standing next to the dusty white fence with her chin lifted and the hair falling in her face, her eyes filled with a glow he'd tried to forget.

She'd been at Lochlain since the fire. She'd led horses to the far pasture. She'd tended to him under the cover of darkness. She'd given him a drink, damn it. She'd soothed shaken members of his staff.

She'd sung to Lightning Chaser, and she'd cried.

Over sixteen hours after arriving, she still wore the same stained, torn clothes. Only her hair was different, no longer stuffed inside a cap, but hanging loose and tangled around her face. In place of makeup she wore soot and fatigue and grief, but somehow, goddammit, she still looked beautiful.

And he wanted to touch. So brutally bad he refused to

let himself move. Because more than touch, he wanted to taste. He wanted to crush her in his arms and bury his face in her hair, to slide his mouth to hers and forget—

For-bloody-get.

It was the word that got him, the word that stopped him. He stepped back and looked toward the hulking remains of Barn B, where his father and Detective Hastings strode toward him, with Beverly Morgan following closely behind. Their expressions were tight, unreadable, and before they reached him, he knew. He knew what the news would be. What the arson dog had detected.

"Thanks for the drink," he said with the politeness typically reserved for strangers. The spark in Darci's eyes went flat, but already he was handing her the glass and turning toward the approaching trio.

His barn complex lay in ruins. He'd lost two horses, might lose several more. Lightning Chaser would never race again.

Now was not the time to wonder if Darci Parnell could possibly taste as sweet as she looked.

"Have that arm looked at," she said quietly, and if there was a note of hurt in her voice, he reminded himself just how dangerous illusions could be.

With narrowed eyes he watched her walk into the glare of the lowering sun as his father drew near, watched her hair sway against her back as she once again headed for Andrew.

"Millie found an accelerant," Hastings said. "Near what your father says used to be the tack room."

Swearing softly, Tyler looked toward the blue-and-white checked crime-scene tape stretched around the barn. In the nearby shade, two of the border collies drank greedily from a bowl of water Darci had brought over.

"There are faint trails leading to both the other barns," Hastings added.

"We're lucky we didn't lose all three," Tyler's father said. "It could have been a hell of a lot worse."

The confirmation of his suspicions sickened him. Someone had torched his barns. Someone had started a fire while the animals were inside, sleeping. If things had only been a little different—

"Someone was supposed to be watching." They had a rotation. Someone was awake at all times, walking the grounds, monitoring the surveillance feed….

Hastings glanced at his notepad. "Fella named Reynard had first shift, but turned it over to a kid named Craig around midnight."

Tyler nodded. Reynard was new to Lochlain; Craig Stevens had grown up there. His father was one of the assistant trainers. Craig was an exercise rider. He wanted to be a jockey.

"He's a good kid," Tyler said.

"Says he heard a noise over by the office and went to check it out. Didn't see anything, so he went to get a drink. He was on his way back when he smelled smoke."

"He sounded the alarm, did everything right," David added. "But he's torn up something awful. His dad is with him now."

Tyler looked at the three of them, Hastings all business, his father grim-eyed, the insurance investigator ominously quiet. She didn't need to say anything. What she was thinking—what anyone would think—was clear.

Only one person stood to profit from torching the barns, and that was Tyler. The insurance policy alone was worth a small fortune.

"The surveillance footage?" Tyler asked. "It show anything?"

Hastings's eyes narrowed. "The CD-ROM is missing."

"Missing?" The word exploded out of Tyler. "That's impossible. That equipment is kept behind locked doors—"

The words fell into a horrible silence. Tyler had been giving riding lessons to Detective Hastings's daughter for almost a year. During that time the men had been cordial, polite. Tyler had always sensed a reserve in the other man, but nothing like the icy wall now encasing him. Hastings was all cop now, with the hard, assessing look only cops had.

"We're going to need an explanation for that," he said. "Because right now, I have to tell you, it's not looking very good."

"What the hell are you saying?" David asked, his chest expanding as it always did when his temper spiked. "You can't really think—"

"We don't know what to think yet," Hastings finished before David could. "But let me tell you what we know. We've got two barns down. An accelerant has been found. The kid who was on watch went to investigate a noise. And now the surveillance footage is missing."

It sounded pretty damned incriminating. Surveillance equipment was in the main building, which was kept locked. Outside the Lochlain staff, no one had access.

"There can be no settlement," Beverly Morgan added. "Not until we know exactly what happened here last night."

Without the insurance payment, there could be no rebuilding. They had a little cash in reserves, but nowhere near the amount necessary to run an operation like Lochlain on a monthly basis.

"My horses have been threatened," Tyler said through clenched teeth. "I gave you the bloody note."

"You did," Hastings acknowledged. "And whether it's a threat or not remains to be seen. We'll run it for prints, see if we get a match."

"But the note doesn't rule anything in or out," Beverly pointed out. With her clean blond hair and starched linen suit, she looked ridiculously out of place at Lochlain. Instinctively Tyler found himself glancing toward the paddock, where Darci stood with Daniel and Shane.

He didn't understand why the hell she wouldn't go home.

"You're both out of your minds," David said. "If you think for one minute my son, or anyone who works for him, would do anything to endanger the horses—"

Hastings's eyes remained flat. "I'll be interviewing the staff. Your office manager—" he glanced down at his notes, then back up "—Peggy. Make sure she has all staff files ready for me in the morning."

Tyler met his gaze. "We have nothing to hide." But someone did, Tyler added silently.

Someone had breached the sanctity of Lochlain. Poured an accelerant, struck a match.

And someone was going to pay.

Arson.

The word wound through Darci like the thorny vines that had once tried to choke out her mother's roses. She kept her back to Peggy, pretended to review a checklist while Tyler's office manager spoke quietly into the phone.

Fire happened. Darci knew that. Barns were dangerous places. Back before her mother died, Darci remembered finding her weeping one morning. The newspaper had been in her hand. She'd refused to tell Darci what she'd read, but that night Darci had pulled the crumpled pages from the trash. There'd been a fire in the Valley. Seventeen horses had been lost. The cause…the storage of damp hay. It had combusted, devoured the barn before anyone could rescue the horses.

But arson… Someone had poured turpentine outside the tack room. Someone had created an inferno and walked away, while over fifty horses were inside, closed in their stalls, sleeping.

The thought chilled.

Horse racing wasn't without scandal. She knew that, too. Races got fixed. Horses were switched, disguised, disqualified. The greatest Australian racehorse of all times had just…died. The picture of strength and health, Phar Lap had been on his maiden voyage to America. He'd just won his first race there. His future had been bright, until the morning his trainer walked into his stall and found him dead. The official cause was an illness from grazing in wet alfalfa.

Many Aussies maintained that the big horse had been murdered.

But a deliberate fire in a horse barn…that was without precedent, and it sickened.

"Is there something else you need, Miss Parnell?"

Darci looked up from her notebook and turned toward the impossibly efficient woman who ran Lochlain with an amusing combination of charm and grit. With her long gray hair, Peggy looked like a kindly grandmother who should be baking cookies, but her dark brown eyes glimmered with intelligence and strength.

To keep a stud full of men running smoothly, she had to have both.

Somewhere during the day she'd changed from her nightclothes to a pair of gray slacks and a black shirt, her hair now pulled into a loose ponytail. She and Darci had been working in tandem much of the afternoon.

"Not tonight," Darci said. She'd drafted a press release and placed calls to everyone involved with Andrew's fundraiser. "Anything else can wait until morning." To the rhythmic pulsing of the Hindu chant playing softly through the intercom, she glanced out the large window overlooking the barn complex. With sunset, activity had finally quieted. Most of the fire brigade had gone home. The last of the neighbors had left almost thirty minutes before, hauling behind them three trailers full of horses. Only Detective Superintendent Hardy, Detective Hastings and a few of the veterinarians remained.

Two were there to query, the others to heal.

"Do you see him?"

The question was wise, knowing.

Glancing over her shoulder, Darci found Peggy watching her through speculative eyes. She didn't bother asking who. Both women knew.

"How did you know?" she asked instead.

Peggy crossed the lavender-scented room and joined her at the window. She had more candles burning than St. Mary's in Pepper Flats, allowing only a trace of the pungent scent of smoke to infiltrate the sanctity of her domain.

"I'm not blind, girl. I've seen you today, trying to fade into the shadows but watching him, tending to him when he pushed too hard."

Darci shifted. Cool air blew from the floor vents, but heat lifted through her. "Lochlain is his life," she whispered. "Lightning…" Closing her eyes, she could see Tyler as he'd been the day of the Queensland Stakes, when a camera had zoomed in on him giving Lightning Chaser a kiss a few minutes before race time. "How does someone survive this?" she asked as he came into view, silhouetted against the blood-red glow of the vanishing sun. "How does someone—"

"He'll survive because he has to." Peggy's voice was as strong and true as her words. "He'll survive because he's a Preston. That's what they do. It's in the blood."

Something deep inside Darci shifted. Peggy was right. Tyler Preston was a survivor, not a victim. He knew how to work a situation to his advantage. He knew how to make sure he always, always came out on top.

"After all, Miss Parnell," Peggy added soberly, "this isn't the first time Lochlain has been compromised."

Darci stiffened, felt the ugly truth of Peggy's words wind through her. She turned from Tyler, who was swiping off his hat and wiping his forearm against his face, and back to Peggy. "You know who I am, don't you?"

The office manager's chin came up. "Aye," she said in an oddly lyrical voice. "I know who you are."

Darci wanted to look away, but refused to let herself. That was the coward's way, what the girl would have done. "I never meant for him to get hurt," she said quietly. "I just wanted…"

Him. She'd wanted him. But she'd known he would never want her, not if he knew how old she was.

Or rather, how young.

To a man in his twenties, a seventeen-year-old was just that. A teenager.

A child.

"You don't owe me any explanations," Peggy said, and then she was turning briskly and returning to her ridiculously tidy desk. "You just need to know that whoever poured that turpentine last night isn't the only one playing with fire."

Darci knew that. Only now, the analogy took on an ugly hue.

"I just want to help," she said. "That's why I'm here. Andrew is a good man. He's exactly what the racing com-

munity needs." If there'd been any doubt, the fire at
Lochlain drove that fact home. Too much scandal was
scarring the sport. If the industry was going to survive,
someone needed to clean it up. "If we can build support
for him in Australia, he stands a good chance of taking over
the federation."

Peggy pulled open a drawer and withdrew two more
files. "I can't disagree with you on that."

"That's why I chose Lochlain for his inaugural fund-
raiser. To show how thick the Preston blood runs."

Peggy's mouth twisted. "I'm not so sure that's a good
idea anymore."

"Oh, but it's a perfect idea," she said. "What better way
to demonstrate what the Prestons are made of? How they
stick together and rise from the ashes and—"

From behind them came the scuffle of boots against
hardwood. And a voice.

"So that's what this is all about? Your party?"

She spun, found him standing just inside the reception
area, tall, grimy, his old dog at his feet and his bush hat in
hand, leaving dark hair flat against his head. He looked…
tired. "Tyler."

"You just don't know when to quit, do you, sunshine?"
With the question, the dark green of his eyes glowed. "I
would ask if they'd taught you that over at Oxford, but the
Parnell princess has always known how to spin a situation,
hasn't she? She's always known how to take the impossible
and make it possible."

"You don't understand—"

"Oh, but I do," he drawled in that disturbingly calm
voice, the one under such tight control that she wanted to
rush over and shove at him, do something, anything, to
bring a spark of life to him. He was exhausted, she knew

that. He hadn't slept in almost two days. He'd been work-ing nonstop, had faced questions that rocked, answers that chilled.

But this was beyond exhaustion.

"You want to take what happened here today," he rolled on, "and turn it into some kind of freak show. Parade as many benefactors through Lochlain as you can, using what happened here to win votes for my cousin." Slowly he pushed from the door. And slowly he started toward her. "Tell me something, love. Where are you planning on putting the collection plate?"

As Peggy gasped, Darci stiffened, but refused to let herself show any further reaction. "You're frustrated, I understand that, Tyler. But this is me. You knew me. You can't really think I'd try to exploit your family."

They'd spent hours talking. At first. He'd brought her here, to Lochlain. Together, on the back of a tall black gelding, they'd ridden out into the rolling hills, separating themselves from everyone and everything. There, they'd been under the big Australian night sky, on their backs and counting the stars.

Then their mouths had met and Tyler had shifted. She'd remained on her back, but he'd been doing anything but counting. And when she'd rolled him onto his back—

He stopped beside a white wicker chair a few meters away. His left arm still hung oddly at his side. "Are you denying it then? Are you telling me that I heard wrong? That when I walked in you weren't telling Peg here about your plans for the big party at Lochlain?"

He made it sound so mercenary. "I'm just trying to help—"

"You can't, Darci." His eyes locked onto hers. "You can't help."

Because he didn't want her to. It was there in every hard line of his body, there in the tight lines of his face. At some point he'd taken a cloth to his cheeks, but whiskers now darkened his jaw, accentuating the grime that remained like the residue of a wipe-on tan.

"But I know people," she said, and her throat tightened on the words. "I have connections. I can—"

"Don't." Just the one word, that's all he said. But it stopped her cold.

"I'm well aware of your connections," he reminded, shifting his right arm to cradle his left. "And trust me, I can do without them. There's nothing you can do here. Go on back to Sam's…" His voice trailed off, leaving his gaze to rake from her face down to her soot-covered sweatshirt and jeans, the dirty boots her father had paid way too much for at Harrods.

"Have a shower," he said. "Wash your hair in that expensive shampoo of yours and get some sleep…." His eyes found hers again, and his mouth curved into the faintest of smiles…not carnal like the ones she remembered, but slow, mocking. "Dream those Parnell dreams," he drawled, "all nice and pretty and…uncomplicated."

Her throat tightened. "You're wrong," she said, but he was already turning and striding toward the door. "If you really think I can go home after what happened here today and just go to sleep…" Then Tyler Preston didn't know her at all.

The door hung open. He was two steps into the warm haze of dusk when he stopped and turned.

"And when you wake up," he said in a voice that was more quiet than flat, more resigned than cruel, "maybe then you'll realize how bloody preposterous it is to think there's going to be a party here next week." Beyond him, the border collies darted from behind the surviving barn. "You need another target, sunshine," he said with that same little half smile. "This time I'm not your bloke."

And then he was gone, stepping from the cool candlelit room into the shadows of twilight.

They were not going to lose another horse.

Russ Chaplain turned away from the last of the X-rays to the stack of pages waiting on the fax machine. For the past fifteen minutes the lab in Sydney had been sending over test results, courtesy of a rush job an old friend had miraculously pulled off. Picking up the results, Russ strolled over to the small desk and sat for the first time in...

He didn't know. Maybe the first time all day.

The three veterinarians who'd rushed to Lochlain from Scone and Tamworth to assist had left with sunset, each of them accompanying a trailer of horses to their new, temporary home. Horse people came together like that. Even long-standing rivalries meant nothing in the face of animal welfare. Only Louisa Fairchild had failed to offer help.

Russ's colleagues would stay with the horses through the night, just as he and his son-in-law would do here at Lochlain, where the most seriously injured horses were being monitored.

Smoke inhalation was tricky. Horses could appear fine for several days before crashing. Fluid could build up quietly in the lungs. They would have to watch closely.

From the back room, he heard Owen crooning to Lightning Chaser, and for the first time that day, emotion punched through the professional wall Russ had hammered into place. He'd been driven, focused, going from one horse to the next, doing what he could, as fast as he could. They'd lost two. One of them a sleek, young, jet-black two-year-old who'd had a weakness for carrots. Russ had treated the colt early in his short life for an infection, and had had a soft spot for him ever since. Hero's Dancer, his name was, and when one of the grooms had dragged Russ over to tend a horse that had gone down...

He'd almost gone down, too. He'd seen Hero's Dancer writhing in the horrible red glow cast by the fire, seen the white of the bone protruding through flesh, and he'd known. He'd known what had to be done.

But in the end, it had been Owen who'd lifted the hypodermic needle to the young animal. Russ had kneeled, cradling Hero's head. And when the end came and the animal's pain-filled eyes had drifted shut, Russ had pressed a kiss to the side of his beautiful face.

His throat burned. Looking up, he blinked against the sting of his eyes and cleared his vision, gave himself a moment before returning to the lab work. But he knew, despite all his training, about being objective and not getting involved, he'd never again be able to slip a young horse a carrot without thinking of the spirited black colt they'd lost too soon.

Because of arson.

The thought ground through him. He was a man sworn to heal. All his life, he'd been driven to help. His father had been a surgeon, his father before him a country doctor. But Russ's love of animals had driven him to veterinary medicine. A fascination with horses had turned his focus to all things equine. He could no more imagine intentionally hurting an animal—

Red caught his eye. He blinked and narrowed his gaze, focused on two sentences in bold text at the bottom of the third lab report.

"Bloody hell," he muttered, standing. Quickly he strode toward the back room, where Lightning Chaser stood with an eerie grace, while Owen shared an apple with the cream sorrel, Anthem.

Heart pounding, Russ approached the bay colt and lifted a hand to his neck, stroked. "How's everyone doing?"

His son-in-law's grim eyes met his. "Stable for now."

Russ understood. For now that was all that could be said. Turning back to Lightning, he looked into the colt's wise, knowing eyes, alert and eager, despite all he'd suffered. "And our boy?"

"You know LC," Owen said. "He's a trouper."

But he was also hurt. He'd been in the barn too long. He'd drawn in too much smoke. A fiercely intelligent animal, he hadn't wanted to walk toward the fire, even if walking toward it was the only way to get away from it. If Tyler hadn't gone in after him—

Russ swallowed hard. "Sweet God," he muttered.

Owen pivoted. "What's wrong? Has he—"

"No," Russ said. "Nothing." Not now anyway. But if the lab results were true...

"Why don't you knock off for a while," he suggested to Owen. "We'll pull shifts tonight."

His son-in-law, a tall lanky kid who hardly looked old enough to be a father himself, but would be before the year's end, scrubbed a hand over his jaw. "I can go first," he said.

"Nonsense." Russ forced a smile, didn't want Owen to suspect anything was wrong. Didn't want anyone to suspect, not until he'd confirmed what he'd read. Then he would tell Tyler first. He owed him that.

"Give me an hour then," Owen said with one last slide of his hand against Anthem's side.

Russ watched his apprentice head for the small office, waiting until the light went off before making his way to the exam room. There, he retrieved a needle and test tube.

He was hurrying back to the sterile holding area when the outer door opened, and footsteps sounded.

Fumbling, he stashed the equipment in the pocket of the third lab coat he'd worn that day as he turned to find Dylan Hastings striding in. "Detective," he greeted.

The big, somber cop frowned his greeting. "How's my daughter's horse?"

"The loss cannot be measured in dollars alone. While the financial toll is sure to climb into the tens of millions, the emotional price will be far worse…."

Alone at Whittleson Stud, Darci stood in the doorway separating the bathroom from the guest suite. Behind her the shower still ran. She had a towel pressed to her body, but water dripped from her hair and slid down her legs, puddling on the hardwood floor. She'd turned the volume on the small television as high as it would go. The second she'd heard the evening news begin, she'd scrambled from the tub.

"Horses were lost," the young anchor with the perfect makeup and hair said as the picture shifted from the news desk to Lochlain. "Careers ended, promise extinguished…"

She'd scrubbed. She'd gone for the shower the second she'd returned to the big quiet house, turning on the water, not hot but cold. She'd been hot all day. Hot and sweaty and covered in smoke and dust and grime. Now she wanted it gone. She'd grabbed the bottle of soap and squeezed, over and over again.

Now the bottle lay empty beneath the hard spray of the shower, and despite the lavender fragrance that had delighted her the night before, it was smoke that still burned her lungs.

"It's yet another setback for the illustrious Preston family," the anchor continued, her voice somber, "with branches both here in the shire and in America."

It was all Darci could do not to grab the bottle of lotion and hurl it toward the television housed across the room in an old teakwood armoire.

The footage cut from the smoldering remains of the big H-shaped barn to the closing seconds of a horse race Darci had seen too many times. "A Lochlain horse, you may recall, was at the center of the controversy stemming from the Queensland Stakes." On the screen, two animals ran neck and neck, beautiful. Free.

Innocent.

"Front-runner More Than All That was disqualified after performance-enhancing drugs were detected in his system."

The image of the two horses dissolved into a tight shot of Tyler with his hand on Lightning Chaser's back.

"The Lochlain horse ended up with the purse, but the shadow of controversy overrode what should have been a moment of great triumph."

Darci's fingers clenched the thick burgundy towel. It was a news story for the network, but for the men and women of Lochlain, it was their life.

"Now the Prestons have essentially been eliminated from contention for the coming year, until they can acquire new horses or their youngest prospects mature."

Her eyes burned. Her throat worked. She tried to scrape the last sight of Tyler from her mind, standing there in the doorway of the small stone office, quietly and politely telling her to go to hell.

But even when she closed her eyes, the image remained.

"If there is any small blessing to this tragedy, it is that the yearlings, housed in the sole barn untouched by fire, were spared."

Now the horses filled the screen, mothers and their leggy colts and fillies, milling anxiously in the far paddock.

"But it will be months before they are ready to pick up the banner once carried by Lochlain horses such as Lightning Chaser and his grand sire Lightning's Match…"

Someone had done this. The thought churned through Darci, bringing with it the disturbing memory of her father's words from the day before: *Now is not the time to be getting involved with the Prestons, not even Andrew. I'm hearing things—*

Darci stiffened.

Someone had done this on purpose. Someone had tried to destroy Lochlain. Someone had killed and injured horses. Someone had gone after Tyler…tried to strip away his greatest passion.

But someone did not know Tyler Preston.

The thought gained force as she hurried back to the shower and turned off the water, ran for her clothes. Someone didn't know Tyler, that was true. But they didn't know Darci Parnell, either.

Now they were about to.

Broken.

In the light of a single lamp, Tyler fought to pull a T-shirt over the bulky cast encasing his left forearm. He'd had no intention of having it looked at, but when he'd finally walked into Lochlain's kitchen, his mother had sat at the big farm table with Dr. Baker.

An hour later, the cast had been in place.

After wrestling with his jeans, he frowned at the small bottle of pain pills the good doctor had left for him, then strode from his bedroom.

The sun had yet to rise. The house was quiet. But from outside came the low buzz of the stud coming to life. And from the kitchen came the soft sound of humming.

Tyler doubted any of them had actually slept.

Shane had gone home, but his parents had stayed. It was his mother he found in the kitchen, lowering herself into a chair at the big table where a grim-faced Russ Chaplain sat. Dark circles shadowed both their eyes.

The two looked up, and instantly his mother, wrapped in a pale pink robe, started to stand. "Tyler," she said, but before she could move from her chair, he motioned for her to stay seated. "There's coffee ready… I thought you could use something stronger than tea this morning."

He glanced toward the tiled counter, where the mug he always used sat waiting. "You don't need to be up this early," he said, but knew his words would fall on deaf ears. "Lucinda can—"

"I know she can," his mother said before he could finish. "But she's not your mother, and I am."

His smile was automatic. Sarah Preston presented a soft feminine image to the general public, but her sons had always seen the steel. She'd rolled with the punches, had never hesitated to push up her sleeves and pitch in. She'd always been right there with her boys, rain or shine. She never asked them to do anything she wouldn't do herself.

It was easy to see why his father had fallen so hard and so fast.

Tyler detoured, sweeping by the table to press a quick hard kiss to her cheek. "You spoil me."

Her smile softened, filled with the pride she always gave her sons—even when they didn't deserve it.

He straightened. Normally nothing would have gotten between him and the scent of dark roasted coffee, but Russ sat there so quietly. So still. "Lightning?" Tyler started, and before the veterinarian could answer, adrenaline pooled.

"Stable," Russ said, but Tyler didn't relax, couldn't

relax, not when Russ sat in his kitchen in the predawn quiet. Coffee sat in front of him. It hadn't been touched.

"Lord of Spirits…" Tyler started, mentally inventorying the most significantly injured horses. "Shadow Flirt…"

Russ shook his head, stood. "All holding their own," he said in a curiously monotone voice. From the table he retrieved a single sheet of paper and handed it to Tyler. "But there's something you need to know."

Chapter Six

Tyler pounded on Sam's door. The sun had finally broken through the clouds, bathing the morning in a blistering, hazy heat. Already the cotton knit of his shirt clung to his back. The moisture gathering inside his cast was worse. It slipped and crawled like a mob of ants emboldened by the knowledge they could not be reached.

He lifted his fist and tried again. He'd been here for five minutes. Normally the door would have been opened by now. The housekeeper Mae was prompt like that. She never kept anyone waiting. But like Sam, Mae was on vacation.

Frowning, Tyler knocked harder.

Over the rustle of the warm breeze, Russ's words kept right on echoing. Tyler had stood there in the brightly lit kitchen, staring at the lab report—both of them. Russ had run the tests twice, just to be sure. Each time, the result had been the same.

Someone had drugged Lightning Chaser.

Cold fury boiled through Tyler. Someone had drugged his horse. Someone had pumped the big bay colt with a sedative, made him groggy, almost guaranteed he would never make it out of the barn alive.

They'd called the authorities. They'd filled in Hastings and the lead arson investigator, notified Beverly Morgan. They'd all made note of the information, but in their well-trained eyes, the presence of the narcotic didn't change their investigations. Anyone at Lochlain could have drugged the horse. In fact, Hastings pointed out, who else had that kind of access?

But for Tyler, the discovery changed everything.

He curled his fist and raised his hand, but before he could make contact, the door opened, and there she was.

She stood just inside the rustic foyer, with her blond hair tangled around her face and a huge, soft, pink T-shirt hanging from her shoulders. Her legs and feet were bare. But it was her eyes that got him, huge and bruised and glowing with a dark light that cut to the quick.

So did the scratches. The thin angry welts started at her jaw and streaked down the side of her neck, criss-crossed her arms.

He hadn't noticed them the night before.

"You're hurt," he said now, moving before thinking, stepping into the cool entryway and reaching for her. "What the bloody hell happened…"

Her eyes met his, and the rest of his question died.

They both knew what had happened.

"I'm fine," she said, but the rough edge to her voice told him her throat remained as raw as his. Dr. Baker said the discomfort could linger for days.

"Your arm," she said quietly, glancing at his cast. "I see you had it looked at."

"Broken," he confirmed.

She frowned. "I'm sorry."

"Look," he started, swiping the hat from his head. "We need to talk."

Her eyes sparked. It was the damnedest thing, but the soft little light punched him in the gut. "After last night—"

"Forget last night." The words scraped. "I was…" It was all a blur. The lead arson investigator had just finished questioning him. He'd checked on Lightning, was headed to the main house when he noticed the glow of lights from the office. And then he'd seen her, Darci, silhouetted through the window, and something inside him had tightened. She'd been there over eighteen hours. She'd stepped in wherever needed. Not once had she complained. Not once had she—

The dichotomy had rocked him. The spoiled girl he remembered from all those years ago…she'd been a master at finesse. She'd known how to work any situation to her advantage. Consequences had not mattered.

With the sun setting he'd pulled open the office door and stepped into the cool air-conditioning. He hadn't been sure why. He'd just wanted to see—

Her eager offer to make sure the party went on had stopped him cold.

"I was tired." He realized that now. At the breaking point. He'd been spoiling for a fight. And she'd been in the wrong place at the wrong time. "Not thinking clearly. I was out of my—" Mind. The word stuck in his throat.

But the understanding in the soft blue of Darci's eyes told him she knew exactly what he'd been about to say. "And now?"

She still had her hand on the door. It still stood open. She'd yet to ask him to stay.

"Now I'm thinking clearly," he said, crossing the hardwood floor to where she stood. Gently, he took the big oak door from her hand and eased it shut. "And I'm not going to run."

Blond hair spilled into her face. She pushed it back and looked up at him, somehow seeming small and fragile despite the stature she'd inherited from her father. Even as a teenager, she'd towered over her friends. "Run?"

That's what he'd been doing, he realized. Running... playing straight into someone else's hands. "We were warned," he told her, but even with the words, the memory, he couldn't quit staring at the freckles sprinkled across her nose, or the eyes without a trace of makeup. Blond, he noted. Her eyelashes were as blond as her hair.

It was the first time he'd seen her without makeup.

"We were warned to withdraw Lightning from the Outback," he said, finally making himself look away, beyond her to the main room of the house and the wall of windows to the rolling hills of Whittleson Stud. Sam had purchased the property several years back and had been carving out a nice niche for himself. Then Louisa Fairchild claimed ownership of Lake Dingo, Sam's main water source, and More Than All That was disqualified after the Queensland race.

"Someone thinks they can bully us," Tyler said. The way Sam had been bullied. His life had been trashed. According to Daniel, his father was on the verge of filing bankruptcy. "Someone thinks they can back me into a corner."

Darci stepped closer. "You were threatened?"

"Whatever you need," he detoured. He'd talked it over with his father and Andrew. They'd all agreed. "There *will* be a party at Lochlain," he said now, and the dark glow in Darci's eyes fed some place deep inside of him—some place he'd told himself he didn't want fed.

"The night after the Classic, Lochlain will be alive," he added, "and everyone will know fires can burn, but they cannot destroy."

Darci's smile was slow, hypnotic. For a long moment she just stood there in that oversize T-shirt of her alma matter, Oxford, so obviously just out of bed, and looked at him. Then she held out her hand. "Come with me."

More Than All That galloped around the exercise track. The racing board had banned the impressive black colt from competition, but Daniel said his father had not given up. Sam was convinced his horse had been targeted.

Just like Lightning Chaser.

The thought tightened through Tyler as Darci worked her way through scorched brown grass in need of mowing toward the far pasture where a sleek chestnut filly grazed. Darci hadn't spoken since she'd led him from Sam's house into the bright sunshine. She hadn't released his hand, either.

Five horses. That's all Tyler counted. The last time he'd been at Whittleson, the previous winter after the dispute between Sam and Louisa Fairchild had turned violent and Sam was short, there'd been over forty horses stabled here. More Than All That had been the crown jewel, but there'd been others with promise. The energy level had been palpable.

Now, it was almost a ghost farm.

The staff had been reduced. And the horses... In a cash-flow pinch after losing many of his boarders, Sam had been forced to sell the majority of his two- and three-year-olds, as well as three pregnant mares with distinguished bloodlines.

Tyler had tried to help. He'd purchased the mares, had made it known he would sell them back when Sam was ready. But Sam had just turned and walked brokenly away.

"It's sad, isn't it?" Darci asked, leading him toward the weathered white fence on the south side of the pasture. In the distance the land sloped, giving way to shade trees lining a dry creek bed. "Everything here just feels so… broken."

Tyler let out a rough breath. "Because it is." Whittleson Stud was on its last legs.

It was little secret Louisa Fairchild was waiting in the wings, ready to swoop in and stake claim to the beautiful slice of property separated from hers by only a lake—a lake, she claimed, that was on her property, not Sam's.

"You sound…" Darci stopped and turned, tilted her face toward his. "Oh, my God," she whispered, and he could see the light dawning in her eyes. "You don't think Uncle Sam did it, do you?"

He looked beyond her fiercely tilted chin to the overgrown pastures. Once the place had been meticulous. After working for other owners the majority of his life, Sam Whittleson had taken great pride in finally owning his own place, his own horses. And with the scandal, he'd lost more than just financial holdings—he'd lost the reputation he'd spent a lifetime building. His dream.

And there were those who maintained Tyler was responsible. That Tyler and Lochlain had been behind the drugging of More Than All That. That it had been the only way to ensure Lightning Chaser won the purse.

"Sam's not here," he muttered, looking back at the way the hot breeze played with Darci's hair. If he lifted his hand, he could catch it… "And I suppose there are those who would say that's awfully convenient." That Sam had gone on safari the very day of the fire at Lochlain. The arson investigator had insinuated as much.

"But he's also a horseman," Tyler said, and something

flickered in Darci's eyes. Once, Sam Whittleson had trained for Darci's father. That's why she called him uncle. There was no blood relation, just a warm affection left over from childhood.

"They're his life," she whispered with the wind pushing the hair over the scratches along her jaw.

"They are," Tyler agreed. Just as they were his. And they always had been. From the time he'd been a small boy, he'd had horses on the brain. All he'd ever wanted was to run Lochlain, to build on what his father had begun and establish the Preston name with the same pre-eminence it enjoyed in America. He'd never lost focus, never lost—

Except once. Once he'd lost focus.

"And I just can't see it," he said now. "I don't care how bloody damning the timing looks, there's no way Sam Whittleson would take his revenge out on my horses." The thought of Sam—of any horse person—lighting a match to a barn full of innocent horses just didn't compute.

"No, he wouldn't," Darci said. "He'd never do anything to jeopardize a horse—not yours, not his own."

"But someone did," Tyler said. "Someone drugged More Than All That—and someone drugged Lightning Chaser."

Her smile fell. "No…"

"Just found out this morning." He wasn't sure why he told her, but the words kept coming. "A sedative."

"Before the fire?"

He nodded.

"Dear God," she whispered. "Is that why he…"

Her words trailed off, but they both knew. They knew the question, and the answer. Yes. That was why Lightning had stayed in his stall.

"Tyler." She stepped into him and lifted a hand to his

arm. "I don't even know what to say. Who could do such a thing—and why?"

He looked beyond her to the sleek little filly in the pasture, and the first traces of recognition surfaced. Those white legs… "That's the question. The arson investigators are interviewing everyone at Lochlain." Taking fingerprints, checking backgrounds. The thought of someone on his own staff…

His arm, closed up in the cast, started to throb. "One of the grooms claims he saw a dark truck leaving just after the bullhorn first sounded." Driving fast, recklessly.

"Claimed?" Darci asked.

Tyler couldn't look away from the filly. She was a beautiful animal, tall and regal, with a tail a shade or two darker than the rest of her coat. She had her face up to the wind, almost as if she could hear what they were saying, and understood.

"No one else saw it," he said.

"Oh." Disappointment dulled Darci's voice. "But they're looking into it, right?"

"They are." The arson team had already asked Dylan Hastings to assemble a list of anyone in the Valley with a dark truck. They were also reviewing security feed from the previous two days. Anyone who'd visited Lochlain would be questioned and fingerprinted, as well.

"The grass should be greener," Tyler said, breaking from Darci and striding toward the shoddy fence separating them from the overgrown pasture. "You need to make sure someone runs the irrigation system."

Darci came up beside him. "They're down to once a week—it's not enough."

Lifting a boot to the bottom rung, Tyler watched the frisky chestnut dance with the wind. That was the only way to describe it. "That's her, isn't it?" The brash three-year-old Thoroughbred who was undefeated among her own gender. She crossed the dark gold grass and lowered her head toward Tyler, flirted with his hand. "That's your girl."

Darci joined him on the lowest plank and leaned forward. "She is," she said, taking the horse's face between her hands and pressing a kiss to the tip of her nose. "Sam's been training her the past few months."

Tyler eased back and watched them, wondered how it was he hadn't heard a word about a million-dollar racehorse arriving at Whittleson. As a two-year-old, she'd run exclusively with the girls, and won every time. She'd been a sure thing for Filly of the Year honors. Now, as a three-year-old, she'd only entered one race—a race she'd won running away.

"Word on the street is you won't go through with it," he mused, watching Darci slip the animal a peppermint—he didn't know when she'd picked it up. "Hear you're going to scratch her come race day." Speculation had it that the filly's entry in her first male-dominated race was just a publicity stunt.

Darci twisted to look at him, eyes glowing, that blond hair still smacking against her face and hiding any trace of the fire. She'd been pale when she answered the door. The scratches had looked garish against her face. But now, outside, with the sunshine glaring down on the two of them, the heat had brought color to her face. And her smile…

It was the same dare-me smile he remembered from all those years ago.

"Then they don't know me very well," she said, lifting a hand to Tyler. "Here," she said, producing another peppermint. Only then did he realize the oversize T-shirt concealed a pair of denim shorts. "You try."

* * *

She watched him. The bush hat shaded his face, but did nothing to protect the rest of his body. His white T-shirt clung damply to his body. With his faded work jeans riding low on his hips and the knee-high grass obscuring his boots, he lifted his hand to the horse her father had given her for her twentieth birthday, and waited. There was a still- ness to Tyler. Not the same awful shock from the day before, but a communion with the animal, a gentleness that stirred something inside her.

Darci's Pride wasn't as easy a mark. The filly with the attitude sniffed twice before lifting her big brown eyes to Tyler. She eyed him for a long charged moment before snatching the candy and turning back to Darci.

The laugh spilled out of her. "Brat," Darci said, running her hand over the filly's mane. She'd brushed her last night, long after Whittleson's remaining staff had gone to bed. She'd gone down to the stable and led the filly into the paddock, talked to her as she'd brushed. She'd wanted to ride—she'd *needed* to. The itch had almost been a pain.

But with the upcoming race, she knew better than to take her horse off routine. A ride at night was out of the question.

"She's ready," she said, loving the feel of DP's mane between her fingers. She'd hated being apart from her these past six months, while the horse had been training with Sam. "She wants to run with the big boys—show them what she's made of."

The second the words left her mouth, regret stabbed her. She looked from her horse to Tyler, and felt something inside her shift. He stood without moving, much as he had when he'd tried to woo Darci's Pride with a peppermint. Then his eyes had gleamed. Now, they burned. He stared beyond the horse to the parched, rolling hills of Whittleson Stud—hills much like those at Lochlain. But Darci knew he didn't see the trees and the brown grass, the glimmer of the lake against the hazy horizon.

He'd be seeing the boys, as she'd so callously referred to them. *His* boy. Lightning Chaser. Grazing quietly in a perfectly maintained pasture. Running with the wind. Standing tall and proud while a garland of roses was placed around his neck—

Her throat worked. "Tyler?"

He didn't move, just kept staring toward a cluster of gum trees. His shoulders were tight, his biceps tensed. She couldn't even begin to imagine what he had to be feeling, the horror and the loss, the grief. The fury. He would never say anything. He would never want anyone to know he was hurting. He was a man of focus, action. He would take all that boiling emotion he didn't know what to do with and refine it into something he could use.

His arrival at Whittleson Stud proved that. His surprising decision to move forward with the party. Most men would have—

Tyler Preston was not most men.

She knew better than to reach for him. She knew better than to touch. But she could no more just stand there and watch than she could force herself to stop breathing.

"Tyler," she said again, this time softer. Quieter.

And with the words, she touched. She lifted a hand to his, curled so tightly around the top fence rung, and squeezed. "I'm sorry."

His jaw, shadowed by a scattering of brown and gray whiskers, tightened.

"Maybe I shouldn't have brought you here," she pushed on. She hadn't been thinking, had just been reacting. When the urgent knocking had pulled her from sleep, she'd yanked on a pair of shorts and hurried down the stairs, never expecting to find Tyler standing on Sam's faded welcome mat. She'd spent the better part of the night preparing for the next time she saw him, but the sight of him standing there—

Her well-laid plan had crumbled.

Swallowing, she stepped closer. "I just thought—"

"Don't." His breath was harsh, the rise and fall of his shoulders tense. "Don't feel sorry for me, Darci. Don't think you have to treat me with kid gloves—"

"I don't."

He pivoted so quickly she had no time to prepare. From beneath the smoke-darkened rim of his hat, the deep green of his eyes burned. "Then why the bloody hell do you keep looking at me like that?"

Instinct told her to take a quick step back. Something else, a core of pride and determination forged by six long years in exile, would not let her. "Like what?"

The hot wind sweeping down from the bush pushed against him, but Tyler Preston was not a man to be moved. "Like you think I'm going to fall apart," he rasped, and his voice was lower than before, so rough and hoarse it hurt to hear. "Like you're scared that if you get too close—"

"I'm not scared." To prove her words, she stepped into him, as close as she could. The fronts of their legs brushed. The heat of his soaked into hers—the strength. "And I don't think you're going to fall apart."

He didn't step back, as she'd expected him to. He made no move to put even a sliver of space between them. He just stared down at her from beneath the brim of his hat, looking as if he had no idea whether to mutter in disgust, or crush her in his arms and kiss her until her bones melted.

He'd done that before—crushed her in his arms, kissed

her. Melted her bones. Her heart. And so much more. In his arms she'd forgotten everything she knew about common sense, everything she knew about right and wrong. She'd just…wanted.

Now, six years and so much growing up later, she'd promised herself she would never let anyone distract her like that again, not when she finally had her chance to take control of her life, to establish a career and earn respectability.

But she'd never counted on an inferno at Lochlain. And she'd never counted on Tyler Preston standing so close.

Or what she was about to do.

"That's why you're here," she said. "Because you're not going to let anyone drive Lochlain into the ground." Never looking away from his eyes—not sure she could if she tried—she slipped a hand beneath her shirt and withdrew the sheet of paper she'd grabbed on the way outside. The pen came next. "And I'm going to help."

His eyes narrowed. "Who are you?" he muttered softly, and for some crazy reason, she smiled.

Who was she? He was about to find out.

So were a lot of other people.

"If you'll just sign here," she said, folding the paper and pointing to the line with the X at the bottom.

He eyed her a long moment before obliging.

She watched him, watched the way his long, work-callused fingers curled around the pen, watched the strong, steady strokes of his penmanship.

"What is this?" he asked with just a hint of that roguish suspicion creeping into his voice, the kind of playfulness she remembered from his days as host of his own horse-manship show. He'd literally charmed the whole country. "Just what am I signing away?"

She swooped the contract from his hands and tucked it under her arm. "I'll tell you," she said, feeling the excitement shimmy into her eyes. "But it'll cost you."

His mouth flattened. "Cost me?"

"One dollar." She tilted her face toward the sun, felt the smile tug at her lips. She'd rehearsed it all the night before, the speech she would make, the case she would set forward.

She'd never imagined they would be like this, standing body to body, eyeing each other with a combination of suspicion and intrigue.

She'd never imagined that for a moment it would all fall away—the fire. The past.

She'd never imagined that it could.

"Can you handle that?" she found herself asking, smiling as she'd smiled at him so long ago, before everything had become so complicated. "A simple dollar?"

Eyes gleaming, he slipped a hand into his front pocket and pulled out a handful of change, isolated one dull gold coin. "That's not very much," he drawled. "Are you sure you don't want more?"

The curl of heat surprised her. "Just the coin."

He made a big show out of extending it toward her, handing it over.

She snatched it, shoved it into her pocket. Her heart slammed and her throat tightened, but she swallowed and pivoted back toward her horse, standing there so patiently, her ears perked, her tail swishing in the breeze. "She'll look good in blue and gold, don't you think?"

Beside her, Tyler stiffened. "I'm not following you."

She would not cry. She'd told herself that repeatedly. She would not let emotion seep into the detail. It was business, pure and simple.

"Darci's Pride," she clarified, and if her voice was thicker than she wanted, she blamed it on the lingering burn of smoke. "She'll look good in Lochlain colors."

Tyler's eyes met hers. Silently he reached for the paper tucked under her arm, and silently she handed it over. He looked down and unfolded it, started to read.

Chapter Seven

The wind kept blowing. A few birds chirped from a ghostly eucalyptus nearby. But other than that, there was only quiet, an odd tense quiet, broken only by the slam of her heart. She watched Tyler read the one-page contract she'd drawn up during the dark still hours of the night, when she'd finally given up on sleep. It wasn't until she'd committed the words to paper that she'd been able to let go and drift off.

Shoving at the hair slapping against her face, she lifted her chin and took a deep breath. "You need a horse, Tyler Preston," she said, and with effort, she forced the emotion from her words. "And I have one."

He looked from beneath the brim of his hat, his eyes dark, unreadable. "I can't accept this."

Beside them, Darci's Pride neighed curiously, and Darci's throat went a little tighter. She didn't look, though, didn't trust herself to. "Of course you can," she said briskly, professionally, as if they were discussing a simple business arrangement and not the sale of half ownership of the beautiful filly sired by the stallion who'd brought Darci's mother so much joy.

"Lochlain's going to have more than a party," she said, lifting her chin. "Lochlain Racing is going to have the winner of the Outback Classic."

Tyler's face remained unreadable. "My assets are frozen. I can't begin to afford—"

Before he could do something stupid like rip it up, she snatched the contract and held up the gold coin. "You just did."

Finally recognition narrowed his eyes. "Are you out of your mind? Darci's Pride is worth a million dollars, if she's worth a cent. You can't sell her to me for a—"

"Partial ownership," she corrected, refusing to feel the sting. "Fifty-one percent." Enough to let Lochlain take the glory. "And for the record," she added, "I've never been more serious in my life. I watched you yesterday." He'd been the quiet center of strength at Lochlain, keeping everyone strong and steady when it would have been easy to let things lapse into chaos. His family had been there for him, his parents and his brother, but in the end, it had been Tyler who'd been there for them.

She'd never felt more helpless in her life. But this she could do. This she could contribute. "I know how much you love your horses," she said. Any speculation that he was responsible for the fire was ridiculous. "You would never hurt them—or mine."

He turned from her, glancing toward the pasture where her prized three-year-old watched with great interest. "But Darci's Pride—"

She cut him off with a finger to his mouth. That's how close they still stood. She put her index finger to the fullness of his lips and pushed up on her toes, looked straight into the volatile green of his eyes.

"She'll do right by you," Darci said. "That I can promise. She's a tough girl. She'll make you proud."

Slowly he moved. Slowly he lifted a hand to her face and eased the hair back behind her ears, baring the scratches she knew not even makeup would hide. The backs of his fingers brushed the tender flesh, gently.

"I want you to be sure," he said quietly, and something inside Darci started to crumble.

She looked up at him, at the shadows playing in his eyes, the sliver of sunlight finding his mouth. Earlier, it had been a hard grim line. Now it looked wide and sensuous—just as she remembered. "I am."

Crazy, she added silently. She was irrevocably out of her mind to stand with her body pressed to his, so close she could feel his breath, the hard strum of his heart—and everything else, every hard muscle, every swell—

His hand slid deeper into her hair, and then he was moving, lowering his face toward hers as the cast encasing his left forearm slipped around her waist and urged her toward him.

Shock swept through her. Desire came in a hard, fast surge. The urge to lean into him and—

It had taken strength to sell Tyler partial ownership of Darci's Pride. It took something far more brutal to twist away and step back, to wrap her arms around her middle to hide the way her hands shook, and keep her voice brisk and airy, professional.

"I'll let you get back to Lochlain, then," she said, forcing her best all-business smile. "I know you have a lot to do, and

Andrew will be here soon." That was true. They had a strategy session. "I can't have him finding me like this, can I?"

Half-dressed in his cousin's arms...

Tyler's eyes darkened. "Would it matter?"

Briskly folding the contract, she looked up. "What?"

"Andrew." He swatted at a fly that had taken a sudden interest in his hat. "Would it really be a shock if he saw you like this, before you were dressed?"

The insinuation hung there between them, leaving a wobbly chill where moments before heat had smoldered. "He's my boss," she said simply. "I don't typically have business meetings in my pajamas."

The lines of Tyler's face tightened. "Somehow I don't think he'd fire you," he said, and for a stunning heartbeat, she wasn't sure if he was teasing or condemning.

"You're going to be okay, sweet girl...I just know you are," Heidi Hastings said. She stood with her arms around her cream sorrel, holding the filly with all the love and tenderness a parent would bestow upon a sick child. "You're a fighter," she whispered, and though she kept her voice strong, stoic, emotion leaked through. "You've always been a fighter."

Three hours after returning from Whittleson Stud, Tyler stood in the doorway to the equine-clinic-turned-sterile-I.C.U., where the most seriously injured horses were being cared for. Detective Hastings stood with his daughter while, two stalls over, a tall Spaniard gently brushed Lightning Chaser.

"Such a strong boy," Marcus Vasquez murmured. One look at the lanky trainer with the chiseled face and it was obvious Spanish blood ran in his veins. But his upbringing had been too continental for a distinct accent to form.

Only occasionally could Tyler detect it, when emotion swamped the normally reserved man who'd stood with Tyler three years before, when Lightning Chaser had been all gangly legs and newborn awkwardness. They'd watched the foal gallop away from his mother for the first time, and they'd both...known.

Much as Tyler had known the first time he'd seen Darci's Pride run. She was an impressive filly with the kind of raw athleticism that made a trainer's heart sing.

You need a horse, Tyler Preston—and I have one.

"That's my boy," Marcus crooned, tending Lightning with the same loving care Heidi lavished on Anthem. "I'll admit you had me worried, but I knew you'd fight like the champ you are."

Marcus had driven straight to Louisville the second he'd heard about the fire. He'd boarded the first flight possible. Once in Sydney he'd headed straight for Lochlain. All told, less than three hours had passed since he'd landed.

"There's nothing wrong with accepting a little TLC," he muttered, his strokes steady, sure.

In response, the big bay colt lowered his head and rubbed the side of his face against Marcus, just as he'd done every morning and evening for more than two years.

"Just a few more minutes," Tyler heard Detective Hastings tell his daughter. "Anthem needs her rest."

"Da..." Her voice, normally so resilient, bordering on adolescent defiance, wobbled on the word. "I can't just leave her—she needs me."

"She's getting the best care possible—"

"How could this have happened?" Long braids swinging, she pivoted toward her father. Tyler was pretty sure she didn't see him standing in the shadows. "I trusted them—I trusted *him*. How could they let this happen? How could a fire—"

"Easy now," her father tried, but Heidi was on a roll.

"I heard you on the phone," she blurted out. "I heard you talking about arson. Someone did this on purpose, didn't they? Someone tried to kill the horses—*my* horse."

Marcus froze.

Hastings moved closer to his daughter. "It is true there is evidence of arson," he said quietly. "But it's too soon to know anything definite yet. Every angle is being explored."

"You don't think he did it, do you?" The question practically exploded out of her. "Mr. Tyler? That's what Zach said, that his dad told him Mr. Tyler is at the top of the list of—"

"Heidi." Hastings's voice was hard, more that of a cop than father. "Not here."

Her chin came up in protest, but she said nothing, just glared at him a long moment before turning her attention back to the filly she'd rescued from a sure trip to the slaughterhouse the year before.

Hastings didn't move, didn't say another word, but Tyler had no doubt the by-the-book detective knew good and well that Tyler stood a stone's throw away and had heard everything. He watched father and daughter a second longer before crossing toward his former trainer. "How's he seem?"

Marcus shot Tyler a quick glance, but when he spoke, it was to the horse, not the man. "You get some rest now, big guy, you hear me?" He ran his hand toward a spot between the horse's ears, then scratched. "I'll be back before you know it with a surprise."

The big colt lowered his head, and after a long moment Marcus pushed away and strode toward Tyler. "Have you seen the office?" he asked, heading toward the back door of the medical facility. "It's like a bloomin' Hallmark store in there."

Tyler had never actually stepped foot in a Hallmark store, but he was familiar enough with the American card retailer to laugh. He *had* been in the racing office and he *had* seen the huge stack of cards and gift baskets overflowing Peggy's desk, and every other perch available. They were pouring in at a stunning rate, from all over the country. Schoolchildren had drawn cards with get-well messages. Racing fans had sent flowers and fruit baskets. There'd even been a delivery of muffins and scones that morning, for the exhausted staff.

Tyler had never seen anything like it.

But he had noticed his friend's evasion. "You didn't answer my question," he said as they exited the clinic into the afternoon sunshine. Wind blew hard down from the bush, for the first time allowing Lochlain to breathe without choking on the lingering stench of smoke. "What's your take on Lightning?"

Marcus stopped and turned toward the pile of charred rubble being picked over by the arson squad. It would be another day or two before the demolition team would be allowed to haul everything away.

"That horse is too smart," Marcus said. He'd always had a mysterious way with animals, part trainer, part whisperer. "Didn't want to scare him."

"You're worried."

"He's tough," Marcus said. "Always has been. But smoke inhalation is tricky. I've heard of horses appearing fine for four, five days before crashing."

Tyler's jaw tightened. "He's not going to crash."

"Of course he's not," Marcus said. "But the Hastings horse…" He shook his head. "That girl breaks my heart. She was singing to Anthem earlier, trying so hard to be brave, but I could hear how scared she is."

The girl had already lost too much in her short life. "She took in a lot of smoke," Tyler said. "It's a miracle she even made it out of there. The two horses we lost were in the stalls on either side of Anthem."

Marcus swore softly. "Bloody hell."

Tyler wasn't sure how Heidi's horse had made it out at all.

"Will you look at Shadow," Marcus said on a low whistle. "He's really coming along."

Tyler turned toward the paddock, where one of his youngest colts, a sleek snowy-white Thoroughbred born just that spring, frolicked with three small white butterflies. The land was parched, any grass without the luxury of an irrigation system was brown, fires were breaking out in the bush with alarming frequency. But Peggy had insisted on cultivating a patch of starflowers. She'd poured the seed and did the watering herself, nurturing the seedlings into big showy blooms of red and orange and yellow, growing wildly only a few meters from where Barn A had once stood.

And somehow the butterflies had found them.

The leggy colt ran freely around the perimeter of the paddock, his steps still on the gangly side, but Tyler could see the grace and promise just around the corner. "Loves to run, that one does," he said. "Daniel's got a real soft spot for him."

"As he should," Marcus said as the crunch of tires against gravel sounded from the long drive. "Give him a year or two and Lochlain will be right back at the—"

His words broke off, his eyes seeming to burn from the inside out. "Christ, Ty, who could do something like this? We worked so damned hard to build Lochlain, and now…"

Tyler glanced toward arson squad investigators, sitting in the shade talking to the new handyman. Reynard had repeatedly risked his life leading horses out of the barns, but because he'd only recently come to Lochlain, the investigators had taken a special interest in him. Beyond, in the parking area, a svelte little convertible eased to a stop, and Andrew slid out from the driver's side.

"We're not out of it yet," Tyler said as Darci emerged from the passenger seat, all fresh and showered, her hair shiny and twisted back into something smooth and stylish.

From this distance, he couldn't see the scratches.

He should have said no. Absolutely not. He should have torn the contract to bits and released it to the wind, walked away. That was his first reaction. He didn't need pity. He didn't need charity. He didn't need—

Her.

But then the horseman in him—the businessman—had taken over. "I bought a horse this morning," he told Marcus as Andrew put a hand to the small of Darci's back and steered her toward the office. "A filly."

He'd looked at the beautiful Thoroughbred he'd admired for over a year, and known what she could do for Lochlain. Darci was right. The stable needed a horse. Insurance money was frozen, and without barns, his boarding business was sidelined. And without cash flow there was no way to rebuild.

But with a horse in the Classic…a horse that had a legitimate chance to win…

Squinting against the hazy sky, Marcus eyed him. "You don't say."

He would sell her back. When Lochlain was up and running again… He would not be like Sam. He would not let stubbornness obscure his business sense.

He would not let pride destroy.

"Darci's Pride," he told Marcus, and though the big Spaniard rarely showed any emotion, his eyebrows lifted as he let out a low whistle.

"Last I checked it was hot enough to fry up an egg out here," he muttered. "Hardly the cold day in hell—"

Tyler killed the words with a freezing look. Marcus had been there six years before. He'd met Darci. He knew.

"You saw her then," Marcus said as Andrew emerged from the office and started toward them. Alone. "Somehow I'm guessing it wasn't old man Parnell who—"

"She's staying at Sam's place." And yes. He'd seen her. He'd seen her two days before in his office, looking beautiful and elegant, so bloody refined his breath had caught. Then he'd seen her the night of the fire, the morning after, dirty and grimy and dressed like a boy, and more than his breath had caught.

"That's right," Marcus said, lowering his voice as Tyler's cousin neared. Like Darci he'd cleaned up, his button-down shirt and slacks crisp and ironed, his face shaven.

"I heard she joined up with Andrew."

Tyler's jaw tightened.

"Andrew," Marcus greeted, extending his hand to his future brother-in-law.

"Is Mel here?" Andrew asked about his sister, the Kentucky Derby and Preakness winning jockey who'd fallen hard for the elusive Spanish trainer.

"In Kentucky, I'm afraid," Marcus said. "She sends her love but couldn't get away." With the Derby only a few months away, Melanie Preston was working hard to join the elite club of jockeys with multiple Derby wins.

Andrew nodded. "Something To Talk About really is," he said, referring to the horse Melanie had already ridden to several victories. Then, with his mouth pressed into a grim line, he dispensed with the small talk and turned toward Tyler.

"You need to see this," he said, handing over several sheets of paper.

Tyler took them and looked down at the neatly printed black words, started to read.

"Darci found them a little while ago," Andrew explained. "She was online checking something and ran across this blog...."

But one has to wonder. Given the scandals that have followed the Preston family around the globe, is a fire just a little too convenient? The Lochlain horses will never race again. Lightning Chaser will go out an untested champion. He'll never have to prove he won the Queensland on talent and determination rather than fraud. There will be no more races, no subsequent blood tests. No DNA tests. The Prestons will never have to prove the bay colt—or any of their horses—really are who they say they are.

Tyler looked up, wanted to slam his fist into something hard. "This is bullshit."

Marcus reached for the top page and let out another low whistle. "Goddamned vultures."

"A cover-up?" Tyler muttered, reading follow-up message board postings printed on the second page. The blog author was a well-known cynic of the horse racing community who never missed an opportunity to point out how crooked the sport had become. It was easy enough to ignore him. But the fact that other people actually believed him, thought a horseman would torch his own horses to cover his so-called tracks—blew him away:

* That whole family should be banned from racing, permanently, one poster wrote.
* Cowards, every one of them, another poster had added. Just in it for the money.

* The Americans let the Preston family off the hook. Justice won't be so paltry in Australia.

"I suppose it's to be expected," Andrew said, sounding every bit the candidate. "Even in America there are those who don't believe the family had no idea Leopold's Legacy was not sired by Apollo's Ice."

The scandal had rocked the Kentucky Prestons for months. Melanie had ridden her heart out in the Kentucky Derby and the Preakness, bringing a long-held dream home for the family, only to have it destroyed when a DNA test blew everything to hell and back. The horse had been stripped of its titles, the family banned from racing—until Andrew's brother Brent proved the deceit had originated elsewhere.

"Convenient my arse," Tyler bit out. Two and two were not adding up. His horse had been threatened, drugged. Even if Lightning Chaser had somehow escaped harm, the sedatives in his system would have ruined his chances at the Classic. And now some idiot was churning the rumor pit, trying to convict Tyler in the court of public opinion before the authorities could even finish their investigation.

There was a cover-up in progress, all right, but it wasn't Tyler doing the covering.

"Where's Darci?" he bit out, but before either man could answer, he was already striding toward the office.

Chapter Eight

They'd worked until midnight. They ordered DNA testing on Lightning Chaser and Shadow Flirt and Morning Glory, all the Lochlain horses who'd ever run publicly. Dr. Chaplain was transporting samples to the lab in Sydney himself.

Shortly after seven, Daniel's wife, Marnie, a public relations specialist, arrived at the office, and together, they drafted a press release. That's how Darci and Marnie viewed it.

To Tyler, it was a cold hard dare.

"We're going to smoke them out," he'd quietly promised, going on the offense rather than staying on the defense. He'd rolled up his shirtsleeves and carefully considered every word Marnie and Darci crafted. He'd reviewed the guest list for Andrew's gala, adding several key members of the media. He'd beefed up the menu, requested that an additional photographer be on hand.

And all the while, Darci had kept a brisk, professional

persona in place, just as she did while working with Andrew. But deep inside, surprise had quickly given way to something far more unsettling.

He'd come for her. After he'd read the negative message board postings she'd pulled from the Internet, his first thought had not been to find Peggy or Marnie…but Darci. He'd told her his plan. He'd wanted her opinion. Her assistance.

He. Tyler. Had turned to her.

Even as the sun began to rise the next morning, the memory of him striding into the small conference room with his hat low on his head and his jaw unshaven, his clothes sooty and his boots covered with dust, still made her heart beat low and hard and fast. Once Tyler Preston had dominated her world, but she realized now it had been the thought of him more than the reality, the roguish image he'd presented through his cable show on horsemanship. Their affair had been brief and daring and forbidden. They'd been lovers, but strangers in so many ways.

This, she realized, watching Tyler in quiet conversation with Daniel and Marcus near the paddock, where a gangly chestnut foal named Dare Me frolicked with his mother. This quiet, grown-up intensity was far more dangerous than all the fireworks in the world.

As if sensing her thoughts, he looked up and caught her eyes, broke from the two trainers and made his way toward the parking area. "You're early," he said by way of greeting.

She found her best all-business smile and opened the door to the horse trailer. "Wanted to get her here before it got too hot," she said as Darci's Pride turned around and moved cautiously toward the open door. The filly stretched her neck and looked around, but made no move to exit.

"Well, good morning there, gorgeous," Tyler drawled, his voice still rough from smoke. "I'm thinking I must just be the luckiest bloke in the whole Valley," he went on, slipping a hand into his front pocket and pulling out two peppermints.

He'd remembered.

"Got up before the sun this mornin' to make sure everything was just perfect for you," he added as he offered the filly one of the treats. She sniffed once, then snatched the candy before lifting her big chocolate eyes to Tyler.

Yesterday she'd been cautious. Yesterday she'd been standoffish. She'd held herself back from the man, not just another pretty face to succumb to his charms. But this morning...

This morning Darci's Pride was all his.

"What a good girl," he kept on, his hands joining his voice. He touched her now, ran his hands along her shiny coat slowly. Softly.

Skillfully.

And the band around Darci's chest tightened. This was what they'd agreed on, that the horse would relocate to Lochlain. It was more of a statement that way, made the deal more real. And she'd get better care here, more attention. With Sam on safari, only a skeleton crew remained at Whittleson Stud. Despite the loss of two barns and all the horses that had been relocated to neighboring farms, Tyler was determined not to lay off any of his staff. Lochlain was swarming with talented horse people just waiting to cater to Darci's Pride's every whim.

Bringing her here, leaving her here, was the right thing to do. Darci knew that. But something hard and sharp lodged in her throat anyway.

"How 'bout I show you around?" Tyler asked as he kept right on stroking the animal. "Help you get settled in?"

The memory struck, rolled through Darci like hot lazy

waves on a warm summer day. Those hands, large with blunt-tipped fingers and square palms—talented. Gentle. Moving along her body, featherlight. Stroking. Teasing.

Possessing.

"All ready?"

She blinked, and by sheer force of will made herself look away from his hand, battered now, still covered by scratches and a few minor burns.

"Looks like my pep talk worked," she said with the cardboard smile she'd perfected in London, standing in a stupidly expensive gown and welcoming her father's guests into their Hyde Park townhome, trying not to think of who *should* have been standing by her father's side....

Tyler's eyes met hers, and for the first time since she'd surprised him in his office several days before, the dark green glimmered with something that could only be called warmth.

"Darci," he said, and the rhythm of her heart changed, deepened. "I need you to be sure."

Early-morning sun beat down against her neck, bared by the long braid hanging down her back. Already, her skin burned.

"I am," she said, just as she had six years before, when he'd leaned over her, hot and hard and spectacularly naked. Then he'd held her hand, his fingers curled with hers.

The memory glowed in his eyes, but before he could say anything, the moment passed and Daniel and Marcus were there.

"Well, hell, Tyler," Marcus said, producing a peppermint from the pocket of his handyman-like vest. "You told me she was a looker but you didn't tell me she was a heartbreaker."

Daniel, too, couldn't keep his hands off the horse. "You're a lucky girl," he cooed. Along her neck, his strokes were steady and sure. "We're going to take such good care of you at Lochlain."

Darci stepped back and watched, slid the sunglasses from the top of her head over her eyes…so no one else could see. She didn't want them seeing her, didn't want them seeing the moisture flooding her eyes as the three men led her horse toward her new home.

But to see, one of them would have needed to glance back—and none of them did.

She stood there with the warm wind swirling dust around her, until one of the last tangible links to her mother disappeared inside the barn…and her phone started to ring.

Absently she brought it to her ear and pushed the talk button, expecting to hear the caterer's voice, or that of journalist Julia Nash who'd recently completed a favorable piece on the Kentucky Prestons. Marcus's fiancée, Melanie, had arranged for her friend to write a follow-up piece on how the Australian Prestons were working to overcome the fire.

"Hullo," she greeted, but the second she heard the distinguished voice boom out her name, she braced herself, knowing all hell was about to break loose.

The afternoon passed in a blur. The arson team completed their assessment of the rubble, clearing the way for demolition to begin. By five o'clock the heavy equipment arrived, a dump truck and an excavator, as well as several other smaller motorized vehicles. With Tyler and the lead arson investigator, the foreman walked the perimeter of the area still cordoned off with crime-scene tape. There was a process for removing the debris. Everything would be taken into Pepper Flats, where it would be stored until the investigation was closed—just in case.

By six o'clock the excavator began scooping up the remains of Barn A.

It all seemed so matter-of-fact.

"I'll want pictures of the barns before," Julia Nash, his cousin's journalist friend, said sometime later. With the long shadows of early evening falling around them, she stood with Tyler, a hand lifted to shield her eyes from the setting sun. Soon work would stop for the day. "Showing before and after pictures will drive home the magnitude of what happened here."

Tyler nodded. They had pictures. His mother had taken them. They lined the walls of the short hallway in the office, documenting Lochlain's evolution from a virgin parcel of rolling hills through the construction of first one barn, then another. Then, finally, the third. "Peggy can help you with that."

"This is a beautiful place you have here," Julia said, glancing around. "I'm sure my readers will be quite sympathetic."

It wasn't sympathy he wanted. Rather, he had a statement to make. But he didn't say that. Julia had traveled halfway around the world to help. He didn't need to alienate her—no matter how trite he found all the posing for pictures he'd been doing most of the afternoon.

Around him, the day wound down. Sulphur-crested cockatoos screeched in the paling sky, kookaburras made their raucous laughing call as they settled. The rare bull-frogs made the owl-like call as the crickets bade the sun good-night.

Marcus stood alongside the practice track, where Daniel worked with one of the older colts. He was still half a year away from racing, but it was a start. Peggy remained in the office, buried by the mountain of get-well cards and gift baskets for Lightning Chaser. His parents and Andrew had headed back to Sydney, while Darci…

He didn't know where she was.

The last time he'd seen her…

He wasn't sure when that was, either. She'd been with Peggy earlier, and Andrew before he'd left. But—

He frowned. Her horse trailer remained in the parking area….

"…such a tragedy," Julia was saying when his mobile phone started to ring. He grabbed it and glanced at the caller ID box, went very still when no name or number stared back at him.

"Talk to me," he said by way of greeting.

The voice that replied was sexless, almost mechanical. "Don't do it."

He turned from the journalist and took a few quick steps toward a gum tree. "Do what?"

"Darci's Pride…don't do it." And then the contorted voice fell into silence, and Tyler stared into the gathering darkness.

Game. On.

She needed to go. The sun had set, the day was over. She'd done what she'd come to do. She'd brought Darci's Pride to Lochlain. She'd made sure she got settled in. She'd stood back and watched, approved of what she'd seen.

Now it was time to go.

"You're going to be just fine," she promised the mischievous filly who'd fallen under Tyler Preston's spell in less than twenty-four hours. He'd saddled her earlier and taken her for an easy ride around the exercise track, just to get a feel, he said.

Now, in the shadows of the spacious stall Tyler had

given her horse, Darci ran her hands along the filly's face and knew she had to leave.

"Tyler will take wonderful care of you," she said. "You'll be the princess of Lochlain." But even as she spoke, her father's words burned. He'd been incredulous at what he called an ill-advised stunt. He'd demanded that she break the deal with Tyler and return Darci's Pride to Whittleson Stud. He'd accused her of playing games—just like before.

Quietly, she'd reminded him that Darci's Pride was her horse, not his.

But saying goodbye… She closed her eyes and sucked in a deep breath, stepped into the horse and curved her arms around the filly's neck. But in the darkness of her mind, it was another horse she saw, another woman who embraced it.

"I'll be back in the morning," she promised, just as her mother had. But there would come a day when she would have to say goodbye for good.

Just like her mother had.

Darci's life was not in the Valley. Her life was…

She wasn't sure where her life was anymore.

But it wasn't here. She did know that.

"You just get some sleep now, okay, sweetest-heart? And when you wake up, Tyler will be here—"

The quick streak of longing stunned her. She'd woken up to Tyler once. She'd awakened to the warmth of his body beneath hers, his hand skimming along her back, his mouth pressing a soft kiss to—

"Darci."

Just her name, that was all he said, but the sound of his voice, quiet, rough, curled through her like the shot of brandy she'd sneaked from her father's liquor cabinet on her fifteenth birthday.

She stood there a long moment, not trusting herself to

turn, but knowing she had to. Earlier she'd had her sunglasses. Earlier she'd been able to shield her eyes from him. Now she knew the second she turned, he would see.

"Look at me."

Her throat tightened. Before, his quietly coaxing words had been for her horse. Now they were for her.

She didn't want to turn. She didn't want to see. But she knew Tyler Preston. She'd watched him the past few days, had seen the way he managed Lochlain. He wasn't a man to be pushed aside. He didn't back down when he wanted something.

And if she didn't turn around, he would step closer— and touch.

Slowly she pulled back from her horse and turned, found Tyler and one of the border collies standing just inside the stall. Behind them, fluorescent lighting lit the corridor, but beyond, there was only darkness and quiet. Somewhere along the line the awful demolition equipment had fallen silent.

"You're crying."

Her chin came up. She blinked furiously and forced a smile, tried for a laugh. "Allergies," she said, but knew he wouldn't believe her. For effect, she wrinkled her nose. "Smoke."

His eyes, shadowed by the brim of his dusty hat, took on an unsettling glow. "I meant what I said earlier." And then damn him, he started to move. He crossed to her, lifted a hand to the horse's side. "You don't have to do this."

"I know, I know," she said as the dog ambled over and rubbed her legs. "You have plenty of help. One of the grooms can—"

"Darci." This time, with her name came his hand, softly to the side of her face. "Don't."

She stopped and looked up at him, felt her eyes start to burn.

"Don't pretend," he said. "A blind man could see this is killing you."

The walls of the stall pushed in on her. Wedged there between horse and man, she had nowhere to hide. Tyler was too close, and saw too much.

"I was there when she was born," she said, realizing Tyler Preston would accept nothing but the truth. "I was the first human to touch her."

"That's a special bond."

"We were in England," she added. "I was at Oxford." Her father hadn't wanted her to leave her studies, not even for a day. But she'd befriended one of the grooms, who'd notified her when the mare's time was near. "I got to Cheveley Park with only a few hours to spare.

"And as soon as I saw her, I knew," Darci told him, the words coming easier now. Too easy. "It was as if Outback was being born all over again."

Against the side of her face, Tyler's hand stilled. "Your mom's horse."

"Yes," she whispered. Outback Pride had been a gorgeous horse, a chestnut just like his offspring. In his day he'd dominated the racetrack, winning races in England and Sydney and Dubai, running a thrilling race at Churchill Downs only to place second by a breath. Ten years ago he'd retired to stud in England, where he'd sired an impressive array of colts and fillies, many of whom had followed in his legendary footsteps.

The little filly with the sassy tail born that April evening had been his last. The big stallion had succumbed to a sudden case of laminitis less than a month after Darci's Pride was conceived.

"I saw him run once," Tyler said as the dog finally lost interest and wandered off. "In the Golden Slipper."

Swallowing against the rush of memories, she looked up—and Tyler's hand fell away. He'd never told her that before. But then, he'd had no reason to. She'd lied to him all those years ago, told him her name was Tara. He'd had no idea she was Weston and Anne Parnell's daughter—and therefore no reason to talk to her about Outback Pride.

"Ran like the wind," Tyler drawled, and something inside Darci stirred. She was an Aussie by birth, had grown up here in the sunburned land her mother had so loved. But she'd been in England for the past six years, living the life of a diplomat's daughter, with all the unending formality of teas and parties and balls.

But now, here, as she stood in the shadows of Lochlain's remaining barn, the cadence of Tyler's accent—the sound of memory and dreams and home—washed through her.

"My mother loved that horse," Darci said. "His bloodline had been in her family for years. She was there when he was foaled, just like…" She glanced at the horse, standing so quietly, but with her ears perked as if she understood every word they said. "She trained him herself."

"I remember," Tyler said. "My father used to talk about your mom, took me to meet her one time when I was a kid. I—"

Without thinking, Darci grabbed his free arm—and found a cast instead. "How old?"

"How old?" he repeated. "I don't know, fifteen maybe. Sixteen. I just remember—"

"What?" The word practically burst out of her. "What do you remember?"

Darci's Pride whinnied into the silence, but Tyler made no move to acknowledge or comfort her, no move to look away from Darci. "You weren't even ten years old, were you?" he whispered, and all that emotion, all that hard, dark, jagged emotion she'd been fighting all day surged against her throat. She tried to turn away, but his hand caught her arm and held her. "I remember my dad telling me about the accident," he said. "It was autumn…I'd just come in for dinner—we were leaving the next morning for America, to see the Derby." His eyes darkened. "Fourteen years ago."

Deep inside the shaking started, the violent rock slide of memory she'd so diligently walled away, crashing down in full awful force. "I was nine," she said. "She wasn't even thirty."

Shadows played against the lines of Tyler's face, bringing with them a sorrow that rocked her. "She was beautiful," he said, his hand finding hers. "Just like you."

"I…" She closed her eyes, could see the blond hair and thin figure…but nothing else. "I don't remember," she whispered, opening her eyes to Tyler. "After she died…my father took all her pictures and donated her clothes to charity…." Essentially wiping Anne Parnell away as if she'd never existed.

Once Darci had realized what he was doing, she'd sneaked into their bedroom and nabbed the bottle of perfume her mother had worn every morning. For a long time she'd kept it between her mattresses. Then, one morning she'd dabbed it behind her ears. She didn't think her father had noticed, until she'd found him later, hunched over his desk, crying.

She'd never worn the perfume around him again.

"You remind me of her."

She lifted her eyes, felt the echo of longing, deep, deep in her bones. "Tell me."

"Your spirit," he said. "Your tenacity."

"You mean my stubbornness," she corrected.

A grin split Tyler's face. "Stubbornness," he conceded. "Grit, determination—she'd be proud of the woman you've become."

The words swirled around her. "When we moved to London I found a shoe box in the back of my closet. There were cards inside, dating back to the day I was born." She'd sat down and started to read, every single one of them. Even now, six years later, the shock of discovery still had the power to unravel her. "She'd written them—she'd written to me even before I was born."

Tyler's hand tightened against hers. "That sounds like her."

"But I don't remember," Darci said. "I read the words…I know she must have spoken them to me herself…I know she sang to me, read me stories—my nana told me that—but I don't remember. Sometimes at night I still wake up—" Cold as ice because she couldn't remember what color her mother painted her fingernails or her favorite shade of lipstick. "Her voice," Darci whispered. "I don't remember her voice."

Tyler moved so swiftly she had no time to prepare. In one fluid motion he stepped into her and pulled her into his arms, the warmth of his chest pillowing the side of her face. She stood there, stunned, aching, listening to the steady rhythm of his heart, knowing she should step away, but barely trusting herself to so much as breathe.

"It was warm," he said, running a hand along her back. "I remember that. Your mother had a warm voice. When she talked it was as if laughter ran just beneath the surface."

Darci closed her eyes.

"She had a way of making you feel like you were special, that at that moment in time, she was giving all of her attention to you."

Slowly Darci tilted her face to his. "Thank you," she whispered.

Their eyes met, and once again his hand slid to cup the side of her face. "It's not goodbye," he murmured, and she blinked.

"Goodbye?"

"That's why you were crying, isn't it? Bringing Darci's Pride here—*leaving her here...*"

The denial came hard and fast—not because he was wrong, but because he was right. And she didn't want that from him, she didn't want Tyler Preston to see and to know, to understand. She didn't want—

"I have to go," she said, all but ripping herself from his arms. She stepped back from him and pivoted toward her horse, gave the curious animal a quick kiss before reaching for her satchel and slinging it over her shoulder. "It's late and I'm due in Sydney in the morning." She had a press conference planned for Andrew, a speech to write, more appearances to schedule prior to the Outback Classic the following weekend. "DP likes to be brushed in the mornings," she said into the silence. All the while Tyler just stood there and watched with the oddest expression on his face. "I'll call you sometime tomorrow afternoon...."

His mouth curved. "Of course you will," he said, and then, because there was nothing else to say, she gave him a brisk polite smile and slipped past him, into the corridor, the night.

But long after she'd left Lochlain behind, his words whispered through her, and his touch still burned. Biting down on her lip, her heart beating too fast, Darci turned into Whittleson Stud and forced herself to think about what the sunrise would bring, not what nightfall had revealed.

In the morning she would head to Sydney, back to Andrew. She would get to work, do what she'd returned to Australia to do: get on with her life, her career. Show

everyone that she wasn't that reckless, spoiled child anymore. That she was a responsible woman, capable of far
more than planning teas and dinner soirees.

There was no room for Tyler Preston in her plans.

Resolved, she locked up the truck and headed for the
yellow glow of the wide front porch. On the far side sat
several rocking chairs; empty now, they swayed with the
warm evening breeze.

The noise stopped her. She held herself still and listened,
heard nothing but the sounds of the land. A quick glance
confirmed everything was quiet and still. Continuing up the
steps, she reached the door—and saw the note.

A rusty nail held the single sheet of paper to the middle
of the door. A picture of Darci's Pride in full glorious stride
stared back at her, along with three crudely written words:

Don't. Do. It.

Darci's heart kicked hard. She spun around and fumbled
inside her satchel, kept her eyes on the night as she retrieved her mobile phone and stabbed out a familiar series
of numbers.

Chapter Nine

Against the night, the house glowed.

Tyler slammed on the brakes and jammed his ute into Park, threw open the door and ran into the darkness. In the distance bushfires painted the horizon in an eerie orange hue, spewing the faint pall of smoke across the entire Upper Hunter. An abandoned homestead had been destroyed. Hundreds of acres—normally verdant and beautiful, now parched and otherwordly—were at stake. All able-bodied volunteer firefighters had been summoned.

But Tyler veered in the opposite direction.

At the dimly lit porch he took the three steps in one and reached the door, didn't bother to knock or wait for someone to answer. He pushed inside and crossed the foyer—heard the voices.

He found them in Sam's sprawling great room, sitting on the old leather sofa. Darci sat tall, her long braid hanging down her straight back and her knees together, her hands clenched tightly in her lap.

Dylan Hastings sat by her side, talking in a low, soothing voice. "…don't see any sign of anyone on the property," he was saying. Tyler saw the gun in the holster around the cop's shoulder. "But it would be best if you didn't stay here alone tonight."

"She can stay with me," Tyler said, stepping into the room. His boots came down hard against the old tile floor, bringing him around the sofa to where Darci twisted toward him.

"Tyler, what are you doing—"

"Daniel called me." He'd just stepped out of the shower when the phone rang. He'd stood there, wet and naked, listening to his trainer's agitated voice. One of his mates had been at the bushfire with Hastings when the triple-0 call came in, something about a break-in at Whittleson Stud.

"What the hell happened?" Tyler wanted to know, going down on one knee. "Are you hurt? Did—"

"I'm fine."

But Tyler took her hands anyway—and saw the sheet of paper sitting in the plastic bag between her and Hastings.

"Son of a bitch," he swore, looking up to meet the cop's eyes. They'd discussed Tyler's plan to run Darci's Pride in the Classic the night before, had agreed it might be their best shot of flushing out whoever had drugged Lightning Chaser and lit a match to Lochlain's barns. "They weren't supposed to involve her."

Hastings frowned. "She's the one who sold you the horse," he pointed out. "It makes an odd kind of sense."

"Involve me?" Long wisps of hair brushed against Darci's mouth. "Involve me in what?"

"The threats." The words were simple, but the suspicion

in Darci's eyes deepened. A few hours before, they had been the eyes of the little girl who'd lost her mother too early. Who'd forgotten too much—and had no way of getting it back.

But they were a woman's eyes now, dark, intelligent, filled with dread and growing realization.

"We figured whoever went after Lightning might not take kindly to Lochlain having another contender in the Classic," Tyler said, carefully measuring his words. "We wanted to make sure they knew, to draw them out of hiding—"

"Bait," Darci whispered as the color leached from her face. "You're using my horse as bait."

The ugly word struck like a punch to the gut. "She's safe," he assured. "She's under twenty-four-hour surveillance." But Darci wasn't. Darci wasn't safe. He'd left her alone, let her go back to Whittleson, where only a skeleton crew remained. "You have every right to be angry—"

She stood and crossed to the wall of windows, overlooking the red glow on the northern horizon. There, she pivoted back to the men. "But it doesn't make any sense. If someone wants to hurt Darci's Pride, why would they send a note? Why would they *tell* us?"

Tyler pushed to his feet. "When More Than All That was disqualified from the Queensland and Lightning took the purse, a lot of people lost a bundle." And Lochlain had profited.

Enormously.

"You think someone is trying to punish you?" Darci asked.

"Or keep Lochlain out of the Classic," Hastings put in. "Make sure he doesn't have a horse to run...make sure he has no way to recover financially."

"What if it's a warning?" she asked. "What if they were all warnings?"

Tyler and Hastings exchanged a quick look.

"The note you told me about," she said. "The one that came before the fire. And this one," she added, glancing at the plastic bag.

And the phone call he'd received, the one only he and Hastings knew about. Then, that afternoon, it had all seemed like a game.

"What if someone knows something and they're trying to *warn* you, not threaten you?"

"Works the same either way," Hastings said. "If someone makes a move on Darci's Pride, we'll catch them."

Tyler watched the play of emotion across Darci's face, the understanding and the fear, the unease. And he couldn't do it, couldn't just stand there coldly and callously, as if this really were some bloody inconsequential chess match.

"You can say no." He crossed to her and took her hands, hated how cold they were. Hated that she'd come back to Whittleson alone, hated the thought of her finding the note and not knowing—

That she'd turned to Hastings…

"You can say no and we stop. We withdraw Darci's Pride from the Classic and tear up the bill of sale, bring her back to Whittleson. Everything goes back to the way it was—"

"And whoever hurt Lightning goes free." The soft words were hard as steel.

"Not necessarily," Hastings said, standing. "The investigation is still open. We've got several leads on the truck seen leaving Lochlain and are interviewing everyone who was at the farm in the days leading up to the fire. Someone saw something," he added, and his eyes went hard. "There's no such thing as a perfect crime."

"But with Darci's Pride," she said. "If we can smoke someone out…"

Her words dangled in the sudden silence, her eyes meeting Tyler's.

"It's what my mother would have done, isn't it?"

Tyler sucked in a sharp breath. He looked at her standing there in the low riding jeans and loose-fitting cotton shirt she'd worn over to Lochlain that morning, at those wide courageous eyes and the hair slipping from her braid…her dry parted lips and the stubborn tilt to her chin—and saw an ache he'd never seen all those years ago.

He wasn't sure how he'd missed it.

They'd made love. Several times. She'd blazed into his life like a Roman candle, and he'd drunk greedily, taking what she offered, wanting more. Craving more. They'd talked, they'd spent some quiet time together, but now he realized that he'd never really known her.

Never really seen her.

He saw her now, not the heiress or the Oxford graduate, the socialite whose daring smile could electrify a room—but Anne's daughter, the young girl who'd grown up too soon.

"Yes," he said, because she knew the truth anyway, would see through the lie. She knew the truth because Anne had given her that—bravery, loyalty, honor—even if Darci could no longer remember her mother's voice. "It's what your mother would have done."

"Then we move forward," she said, jaw still at that fierce angle, her blue eyes alight with a glow that rivaled that of the bushfires. "We take every precaution, we keep my girl, *our girl*," she corrected, "safe, and we nail the bastard who did this to you."

We. The word slipped through Tyler like something dark and illicit—and for the first time in six years, all that focus, that rigid discipline upon which he relied, blurred.

* * *

"You really don't have to stay here. I'm fine."

"Then get your bag. We've got plenty of room at Lochlain—"

"No. That's not necessary. Dylan said—"

"This isn't about Hastings. It's about you, and me, and a chance I'm not going to take."

The force of the quiet words stopped Darci cold. She stared up at Tyler, at the hard lines of his face and the un-yielding blue of his eyes, and realized she'd have better luck shoving up against a mountain.

"Tyler." For effect, she stripped the defiance from her voice. "I appreciate what you're doing." She did. The sight of him striding into Sam's house, hair damp and curling at the nape, his steps purposeful, still had her pulse humming. "But…"

She'd left Lochlain for a reason. She'd pulled herself from his arms and walked away, driven away, not allowed herself to look back. Because if she'd stayed, if she'd let him touch her for one second longer, the years would have fallen away and she would have been seventeen again, reckless, willful, concerned only with what she wanted, consequences be damned.

Consequences had damned, all right.

"But nothing." Moving past her, he crossed to the rustic kitchen desperately in need of updating. It was done all in browns, and not the pretty modern browns, either. These were dark browns, with a hint of orange thrown in. The range was clean, but ancient. The refrigerator was round-edged and white. Posted to it were newspaper clippings leading up to the Queensland Classic.

But none from the fallout that followed.

Tyler stopped abruptly and turned. "Unless you'd rather me call Andrew," he said with deceptive gentleness, and something inside her twisted.

"He's in Sydney—" she started, but Tyler did not let her slip off the hook that easily.

"He'd come," he said, standing there so still, watching her, assessing. "If he knew you were in trouble—"

"I'm not in trouble."

"If I told him what happened—"

"Don't." This time it was she who moved, she who crossed the cold tile and reached for his wrist. The sleeves of his black button-down were rolled up, bringing her palm in contact with the warmth of his skin. "Don't call Andrew." He was her boss, the first one to give her a chance. He'd hired her to run his campaign—not so he could come riding to her rescue.

"It's me or him," Tyler said into the stillness, and just as it always did when he looked at her like that, all focused and concentrated, as if she were the only woman in the world, her blood heated.

With insidious precision, Tyler Preston had just backed her into a dangerously tight corner.

She couldn't choose Andrew. She couldn't ask Tyler to call his cousin. Because Tyler was right. Andrew would come. He was that kind of man, a Preston down to the bone—caring, loyal, steadfast. He treated his employees like equals. Integrity ran like fire in his veins. That's why it was so vital that he defeat Jacko Bullock.

But Darci did not want him to think of her as anything other than his capable, dedicated campaign manager.

But to say Tyler...to choose Tyler...

She lifted her chin, acutely aware of the pulse point

throbbing in his wrist just beneath her thumb. "Don't call Andrew." Those were the only words she would allow herself to say—what she did not want. What she did want—

"Then you'll come back to Lochlain with—"

"No." Because the word shot out of her, she softened it with a smile. "That's what they want," she said. "Whoever sent that note. To scare us. To bully us. If we play into their hands…" She let the words dangle for a long heartbeat. "They've made their move," she added. "Now it's time for mine."

Tyler frowned. "You make it sound like a game."

"Not a game." Not even close. "But whoever sent that note would be crazy to make another move tonight—and if they do—" she looked up "—we'll be ready."

He let out a rough breath, but when his eyes met hers, they were steady. "You've thought this through."

"I have," she agreed.

And something about him changed, shifted. "Then sit," he stunned her by saying, and with the words he gestured toward the butcher-block table in the breakfast nook. She'd placed a vase of white and yellow wildflowers in its center the day before. Now they'd wilted. "And let me fix you something to eat."

Darci blinked. He made it sound so simple. *Sit. Let him fix her something to eat.*

She *was* hungry. It had been hours since the late-afternoon granola bar she'd shared with Darci's Pride. But this was Tyler Preston dominating Sam's small kitchen, and the thought of playing house—

She'd be better off walking straight into the bushfire blazing to the north.

She'd thought she could skim the perimeter of his life.

She'd thought she could shine a spotlight on Lochlain without brushing up against the man. But that, she realized now, was her fateful mistake.

Lochlain was the man—and the man was Lochlain. It was Tyler's blood and sweat that pulsed like a lifeline through the lush, Hunter Valley farm. It was the man who made Lochlain work, the man who held it all together—and it was the man she faced now in the shadows of Sam's out-of-date kitchen, the man wearing the dark shirt open at the throat, the cast on his arm, the low-riding, ridiculously well-fitting jeans.

But it was the past she had to confront.

"Why?" She hated the harshness of the question but refused to let him see. Let him know. "Why are you doing this?" she asked, gesturing toward the eggs and cheese he'd taken from the sparsely stocked refrigerator. "Why do you…"

Care. The word jammed in her throat—she wouldn't let it out. "…have to be so stubborn."

The corners of his eyes crinkled with a smile that sent her heart into a long, slow free fall. "Because you're hungry?"

She refused to let her mouth curve, even as she silently damned that blunt Aussie charm he had down to a raw art form. She'd dated in England. She'd tried. But no one had made her laugh the way Tyler had…no one had made her feel *alive.* "You know that's not what I mean."

With an infuriating insouciance, he turned from her and opened the drawer beneath the range, fumbled around and pulled out a skillet. The burner came next, the skillet over the flame, three eggs cracked over the edge. "What kind of man would I be if I just left you—"

"Tyler." Her voice was quiet, steel. But her bones wanted to melt. "Stop."

He lowered the heat and put down the spatula, turned

toward her. And while the simple recessed lighting brought highlights to his hair, shadows played like a dare in his eyes.

"You were young," he said without preamble, and her heart slammed hard against her ribs. "Just a kid."

She'd rehearsed this, planned this. Wanted this. She'd wanted to explain, to make him understand. She hadn't meant to lie, hadn't meant to play games. She'd just wanted...

"That's no excuse," she said now. "I was old enough to know what I was doing."

"No, you weren't," he said quietly. "But I was."

That stopped her. That *floored* her. All this time, all these years, she'd never imagined that he might blame himself, hold himself responsible. "You had no way of knowing—"

"Sure I did," he said. "If I'd wanted to. If I'd let myself," he added as he twisted back to the skillet and flipped the crude omelet. He stayed that way a long moment, his big shoulders hunched over the stove, his chest rising and falling with his breath. "But I didn't want to," he said, and in doing so, knocked what remained of the breath from her lungs. "All I wanted was..."

Their eyes met, and the moment froze.

Outside the night sang the song of the summers of her childhood, so different from the cool damp nights in England.

Inside, the eggs crackled and her blood hummed.

"*You,*" Tyler rocked her by whispering into the taut stillness. "All I wanted was you."

For one of the few times in Darci's life, words slipped away.

"I could have stepped back," he said. "I could have asked more questions, paid more attention to the inconsistencies in your story."

Because God knew there'd been plenty. She'd been

making it up as she went along, beginning with the name she'd given him: Tara Moore.

"I could have asked why you never let me pick you up at your place…why you never gave me a number to call."

Because she'd been living with her father, and he'd carefully scrutinized her mobile phone bill.

"I could have taken it slow," he murmured, setting down the spatula and lifting his good hand to the side of her face. There, he slipped a finger against a few strands of hair that had worked free of her braid.

She hadn't had a chance to clean up. She hadn't showered since the night before. She'd been in the heat all day, working at Lochlain, tending to Darci's Pride. She could feel the dried salt on her skin.

She'd never let Tyler see her like that before. She'd never let him see beyond the glitz and the glam, the costume of makeup, couture clothes and designer perfume she'd hidden behind each time they'd been together.

Even when they'd made love, she'd made sure the lights were off.

"There's no way you could have been a virgin," he destroyed her by adding. "Not if what you'd told me was true…if you were really twenty-three years old."

Her lungs shut down. Her throat went dry. "Tyler—"

"That should have stopped me," he said. "When we were in bed that first time, and you turned out the lights—"

The memory curled through her, stripping away the years and the lies, the heartache, leaving only her—and Tyler. "I was scared," she shocked herself by admitting.

"I know." Against the side of her face, his thumb slid to her bottom lip. "You were shaking," he whispered, "and you shouldn't have been…not if you'd been twenty-three years old."

He'd been gentle. He'd been impossibly romantic. He'd carried her to the bed, where they'd slowly undressed each other. With each second that he'd touched her, the need had grown like this massive groundswell within her, an urgent hunger and craving she'd been wholly unprepared for, overriding the fear and the caution, the cold brutal inevitability that she could not hide her identity from him forever.

"But you were so damn sweet," he muttered, and her heart started to bleed. "The way you looked at me with those goddamned blue eyes…"

He'd slid on top and kissed her softly, taken her hand as he pushed inside. She'd tried not to wince. She'd tried not to gasp. But there'd been no way to hide the tightness—or the blood. "I didn't want you to know."

His eyes warmed. "Kind of hard to hide something like that."

So she'd lied. She'd concocted some kind of silly schoolgirl story about wanting to wait until the right man came along.

But within the heart of the lie had been the soul of the truth.

It had been less than a week later that her father found them. In a hotel. Naked. He'd become suspicious. He'd hired a private investigator, had her followed. By the time he'd barged in on his seventeen-year-old daughter in bed with a twenty-eight-year-old man, Weston Parnell had known what he would find. He'd had pictures.

One week later, Darci had been stashed half a world away in England, and Tyler had been on the brink of financial ruin.

"You were just a kid," he said again, his eyes steady on hers as he flipped off the range and slid the skillet from the burner. "But I knew better. I knew what happened when a man took what he wanted, all else be damned. I knew the consequences, the fallout."

He almost made it sound as though he'd taken advantage of her. "But you couldn't have known what my father would do."

His smile was bittersweet. "He loves you. I can't blame him for that."

Weston Parnell had gone after Tyler full throttle. He'd used his friendship with Jackson Bullock to ensure the end of Tyler's syndicated television show on Australian horsemanship. Other connections he'd used to encourage boarders to pull their horses from Lochlain. He'd even convinced Tyler's banker to call his loans.

Overkill, to be sure. But Weston Parnell never did anything halfway, especially when it came to his daughter.

Especially not after losing his wife.

"You can't blame yourself, either," Darci said.

Tyler's breath was slow, rough. "I blame myself for being reckless," he said. "Impulsive."

The word her father had thrown in her face so many times since her mother had died burned through her.

"If I'd been a little less irresponsible," he added, "I might have spared you—"

"Spared me?" *He'd* been the one her father brutalized.

"England," he said quietly. "Exile. Six years is a long time to be away from home."

The ache started low and spread fast, ripped through her like the fire punishing the dry brittle bush. Tyler Preston felt guilty. He blamed himself for their affair. He blamed himself for the actions her father took, for carting her off to England and severing her ties with Australia…except for the horses, for Outback Pride, who'd traveled with them, and Darci's Pride, who'd been born several years later.

"But I'm not that reckless kid anymore, Darci," he said as his hand fell from her face. "And this time, I'm not looking away."

The fires burned. Off in the distance, just east of Lake Dingo, the red glowed against the night sky. The fire brigade was there. All volunteer firefighters had been mobilized. Hastings had returned to help fight the fire that threatened to sweep toward the town of Pepper Flats with the slightest shift in the wind.

But within the confines of Whittleson Stud, there was only darkness.

Tyler prowled the rambling house Sam had purchased for a song after the former owner had passed away without heirs, moving from room to room, looking out the curtainless windows, watching. Daniel had told him where his father kept a stash of firearms. Tyler wanted to be surprised, but wasn't. Australians didn't have the right to bear arms. A license was required, the fallout from a heinous mass shooting in the late nineties. Shotguns in particular had been targeted.

But the new law had not stopped Sam.

Tyler had found the piecemeal collection and selected a shotgun, loaded it. Now he kept the weapon his father had taught him to shoot in his hands and tried like hell to ignore the sound of water rattling through the pipes down the hall.

She'd eaten. Quietly. She'd taken the eggs he'd fixed her and sat at the table, shared her glass of water with the wilted wildflowers before she'd taken her first bite of food. But once she'd started...

Through the window, he saw the glow of memory in his own eyes. Once Darci had started eating, she hadn't stopped until she'd taken the last bite. He'd rocked back on the legs of the chair and watched, refused to let himself move. Touch.

Want.

The water shut off, and his imagination took over. He'd seen the small bathroom before she'd stepped into it. Even though Hastings had inspected the entire house, Tyler had insisted on taking a second look before Darci took off her clothes and stepped into the claw-foot bathtub.

She was exhausted. He knew that. He'd seen it in her eyes, no matter how hard she'd tried to pretend otherwise. He'd seen the fatigue, the struggle, just as he saw so much else.

None of which he'd let himself see before.

Turning from the small room Sam used as an office, Tyler took to the hall and returned to the great room. That's where he stood when the scent of roses and baby powder drifted against the echo of tobacco and leather. He saw her through the window, her reflection ghostlike as she moved toward him. Her hair was wet and loose around her face, combed straight. The last remnants of her makeup were gone. The pajamas she'd slipped into were big and boxy, a soft peach top with a scattering of stars and moons and suns. Matching cotton shorts hung to her knees.

"Tyler," she said, and even her voice sounded fresher, revitalized. "I set out some fresh linens—"

Her voice stopped abruptly, and through the reflection he saw the frozen look on her face and knew she'd seen the gun.

"No," she whispered. "No…"

Tyler turned toward her, felt the burn clear down to the bone. "Go to bed," he said.

But Darci, being Darci, didn't just hold her ground; she kept right on coming. "Where'd you get that?"

"It's Sam's."

Shock blanched her features. "My God…is that why Louisa was so scared—"

"No," he finished before she could ask. "He was unarmed that day." But Louisa Fairchild had been frightened of the grizzled old man anyway. He'd charged into her house in a rage. Some said he'd been drinking. Louisa insisted she'd felt threatened. "The gun was hers."

Darci's chest rose and fell with her breaths. Through the neckline of her pajamas, the arch of her collarbone revealed a spot of unabsorbed lotion.

"You don't need that," she said. "Nothing's going to happen."

She was convinced the note left on Sam's doorstep was a warning, not a threat.

It was not a chance Tyler could take.

"You're exhausted," she said, but like him, did not move. Several meters still separated them, empty space that might as well have been a brick wall. "You need to rest. Let me get you a brandy—"

"No." The word came out harsher than he'd intended, but he made no move to soften it. "Just go on to bed, Darci."

The slight rise to her chin should have warned him. "Not without you," she said, and then she glided through that invisible wall between them and settled down on Sam's old leather sofa, her legs curving beneath her. "You sure I can't tempt you with a brandy?"

He didn't sleep. Not for a long, long time. He stood there at that big showy window, looking out into the darkness. Every so often he would turn toward her, and she would quickly close her eyes.

The mantel clock ticked on, loudly. Relentlessly. Tracking each second deeper into the night. Darci wasn't sure when she finally drifted off, but she knew with unsettling clarity the first time she'd awakened. He'd been there, sitting on the edge of the sofa. His hand had been on her face, smoothing away a few strands of hair with a gentleness that made her heart catch. There he'd lingered. Eyes closed, she'd held herself still, mimicking sleep with her breath.

But she'd been excruciatingly, painfully awake.

Long moments had passed before he pulled away and left—even longer moments until she'd stopped tracking his movements. Maybe she should have said something, let him know she was awake. But the hard-fired determination forged through years of exile would not let her. She'd signed on with Andrew's campaign to stake a claim to her future, not fall back into the past.

When she next awoke it was too quiet, and the first whispers of sunlight drifted in through the window. For several breaths she held herself still, while silently she listened. Only when she heard the deep rhythmic breathing of sleep did she open her eyes—and see.

Sometime between the deepest part of the night and the first breath of dawn, Tyler had quit prowling the house. He'd poured himself a drink and sunk into Sam's old recliner, and finally, at last, exhaustion had claimed him.

Over seventy-two hours had passed since the fire. She knew he hadn't slept that night, and doubted he'd found more than a morsel of sleep here or there since then. He'd been pushing forward, doing what needed to be done, leading, directing, making sure everyone at Lochlain was cared for…shepherding each and every horse as if they were children, not animals.

In the end, they'd lost three, two the night of the fire, one the following evening. The handful who'd run off during the inferno had been found and were now safely at a neighboring farm. Those most seriously injured were in stable condition. Lightning Chaser was being watched closely, but so far was holding his own, thanks to Tyler.

His barns had been torched. His prized horse drugged. He'd been threatened the morning before the fire, accused the morning after the fire. There were those in the press who maligned him, and those in the public who celebrated him.

And now, for the first time in what had to be at least four days, he slept.

Darci slipped from the sofa and wished Sam had some kind of curtains she could close, anything to keep the sun from bathing the great room in light. Because there was nothing, she took the soft coverlet she'd used and crossed to Tyler, draped it over his body. She wanted to pull off his boots—

The memory slipped in hard and fast, of Tyler grinning, pursuing her across a hotel room. She'd backed away, one slow step at a time, until her legs had brushed up against the mattress. He'd closed in on her, going down on one knee as he reached for her right leg and pulled off her flashy red boot.

Now she looked away, from the man, from the past she did not want to see, and realized that while Tyler had poured himself a brandy, the glass sat on the small table completely untouched.

It was all she could do not to pick it up and throw it back herself.

Quietly she left the big room and slipped to the guest room, where she quickly dressed. In a few hours she would head to Sydney, where Andrew waited. Julia would meet her there later in the day. There were interviews with a magazine and news station in the afternoon, a dinner party in the evening. There was a speech to approve, a press release to craft, phone calls to make.

And somewhere in between all that, there was her father waiting to tell her how reckless she was.

Frowning, she dragged a brush through her hair and twisted the strands behind her head, fastened a clip to hold the knot in place. Next came her makeup and the cream pantsuit she'd bought several months before at Harrods. The costume came together, the pearl necklace and matching earrings, the opal ring that had belonged to her mother, the dash of perfume, until finally when she looked in the mirror, it was a poised, elegant, impossibly British-looking stranger staring back at her.

Shortly before eight, the phone rang. She'd been awake for two hours. Somehow, Tyler had continued to sleep. She answered on the first ring, expecting to find Andrew or Julia or maybe even her father.

"Darci," the man said by way of greeting, but it was enough for the sober tone of his voice to register. "Is Tyler still there?"

Instinct—or maybe it was the edge to Detective Hastings's voice—had the first cold whispers of adrenaline burning her chest.

"He's sleeping," she tried, hoping that her imagination was acting up and that the cop would just give her some kind of message to pass on. "He was up most of the night and I think he really needs—"

"I need to talk to him."

She stilled. "Has something happened?"

"I need you to wake him," Detective Hastings said, but before she could even turn, the sleep-roughened voice sounded from behind her.

"Darce?"

She twisted and found him standing just inside the doorway, still fully dressed but with his hair mussed and his eyes heavy from sleep, his jaw in desperate need of a razor.

She'd seen him like that before.

Feeling horribly like the grim reaper, she walked the phone over to him. "It's Detective Hastings," she mouthed, and in that one cruel heartbeat, everything changed. The lines of his face tightened. His stance straightened. Fully awake, he took the receiver and brought it to his ear, announced himself. Then listened.

All the while Darci stood and watched, tried to breathe. She saw his eyes darken, the shadows deepen. She saw the quick flare of shock, the punch of horror. She heard him ask when and where and who, heard the quiet oath, felt the tension radiate from his body.

The call didn't last long. Tyler let out a rough breath as he lowered the receiver, closed his eyes for a long hard moment before opening them to her.

"Tyler?" she asked, but already, without him saying a word, she knew. It was bad. Real bad.

"I have to go," he said, and in the broken silence that followed, she heard the struggle. He didn't want to tell her. He didn't want her to know.

"Something's happened," she said.

The green of his eyes went horribly flat. "They found a body," he said. "At Lochlain."

Chapter Ten

The sun shone hot and hard, creating a vivid contrast between the living and the dead. The stark, charred remains of the barns made the blue of the sky look unnatural. Even the earth kept no secrets, burned grass giving way in an eerie zigzag to patches that were merely brown and thirsty.

"Where?" At the edge of the crime-scene tape, Tyler narrowed his eyes at the white sheet draped over the outline of a body. Not too far away, several grooms and trainers hovered with the border collics beneath the shade of the gum trees, watching.

"Under a pile of rubble," Detective Hastings said. "Back there," he added, gesturing toward the far side of Barn B, where a large piece of demolition equipment stood still.

"That would have been a stall," Tyler confirmed. "Near Lightning's."

Hastings and Sebastian Hardy, the chief arson squad investigator, exchanged a tight look. There were others present, as well, men Tyler knew and men he'd never seen before. Some wore sunglasses and some wore hats. They all wore the identical grim expression.

For three days a body had lain beneath the rubble.

They'd all walked the area. The arson squad had pieced through the charred wood and ash. Crows had circled. Flies had swarmed. Looking for food, they'd all commented....

Everyone was accounted for. Every employee of Lochlain, every firefighter, every neighbor. *Every-bloody-one*.

Except the bloke beneath the sheet, dead for three days but missed by no one.

"And there's no identification?" Darci asked, stepping closer to Tyler's side.

The urge to pull her into his body and hold her there, safe and protected and away from the ugliness that had come to the Valley, burned through him. But he didn't let himself move.

"Nothing definitive," Hastings answered. Even if the victim had carried a wallet, the fire had burned too hot for too long. "There are a few things we need to look into," he added, but refused to divulge what.

A man. That was about all they could tell for certain from the remains, but even that required verification.

"You should go," Tyler said, lowering his voice and turning to Darci. She didn't belong here, all fresh and showered and clean, in that haute little cream suit, standing among the big piles of charred debris with the stench of death and decay overriding the baby powder of the night before. "Andrew's waiting."

"I've already called him. He can get by without me—"

"No." Only a few hours ago he'd watched her sleep. He'd kept his distance for as long as he could, standing at the window, even going out on the patio. But as the night had deepened she'd stirred, and he'd found himself crossing to her. To move the cover back up, he'd told himself. But then his hand had brushed the soft skin of her cheek, and he'd stood there frozen, knowing it wasn't right. Knowing he shouldn't touch. But he lowered a knee to the rug and touched anyway, softly. Gently. Just a hand to the side of her face.

She'd smiled.

She'd goddamn smiled.

She might as well have knifed him in the gut.

"You need to go," he said. *He* needed her to go. This wasn't what he wanted, not any of it. He didn't want Darci Parnell at Lochlain, standing by his side.

He didn't want her crying out in her sleep.

Didn't want her scared.

"You've done enough," he said, and though he meant the words sincerely, they came out gruff, and the flicker of hurt was impossible to miss.

"Tyler," she said, her voice lower, more discreet. "It's not too late to reconsider. I can cancel the party—"

He shot Hastings and Hardy a quick look, then took her hand and hustled her toward a paddock where a young filly chased a small white butterfly.

Once the sight would have warmed. Now there was nothing, just the cold of Darci's flesh soaking into his. "You're scared," he said, and the reality twisted through him.

"How can I not be?" She glanced beyond him to the unidentified body beneath that impersonal sheet. "What if it wasn't an accident? What if someone killed that man?"

Here. At Lochlain. And started the fire to cover up the crime.

It was a sobering possibility.

"What if it was supposed to be you?" she asked quietly, and with the question she pushed up on her toes and lifted a hand to his face.

It was the first time she'd reached out to him, the first time she'd initiated contact, in six years.

It wasn't. That's what he wanted to say. The body was not supposed to be his.

"That's why you need to go to Sydney." Why *he* needed her to go. "Get away from all this." So he could quit worrying about where she was or what she was doing, so he could quit looking.

Quit wanting.

"We can scratch Darci's Pride—" he offered.

But Darci's answer shot into her eyes before the word left her mouth. "No." Her chin came up. "I'm not running scared," she said. "Whoever did this to you…" Her words trailed off. "They're not finished," she said. "DP is our best chance of catching them."

Our. The word hovered there between them, leaving the only truth that mattered.

Tyler didn't stop to think. There was only this hot boiling need inside of him. Everything else fell away, the fire and the investigation, the body. Hastings and Hardy and Daniel and Marcus. There was only Darci…and the way she kept looking up at him, the blue of her eyes drenched with a silent communion that fed some place deep and dark and too long denied.

He reached for her, pulled her close, kissed her. Hard. On the mouth. Sliding his hand to the back of her head, he urged her toward him, brought her mouth to his and took the promise and the sunshine that had walked out of his life too long ago. She tasted so damn sweet, of innocence and sincerity, of the peppermints she'd slipped her filly on the way in—and the coffee she'd grabbed from the Whittleson Stud kitchen as they'd run for Lochlain.

"Go," he said, ripping his mouth from hers. *"Please."*

Her eyes were dark, her mouth damp and slightly swollen from the force of his kiss. She looked up at him, a few strands of hair falling against the elegant lines of her face. *"Tyler..."*

He shook his head. "Not here," he said. "Not now."

The moment stretched. The hot wind blew dust and ash against them. Around them, the crows kept circling, but it was the song of the cockies he heard, and the pounding of his pulse.

"You shouldn't have done that," she finally said, and for the first time since she walked back into his life, a strangled noise rumbled from low in his throat.

"I know."

Daniel took Darci's Pride to Sydney. There, she would train. And there, hidden cameras watched from high in her stall, waiting.

If someone meant the filly harm, if someone *tried* anything, they would be caught.

Tyler stayed at Lochlain. There were endless questions to answer, a different kind of surveillance in progress. For almost a year Dylan Hastings had trusted Tyler with his daughter, but now the cop watched Tyler through cold, impersonal eyes. His questions were matter-of-fact: When was the last time Tyler had been in the barn? When was the last time Tyler had been in the office...in the room with the surveillance equipment? Who else had access?

With the discovery of the body beneath the rubble, the arson investigation had shifted to that of a potential homicide.

It could have been an accident. Hastings conceded that. It was possible. But there were too many irregularities to overlook.

If the death was accidental, then what was some unknown person doing in the barns of Lochlain in the middle of the night? How did they come to be there? Why did no one see them?

And most damning of all, why had the surveillance system been tampered with? The footage of those crucial hours stolen?

Even Tyler had to admit the pieces didn't look much like an accident.

They looked like cold-blooded murder.

But no one was missing. Not one person in the Valley was unaccounted for. Forensics was working with dental records, but that was little more than a shot in the dark. With luck they would determine cause of death, but without a lead or other form of ID the body might never be identified.

Three nights before the Outback Classic, Tyler lifted the brush to Lightning Chaser's side and went to work. His strokes were soft, easy. The horse was holding his own, but Dr. Chaplain said it was too soon to declare the Thoroughbred out of the woods.

The same applied to young Heidi's horse, Anthem, as well as a handful of others.

Quiet throbbed through the barn, broken only by the occasional whinny or sigh. Dr. Chaplain had gone home a short time before. In the morning, Tyler would leave for Sydney, but the veterinarian would stay with the injured animals until the night before the race.

Darci's Pride was looking good. Daniel had rung up Tyler several times reporting on the filly's progress, but

Darci herself remained silent. He'd seen her a time or two, during news segments focused on the Classic. She'd been with Andrew as he gave a speech at a luncheon of horse aficionados. Another time he'd caught her on Andrew's arm at a gala celebrating the upcoming Classic. She'd looked happy, in her element, clean and elegant and…safe.

A far cry from the night she'd stood shoulder to shoulder with the men of Lochlain, dressed like a scrawny teenage boy as she helped fight the fire.

An even further cry from the party girl who'd rocked his world six years before.

With a burn to his gut, Tyler finished up with Lightning Chaser and bade the horse good-night, walked through the darkness toward the big stone house and saw the man waiting on the porch.

"The horses," Andrew said. "At the end of the day, that's all that matters. That's why we're here. Not for sport or ego or pride or profit. It's the horses that matter…the horses we must put first."

Applause greeted Andrew's words. Those in the hotel ballroom surged to their feet, close to two hundred of Australia's finest horsemen and women. They'd gathered in advance of the Outback Classic, the majority of them hailing from the Hunter Valley, but representing Perth and Melbourne, as well.

Darci sat at the head table, smiling as Andrew waited for the clapping to die down. This was their third dinner in three days. There'd been luncheons, as well, two interviews and an afternoon tea. Each had been crafted to bring Andrew into contact with the right people.

They'd only crossed paths with Jackson Bullock once.

Now Darci scanned the crowd of familiar faces, friends

of her father she'd known much of her life, all dressed in tuxedos and shimmering evening gowns. The next generation was there, as well, men and women who would soon take the reins from their parents. Many of them Darci recognized from...

Before.

She'd run with several of them, a fast crowd with too much money and time, not enough sense. They'd gone from party to party, running the streets of Sydney in search of the next big adventure. Toward the back she saw Martha Mathison. A few years older than Darci, Martha had been present when Darci had first set her sights on Tyler. She'd egged her on, advised her on the best lines to use.

She'd even told her how to best kiss a man—because at seventeen, Darci hadn't just been a virgin. She'd never even been kissed.

Now Martha wobbled toward her table with two drinks in her hand. A man Darci did not recognize greeted her and helped her sit before the two shared a sloppy kiss.

"It's criminal," Andrew said as Darci realized just how little Martha had grown up, "how many horses die each year on the track. How many horses break from the gates to do what they love to do, what they've been trained to do—*what we ask them to do*—only to go down. And in that one instant everything changes, all the hope and excitement shatters, just like the bones in their legs. And they die there, on the tracks, trading glory for euthanasia all because someone decided to save a few dollars."

Darci shifted, feeling the stare from half a room away. She turned, saw her father. They'd been playing phone tag since her arrival in Sydney.

"Or maybe they survive," Andrew went on, the fervor in his voice increasing. "They make it through surgery.

They start to recover. Then what? Best case their careers are over. Worst case, they go through day after day, their bones gradually healing, while everyone holds their breath, praying laminitis does not strike."

Weston Parnell exchanged a look with the elegant older woman seated next to him. At eighty, Louisa Fairchild still cut a striking figure, though she was paler than the last time Darci had seen her, with a gauntness that made her look even more severe. As a child, Darci had loved to visit Fairchild Acres. But now that Darci was working for the Prestons, Louisa wasn't even returning her phone calls.

"We've lost too many great ones that way," Andrew said, and Darci knew his thoughts were on the American Thoroughbred Barboro. They'd designed this speech to hit an emotional chord. To the Australian racing community, Andrew was mostly an unknown. And what was known centered around the scandal his family had just weathered and the fire at Lochlain.

"We need more funding," he continued, and Darci couldn't help but glance at the front table, where the Prestons gathered. Andrew's parents beamed with pride. His aunt and uncle smiled warmly. His cousin Shane sat with his new wife, holding hands and exchanging warm, knowing looks. They were all there, all but one.

"We need more commitment," Andrew said as Darci stared at the empty chair, where a small place card sat just beyond a crisp, unused napkin. "We must eradicate laminitis in *our* lifetime…"

Darci lifted a hand to her mouth and pressed her fingers there. If she let herself she could still feel Tyler's mouth…

The quiet force of his need had stunned her. If she'd stayed at Lochlain one day longer…

He should have arrived by now. He'd been scheduled to. But that had been before the body was found…and accusations of arson turned to whispers of murder.

Forcing a smile, she rose as the conclusion of Andrew's speech earned a standing ovation. She scanned the patrons, their smiles and nods, and knew she should feel satisfaction. This was what she'd planned. What she'd wanted.

But the swell tightening through her had nothing to do with pride.

"With only days left before world leaders arrive in Sydney," the morning newscaster announced, "police are bracing for record crowds. Protesters are already gathering in Hyde Park to make sure their global warming message is heard…."

Darci finished fastening her grandmother's pearls and slipped into the taupe flats she'd picked up before leaving London. A glance at the bedside clock told her she had twelve minutes before Weston Parnell would send out a search party.

Her father was a stickler for punctuality.

"And with the Outback Classic less than forty-eight hours away," the broadcaster continued, "city officials are working overtime to ensure racing enthusiasts are not hampered by a scheduled march commencing downtown."

Darci snatched the remote and aimed at the television, but froze when the image transitioned from the attractive redhead to activity at Warrego Downs. Four or five horses worked on the exercise track, while several others stood with their trainers and grooms.

"All eyes will be on the filly," the anchor narrated as the footage shifted to that of Darci's Pride, quietly watching from her stall, "recently acquired by Lochlain Racing."

And then there he was, Tyler. It was a close-up shot, of man and horse, and Darci found herself walking closer to the television. There, she lifted a hand, and touched.

He looked tired. That was her first thought. His eyes, normally so warm and vibrant and wickedly irreverent, were dark and drawn. Shadows circled his lower lashes. And his mouth…

The last time she'd seen that mouth it had been soft and moist and swollen. Now it was a grim tight line.

"With his stables in ruin and a suspicious death investigation swirling around him, Tyler Preston is placing all his hopes on newly acquired Darci's Pride, a filly. Can the girl run with the boys? That's just one of the intriguing questions racing fans are waiting to have answered…"

Darci stepped back from the television. He was here. In Sydney. Tyler was at the track. With Darci's Pride.

The stab of disappointment surprised her. He hadn't promised to call…he hadn't promised anything.

Zapping the off button, she stared at the blank screen a long moment before tossing the remote onto the bed and reaching for her satchel. She was two steps from the door when the phone rang.

She almost didn't answer. She'd see her father soon enough. But an unwanted glimmer of hope pulled her toward the elegant hotel desk, where she reached for the receiver.

"It's not too late."

The distorted words stopped her. She stood frozen, forced herself to speak. "Who is this?"

"It's not too late," the garbled voice said again, and then the line went dead, and Darci was left standing there with a dial tone droning in her ear. And deep inside, she started to shake. Because she knew. She knew what the caller meant—what the warning meant.

Darci's Pride.

It wasn't too late to scratch her from the race.

Or else...

Awful images crashed in from all directions, culminating in the memory of another filly who'd run with the boys. Eight Belles had gone from glory to tragedy in one cruel instant. And now, in trying to help Tyler, Darci had put her horse in danger. This made the third warning—or threat. If they kept the filly in the race, there was a very real chance—

She blocked the thought, wouldn't let it form. Tyler had a plan. Precautions were being taken. Darci's Pride was being protected.

But the cold kept right on bleeding through her, numbing her fingers as she placed the call.

Four minutes later—and with only one to spare—the elevator slid open and she made her way toward the hotel restaurant. Her heels clicked smartly against the marble floor. On her face she had a practiced smile. No one would know. No one would guess how much restraint it required to keep herself from running through the doors and grabbing a cab, getting to Warrego Downs as fast as possible.

Everything was under control. To give the slightest indication otherwise would only jeopardize wheels already in motion.

Not quite eight-thirty, the chic lobby bustled with activity. Between the Classic and the upcoming summit, there wasn't a room to be had. From the coffee shop came the rich aroma of espresso. Men in white suits flanked the concierge desk, while a camera crew set up alongside the hotel's signature fountain.

"There you are!" her father boomed, and as she turned, his arms came around her, pulling her into a tight hug. He was a big elegant bear of a man, the polish and refinement he showed the world at large the perfect disguise for the raw emotions that boiled through him. He'd always been that way, like a typhoon, she'd thought as a child. Blustery whether he was happy or sad.

And then her mother had died, and the bluster had died with her.

"If I didn't know better I'd think you've been avoiding me," he said, and Darci's smile relaxed the slightest fraction. She *had* been avoiding him, and they both knew it.

"As if," she said with obligatory kisses to both his ruddy cheeks. He'd gone completely gray in the past twelve months, but somehow still cut an impressive figure. "The campaign is just keeping me busy."

"The campaign," he echoed, and from behind them, a lightbulb flashed. She spun around, saw the camera crew busily capturing the crowd. "I was sorry I had to leave early last night," he said. "I was hoping for a few minutes alone with you."

"Well you have me now," she said with a smile that was only partially forced.

"That I do." Taking her hand, he guided her into the crowded dining room. White greeted her everywhere, from the cloths draped over the tables to the curtains trying to block the bright morning sunshine and the attire of the waitstaff.

Within minutes they were seated and their orders placed, water served and tea steeping. "Now, Darci," her father began, as she'd known he would. "We need to talk."

This, she'd planned, as well. As a child, she'd let him take the lead. But she was an adult now, and it was time he realized he could no longer dictate her every action. "We do," she acknowledged, then launched her curveball. "I need to know what you know," she said. "About the Prestons—and the fire."

Her father sat back. His brows, silver now, drew together. Around them the buzz of other patrons sounded, but Weston Parnell said nothing, not for a long, long time. He just watched.

It was one of his hallmark techniques: hold quiet, let it become unbearable, and then she would back down without him even saying a word.

Reaching for the dainty porcelain cup, Darci ignored the punch of adrenaline and toyed with the tea bag, meeting tit for tat.

She wouldn't tell him. She couldn't tell him. If he knew about the threats, the warnings, if he had any idea she'd placed Darci's Pride in danger...

"That's not why we're here," her father said at last, and while once Darci might have wanted to scream at his dismissal, now she only sighed.

"It's why I'm here," she corrected. "Last week you warned me not to get involved with the Prestons." She released her tea bag and met her father's stare. "That very night Lochlain burned," she said. "And this week a body was found."

"Advised, Darci-Anne," he corrected. "I advised you to steer clear...and with good reason, wouldn't you say?"

"What do you know?" she pressed, and the knot of dread wound deeper. She wanted to believe him. She didn't want him to know anything. She didn't want him to...be involved.

But once before he'd tried to destroy Tyler. "What have you heard?"

Her father's expression darkened. "Just what you said... that someone deliberately set fire to two barns and in the process killed a man."

"*Dad.*" She kept her voice quiet but firm as she leaned

closer. "I'm serious. If you know something…if you heard something…you have to tell me."

He sat a little straighter. "Darci, sweetheart, I love you. Is that really such a crime?"

"Dad—"

"We've been down this road before," he said, "and no good came of it. I tried to steer you away from trouble, but now look what's happened. *You sold your horse, Darci…* your mother's legacy."

She sat back. Shock jammed the breath in her throat. She bit down on her lips, didn't trust herself to speak. "If you really think that's what I did," she said after a long silence, "then you don't know me at all—and you didn't know her, either."

He winced. For maybe the first time she could remember, her father actually winced. "I know you," he said. "And I most surely knew your mother—"

"Then you know that she was passionate about horses and loyal to her friends. That she was kind and giving and stood up for what she believed in. That she—"

"Weston," came a rich cultured voice from behind them. "Darci…what a lovely surprise."

Chest burning, she glanced up to find Jackson Bullock gliding to their table, the regal Louisa Fairchild on his arm. Darci had been trying to arrange a private meeting with her for Andrew, but as long as the Prestons backed Sam in the dispute over Lake Dingo, Louisa had made it clear she had no use for them.

"Jacko," her father greeted. "Louisa."

"It's been too long," Jackson said, reaching for Darci's hand. She didn't want to offer it to him, but knew that snatching it away would be childish. "I must say you remind me more of your mother every day."

The superficial comment grated, even as her mouth

curved into a smile. "Thank you," she said politely. "We were just talking about Mom."

"A lovely woman," Jackson said. "I still miss her."

A strangled noise broke from her father's throat, but before he could reply, Jackson continued. "Louisa here was telling me about Andrew's speech yesterday, and I just want you to know, Darci, there are no hard feelings."

Darci sat a little straighter as the waiter checked their water glasses.

"I know we all make choices," Jackson said. "Sometimes we're dead-on and sometimes…"

Her father pushed back in his chair and stood. "It's stunning how fast they grow up, isn't it?" he said, and though the words were buoyant, shock quickened through Darci.

He was defending her. Only minutes before, her father had been the one questioning her choices, but now he stood chest to chest with his longtime friend, defending her.

"It is," Jackson said, but of far more interest was what went unsaid, the undercurrent that hummed beneath the surface.

"Good seeing you," her father concluded, and with a firm handshake and a quick nod in Darci's direction, Jackson and Louisa strolled toward a small round table at the back of the room.

"Now," her father said, reaching for his still-crisp napkin. "Where were we?"

The horse was ready. Sassy as always, she waited in her stall, flicking her tail at the occasional fly. She would be groomed and fed, checked over one last time, then left alone for the night.

Except for the closed-circuit horse cam.

Tyler looked away from the visual on his laptop and placed a quick call to room service before confirming with the front desk that no messages awaited him. His mobile phone had rung throughout the afternoon, his parents checking in prior to the evening cocktail party, Peggy with last-minute details, a reporter with several questions, even Hastings with an update on the investigation.

But not once had Tyler heard the voice that refused to leave him alone, the one that whispered to him during the darkness of the night.

You shouldn't have done that....

No. He shouldn't have. He shouldn't have kissed her any more than he should have made love to her six years before. But goddammit, every time his phone rang, something inside him jumped.

Swearing softly, Tyler flipped on the television and worked off his boots, stripped off his clothes as the weather forecaster predicted another day of crippling heat and no rain. The bushfires were contained for the moment, but with the slightest shift in the wind...

He strode to the bathroom and jammed on the water, stepped into the marble tub. There would be no more fires at Lochlain.

In a pulsing massage rhythm, cold water came pouring down against his back and shoulders. He'd been in Sydney thirty-six hours. When not sleeping, he'd been at the track.

Darci had been nowhere in sight.

Grabbing the soap, he jerked it along his body and forced his thoughts back to the race and Lochlain, to the fire and the body and the investigation that featured more questions than answers. They'd found a ring near the body, a large black opal in an unusual sterling setting. Hastings was interviewing jewelers, seeing if any of them recognized it. Victim...perpetrator...either was possible.

Running the soap along his hair, Tyler lathered it up and started to rinse. That's when he heard the pounding.

Swearing under his breath, he stepped from the tub and grabbed one of the big white towels, jerked it around his hips as he strode for the door. He didn't stop to look through the peephole. He just twisted the knob and pulled...and saw her.

Chapter Eleven

Nothing prepared her. Nothing could have. She'd arrived amid a flurry of activity at Warrego Downs only to learn Tyler had left an hour before. She'd told herself to leave well enough alone, that if he'd wanted to see her he could have called.

But she'd rung up Peggy and gotten his room number anyway. Because he needed to know, she told herself. He needed to know about the warning. She'd asked Dylan not to tell Tyler, had insisted she would tell him herself. She wanted to—

Want. It was so not the right word to use in conjunction with Tyler Preston.

He stood there now, just inside the partially open hotel door, wet and naked save for the fluffy white towel riding low on his hips. "Tyler."

He didn't smile, didn't grin, didn't frown, didn't allow

any emotion to crack through his stony face. He just lounged there with one hand at the towel, the other on the doorknob. "You're not room service."

"No," she agreed, trying not to look, to somehow pretend he didn't stand there with suds dripping from his hair to his face, that water didn't slide down his chest to the trail of hair she'd once—

"Don't tell me you're still hungry—" she began. The wash of heat came instantly, swimming like a dangerous drug straight through to her blood. "I mean, I heard there was a banquet at the track…." All the owners and trainers had been there, along with handpicked representatives of the international media. She'd arrived late. "Daniel said—"

"I didn't get enough."

She stood a little straighter and searched for the faintest veil of nonchalance.

"But that's not why you're here, is it?" he asked, and in some traitorous corner of her mind, she would have sworn she caught amusement in his voice. "To talk about my appetite?"

Her heart kicked hard. Her chest burned. "No, I—" Knew. She knew about Tyler's appetite.

But stepped into him anyway, moved without thinking to swipe a finger just above his eyes. Too late she felt him, far too much of him, hot and hard and wet, pressed against the strappy little black dress she'd chosen for Andrew's cocktail party.

"Soap," she explained with what she hoped was a lopsided smile, stepping back as she showed off the suds on her index finger. "It was about to—"

"Darci." He lifted a single brow. "What are you doing here?"

It was like a bucket of ice water. She stepped back and

felt the cool air against her arms, quietly damned him for standing there so nonchalant while she stammered around like a schoolgirl looking at a naked man for the first time.

"We need to talk," she said, trying to shut everything else out, the soap and the water and the chest she'd once rested her head against, the towel slipping lower… "And you need to shave."

His hand came up to the whiskers crowding his jaw. "I'll be downstairs later—"

"No." The word shot out of her. "Here."

"I don't think—"

"But I do," she said, and then she took the decision from him. She nudged the door and breezed past him, strolled past the jeans and shirt strewn on his floor and into his suite.

"Go ahead and finish up your shower," she announced with forced breeziness. "I'll wait."

He found her on the bed.

She'd pulled the laptop over with her, sat with her legs curved under her as she stared at the screen. The little black dress rode high on her thighs, baring too much leg and a little butterfly tattoo inside her ankle that had not been there six years before.

Looking away, Tyler fumbled with the buttons of his dress shirt.

"Who else is watching?"

No one. The words burned his throat. No one else was watching her…just him.

"Hastings's team," he said, shoving at another button. "They're in the office nearest her stall. If anything happens…"

Darci's eyes, huge and dark and filled with a knowing that ate at his gut, met his. "What if they don't get there in time?"

"They will." They had to. "Only three people have authorized access tonight," he said. Besides himself, Daniel and Russ. "The second anyone else steps foot into the stall, Hastings will be on the move."

Thirty seconds. That's how fast they could be there.

Five seconds. That's how fast a horse could be killed.

Darci looked back at the screen, where one of the most anticipated entrants in the Outback Classic stood quietly in her stall. "She practiced well," Tyler said. "She ran easy."

"It's what she loves," Darci said, and in her voice, he heard the twist of love and fear. "Just like her sire."

He knew better than to cross over to her. He knew better than to join her on the bed. But something dark and unfathomable drew him across the room. He put a knee to the mattress and leaned over her shoulder, focused on the horse, and not the soft scent of roses and baby powder drifting from the curve of her neck.

"Darci…" His voice caught on her name. She twisted toward him, damn near slayed him with the glow in her eyes. He'd done this to her. He'd accepted her offer of Darci's Pride, and in doing so, put them all in jeopardy. "It's not too late," he said. "We can still stop—"

"No, we can't," she whispered. "I'm not a coward."

"But you are scared." He could see it in her eyes.

"Of course I am," she admitted with a tentative smile. "But if we stopped now, we'd never know…"

Her words trailed off, and for a long moment he said nothing, just looked at her sprawled a breath away from him, with her hair swirled up and twisted behind her head. His hand came up slowly, his fingers finding the line of her neck and dragging lower, past the pearls to the arch of her collarbone.

"You shouldn't be here," he muttered as his body stirred. "You should be downstairs." Away from him.

With Andrew.

"No," she said quietly as his fingers kept roaming. "This is where I need to…" On a rough breath she pulled away and grabbed his hand, squeezed. "I got another warning."

The quiet words stopped him. And for the first time he saw beyond the refined beauty of her makeup and hair and clothes to the heartbreakingly courageous little girl inside, the one who knew what it was like to lose someone you loved, who knew what it was to hurt, to grieve…but who'd offered him her horse anyway, who sat here even now, watching her horse sit like bait in a trap, while all he could think about was stripping off her clothes and burying himself inside of her.

"When?" The question was soft, lethal.

"This morning."

He jerked to his feet. "What did it say?"

"The same thing you said…that it's not too late."

Something cold swept through him. "Why didn't you call me?" He would have—

The answer registered in her gaze long before she spoke. From the moment she'd left for Sydney, he'd done everything in his power to pretend Darci Parnell did not exist. He could have called. He could have checked in with her. She'd already been threatened, after all. And the horse running under Lochlain colors had been hers only days before.

"I called Dylan," she said, and the truth wound around his chest, and squeezed. "I told him I'd tell you tonight."

"That's why you're here." In his hotel room, on his bed. To keep vigil on her horse—as he should have been doing.

His shirt hung open. Two or three times he'd fumbled with the buttons, but he'd only managed to shove the bottom three through their holes. Each time he lifted his hands, he lowered them seconds later and went about something else.

Darci tried not to notice.

Seconds slipped into minutes. Minutes dragged into hours deep into the night. Cool air drifted in from the open French doors Tyler had stalked through a few minutes before. He was like a big caged animal, all that primal energy pulsing through him, but nowhere to go and nothing to do. But watch.

He was angry. She knew that, too. One minute his eyes had gleamed with raw sensuality as he'd skimmed his fingers down her neck. Then…like a crude slide show transition, he'd pulled back, pulled away.

Because of the warning.

She should go. She also knew that. Her presence in front of the monitor would change nothing. Dylan and his team were in control. They were monitoring the horse cam. The second something happened—

But she couldn't. She couldn't just waltz back downstairs and paste on a smile, meet and greet and pretend that she hadn't a care in the world.

The tentative movement stopped her breath. Into the darkened picture on the computer monitor, a shadow fell, and a drowsy Darci's Pride stirred. "Tyler!"

The shadow became a man, moving in on her horse, and then Tyler was there, leaning over her even as he fumbled with his mobile phone.

Then she saw the syringe.

"Oh, my God!" She surged to her feet as Darci's Pride whinnied—but it was over before it began: Dylan Hastings and two other men swept into the stall, taking out the culprit with a hard tackle before the needle could penetrate the horse's flesh.

Darci sagged and tried to breathe, felt the hot burn of tears. "My God," she whispered against the hard tangle of shock and horror and relief, and then Tyler was there, this time pulling her into his arms and holding her, threading his fingers into the hair swept behind her head.

"It's over," he murmured, and though his words were steady and sure, calm, she could hear the hard slam of his heart. "It's over."

But then Dylan yanked the wiry man to his feet and Darci gasped. "I've seen him," she whispered.

Tyler froze, only his chest moving as Dylan took command of one of Lochlain's trusted caregivers.

Russ Chaplain's son-in-law.

Tyler shaved. He dressed in a crisp tailored suit straight off the pages of a trendy fashion magazine. He combed his hair. He drank tea and ate a scone. He smiled. He laughed. He charmed.

And all the while, Darci's heart quietly broke.

He stood at the far side of the Preston private box at Warrego Downs, commanding the local press with all the wicked Aussie charm she'd so missed while in England. He said the right things, made the right jokes. He invoked his trademark combination of confidence and self-deprecating humor. No one would know. No one would guess that he hadn't slept in close to forty-eight hours. Not a single reporter had the slightest clue that while all the pageantry and tradition of the Outback Classic swirled around them, twelve hours before, a simple syringe had almost changed everything.

"Ah, but a smart man learns to never discount the fairer sex," he countered as lightbulbs flashed. The reporters pressed in for more. "That's a mistake that can only lead to regret."

Laughter. Another question.

"He cleans up well, doesn't he?" joked Julia Nash. Dressed in an amazing lavender hat and crisp white gloves, the handpicked journalist had been shadowing Tyler all day. Of the gathered press, she alone knew about Owen Carberry. They'd told her on the condition that she hold quiet until more details were known and a formal announcement could be made.

"They all do," commented Shane's new wife, Audrey. "I still haven't quite gotten used to it all." Beneath the rim of her bold red hat, her smile widened. "How Shane and his brother can look so scruffy one minute, then…" She laughed. "Sarah must have had her hands full with those two."

"She did." This from Tyler's cousin Hilary, a striking brunette confined to a wheelchair following the accident that killed her parents. "They're a mess," she said as the first strains of the "Advance Australia Fair" quieted the crowd gathered outside. "But a fun mess."

The women fell silent as the music swelled, and over a hundred thousand horse racing faithful began to sing.

The tradition had begun late in the 1800s, when the first races were run at the humble track along the flats of the Maribyrnong River. Steeped in a tradition of beauty, strength and style, Warrego Downs was now known for its wide lawns and beautiful roses.

Darci's breath caught as the horses left the paddock in the post parade, walking before the stands on their way to the starting gate. Led by Sydney favorite Riff-Raff, they paraded along the grassy track as the press of men in suits and women in their finest hats and gloves and handbags swayed to the music.

As it all wound down, Darci glanced from the horses to

the three Preston men standing shoulder to shoulder. They cut an impressive sight in Armani, each with a red rosebud on the left lapel, father and the two sons who had surpassed him in height. Looking at them no one would ever know…

She glanced at her watch. Dylan should have been here by now. He'd called thirty minutes before, had promised he would be there before the race to fill them in on all they'd learned since taking Owen into custody. The detective had been intimately involved in setting the trap, but now the matter rested in the hands of the Sydney authorities. Dylan's access was a simple courtesy.

"Just look at her, would you?" Tyler drawled, and at his words all eyes turned to the grass track below, where Darci's Pride, draped in the blue and gold of Lochlain Racing, walked with the regality of a queen. Her head was high, ears perked, tail swishing. "The boys had better watch out."

"Any further word on the fire?" a reporter from the *Sydney Morning Herald* wanted to know. "Has the body been—"

Tyler lifted a hand. "Not today, okay, Rach? Today is about the race."

Mollified, the pretty young reporter, dressed as fancily as every other woman in attendance, beamed a smile back at him and tossed another question. "Can you tell us about Lightning Chaser? How's his recovery coming along?"

It had been this way since they'd arrived several hours before. If anything, the fire and possible homicide had only increased Tyler's celebrity status.

"I heard there was a watch found," Hilary said quietly. "Somewhere near the body."

"A ring," Audrey corrected. "A black opal, I think."

The sharp intake of breath caught Darci's attention. She turned just as Daniel's wife, Marnie, stepped into the group of women. "A black opal?"

It was something in her voice that made Darci look beyond Marnie's butter-yellow fedora and gloves to the uncertainty in her normally vibrant eyes.

"Shane says it's quite unique," Audrey said. "In a silver setting, I think."

Marnie's eyes grew distant. The conversation danced on, but she remained silent, even as the horses neared the starting gate.

"If you'll excuse me," Tyler said, and though his voice was that of the perfect host, his eyes darted toward the door, just as they'd done every five minutes or so. "My girl is about to run."

The horses moved toward the gate, twelve beautiful three-year-olds eager to run for the roses, and the crowd of over one hundred thousand eager fans roared. Australians took their horse racing seriously. When an outbreak of equine influenza had necessitated the cancellation of several key races a few years before, the racing faithful had been devastated.

Now from the three newly renovated grandstands, they stood and cheered as the first horse was led into the gate. In the midst of the noise, the door to the suite opened.

Tyler tensed, but it was Andrew who joined them. "I didn't think I'd ever get through that crowd," he said, heading straight for Darci. "This is your big day." He gave her a quick, warm hug, and over his shoulder, Darci saw Tyler turn and walk onto the balcony overlooking the track.

"You look great," Andrew said, stepping back. His eyes were warm, confident. "Any news yet?"

She shook her head.

"Let's get outside then." Taking her hand, he escorted her from the air-conditioning into the stifling midafternoon heat. She, too, had dressed with care, selecting her three-piece suit in a light cream fabric, with a straw Breton hat in ice blue to deflect as much of the sunshine as possible. But there was no getting around the requisite gloves and stockings—virtually every woman in attendance wore them.

While the horses were the main attraction at the Outback Classic, fashion was a time-honored sideshow.

Mr. Saigon, offspring of beloved mare Missy Saigon, made his way into the gate, followed by It's About Time and Rebel Yell.

Darci gripped the rail and watched as Daniel led Darci's Pride closer.

The rush of emotion surprised her. She shut her eyes and breathed deeply, but her throat closed up anyway.

"Dear, are you okay?"

Opening her eyes, Darci found Sarah Preston, breath-taking in a soft coral suit with matching fedora, standing beside her. "I'm fine," she said. "I was just…" She forced a smile. "My mother loved the races," she said as the memories rushed from all those dark secure places where Darci tried so hard to keep them.

"Yes, she did," Sarah said, and then she did the most amazing thing. She stepped closer and took the hands of the woman who'd once almost ruined her son, and squeezed. "She's here, you know," she said softly. "When those horses break out of the gate, there'll be angel's wings on Darci's Pride. You just wait and see."

Tears came in a hot rush. "Thank you," Darci whispered as Daniel eased the horse into her gate.

"Thank *you*," Sarah returned with all the elegance and refinement of the wine her family had bottled for decades. "Thank you for doing this for us," she said. "For Tyler. It means a lot."

Darci didn't know what to say. She smiled, and as the last horse, Riff-Raff, was led into the starter, she looked down the row of seats to where Tyler stood with his father and his brother. David and Shane each had binoculars lifted toward the starting line, but Tyler...

Darci followed his gaze back to the French doors leading to the suite—and saw a grim-faced Dylan Hastings standing just inside.

"Here we go!" Sarah Preston cried as the call of the bugle sounded through the grandstands. Darci twisted just as the horses broke onto the track, fans cheering wildly as Riff-Raff bolted to a quick lead, followed by Mr. Saigon and It's About Time.

The quick tangle of horses horrified. Wedged between a large black colt and Rebel Yell, Darci's Pride stumbled. Her front legs went down...and for a horrible frozen moment, everything just stopped. Darci's breath. Her heart. There was no crowd or raucous cheering, no heat or police detective poised just behind her. There was only her horse, the horse she'd fallen in love with from the moment of her birth, struggling to recover.

Silently Sarah Preston and Andrew each reached for one of Darci's hands, just as the horse recovered and surged forward.

It was all Darci could do not to go to her knees.

Wordlessly she watched her filly race forward, finding her way to the inside where she contented herself to run several furlongs behind Riff-Raff and Mr. Saigon.

"Come on, come on," Darci whispered, sliding a glance to Tyler. He stood as stoically as he had all morning, no expression on his face, his body at complete attention as he watched the horses thunder around the track. And for a stunning heartbeat Darci wished...

"Look at her go!" David roared.

"She's doing it!" Shane cried.

Darci could do nothing but stare, nothing but stand there beneath the relentless summer sun, with her hands held by Andrew and Sarah, and watch her horse find an opening between two of the boys and shoot forward.

"And it's Darci's Pride," boomed the announcer, "closing in on Riff-Raff!"

The crowd roared. Those gathered in the Preston suite cheered wildly.

Tyler stood without moving.

"Angel's wings," Sarah whispered with a gentle gloved squeeze to Darci's hand. And deep inside, something quietly shattered. Mom, she thought. *Mom...*

The horses pounded around the last turn, racing along the final furlong of straight track. Darci's Pride ran full out, edging alongside Riff-Raff just as Rebel Yell closed in from the outside. The three horses converged like an arrow to dash for the finish line as the crowd cheered.

"You can do it, you can do it!" chanted those in the Preston booth, but Darci could say nothing, could barely breathe.

Again everything slowed. With the gold and blue colors of Lochlain Racing, Darci's Pride ran with everything she had—and crossed the finish line less than a head before Rebel Yell.

"She did it!" roared David Preston. "By God, the girl did it!"

The crowd went wild. Father crushed son in a hug. Brother slapped brother on the back. Audrey and Marnie and Hilary laughed and embraced.

And Darci... Swept up in Andrew's arms, Darci cried.

Chapter Twelve

It was all a blur. Dylan Hastings stepped back as Tyler and Darci were hustled from the owners' suite to the winner's circle, where roses were draped, and the Outback Classic trophy was presented. Darci's Pride stood quietly, her coat still damp from sweat, while around her photographers snapped wildly.

"Score one for the girls!" the race commissioner declared as he posed for a picture with Darci and Tyler. "Brilliant race!"

Dylan Hastings hovered nearby, while Tyler did and said all the right things. He smiled and shook hands, answered questions and stood for countless pictures. All the while he kept Darci by his side, saying that although he was majority owner, all the credit went to Darci. She was the one who'd overseen the horse's training....

But he wouldn't look at her. And though he had to hold

her hand in one picture, and put his arm around her in another, his touch felt as impersonal as a stranger's.

He'd shut down. He'd closed himself off from her. From the moment she'd mentioned the second warning, a door had slammed completely shut.

For over an hour they were pulled in one direction after another. Champagne flowed. Mobile phones rang with endless praise. Even her father found and congratulated her. Darci was just hanging up with a friend from London when she saw Tyler slip from the banquet room, just behind Dylan.

She found them in a small office down the hall. The door was closed, but she wasn't about to let him shut her out of this. It was her horse who'd almost been drugged...her horse whose career could have been ruined, or worse.

The two men stood in quiet conversation as she stepped inside. They glanced toward her, stilling as she closed the door. Dylan shot Tyler a quick look, as if asking if it was okay for Darci to hear what had to be said.

Tyler nodded. That was all. He just nodded.

Frustration wound through Darci, but she knew now was not the time. She could see the tension in every line of Tyler's body. She knew the toll this was taking on him, the betrayal that still sliced to the bone.

"Carberry confessed," Dylan said. His eyes were grim, shadowed from lack of sleep. "He broke pretty easily."

"But why?" Darci asked, joining them. "I saw him with the horses. I saw him..." With Lightning Chaser and Darci's Pride and even the filly Anthem. At the time, she'd thanked him for taking such good care of the horses.

The memory chilled.

"Money," Hastings said. "Carberry took a big loss when More Than All That was disqualified. He'd bet heavily, didn't have the funds to cover."

Darci frowned. "My God…"

"We found betting records from several offshore operations. He'd put huge sums of money against Darci's Pride."

"Against," she whispered, as the pieces fell together. One loss led to another, then another. Desperation took over. Chances were taken. It was easier to make sure a horse lost than to make one win. "So the drug—"

"A sedative," Dylan supplied. "Carberry says he just wanted to slow her down. With More Than All That and Lightning Chaser disqualified, that left her, Rebel Yell and Riff-Raff as the main contenders. Her odds were good…." A brief smile cut across his face. "Real good," he said. "Congratulations, by the way."

She tried to take it all in. "So he bet against her, intending to make sure there was no way she could win."

"That was his intent with Lightning Chaser, too," Dylan said. "Carberry had just started experimenting with the sedative a day or two before the fire, to gauge its effects and determine how much he should administer."

"Because only the winners are tested," Darci said. The deviousness of it sickened. She glanced at Tyler, saw the horror of it burning in the dark green of his eyes.

"His wife was the one who sent the notes," Dylan said. "She was scared, trying to stop him."

"Warnings," Darci realized, just as she'd suspected. It hadn't made any sense that someone out to harm would announce his intentions.

"Where's Russ?"

It was the first time Tyler had spoken since she'd entered the room, and despite the mound of questions that remained, the one he'd chosen was about his veterinarian...his friend.

"With his daughter," Dylan said. "He wanted to be here, wanted you to know how damned sorry he is, but... Kelly's in a bad way. She's thirteen weeks pregnant."

The lines of Tyler's face tightened. "This isn't his fault."

"I'm not sure he'll believe you on that one," Dylan said.

But Darci knew Tyler would find a way. "So it's over," she said, saying what Tyler wouldn't say, voicing the words that would lift the burden from his shoulders. With Owen Carberry in custody, the shadow of suspicion would finally go away. "Was the fire some kind of accident then?" she asked. "Which would make the body—"

"Owen didn't start the fire."

Darci stilled. "What?"

"Owen Carberry had nothing to do with the fire," Dylan said. The words were flat, grim. "And he has no idea whose body we found in the rubble."

Tyler absorbed the blow of the words, just as he'd absorbed everything else.

"But I don't understand—" Darci stated.

"Separate events," Hastings explained as David Preston stepped into the small office. "We searched his house... talked to his wife.... There's nothing to tie Owen Carberry to the fire."

"Son of a bitch," David swore, joining them. "And you're just going to accept that?"

"We're not accepting anything," Dylan shot back. "The investigation is wide open...but at this point Owen Carberry is not the prime suspect."

Because Tyler was. Dylan didn't say the words, didn't need to. They hung there like acid rain.

"Until we find the murder weapon—" Dylan began, but David Preston cut him off.

"Murder weapon? Since when is this a murder?"

Dylan frowned. "Since forensics confirmed our John Doe was killed by a bullet, not the fire."

Darci closed her eyes, opened them when Tyler's deceptively quiet voice ripped into the stillness.

"Anything else?"

Dylan's expression closed. "Not now."

Tyler nodded, turned toward the door.

"I'd suggest you not plan any trips any time soon," Dylan said into the silence. "Especially out of the country."

Tyler said nothing, just kept right on walking, his father falling into close step behind him.

He didn't come back. The festivities swirled on as evening lapsed into night. Congratulations kept pouring in. Champagne flowed as reporters elbowed their way toward Darci. Photographers kept tabs on her every move. They all wanted the same thing.

Tyler.

"Looks like Elvis left the building," Andrew announced, returning after a thirty-minute absence. "I checked everywhere, but didn't find any of them. I'm afraid they've left, Darce."

She forced a smile, pretended it didn't matter. "Thanks for checking," she said, even as the vise around her chest tightened. First Tyler and his father vanished, then Sarah and Shane and Audrey. Neither Daniel nor his wife had been seen, either.

On the heels of Darci's Pride's greatest victory, the Prestons had closed rank and gone home.

"So have you had a chance to take it all in?" Julia Nash

asked as Andrew snagged two more goblets from the tray of a passing waiter. "I hate to ask this, but it's what everyone will want to know.

"Any regrets?" she continued. "Now that Darci's Pride is the toast of the racing community, do you regret selling partial ownership to Lochlain Racing?"

Darci braced herself, saw her father working his way through the increasingly tipsy partygoers toward her.

"No," she said, with a long deep sip of Cambria Estates' signature Shiraz. "No regrets."

But in that dark quiet place, the place that couldn't stop longing for the touch of a man who'd taken what she'd offered then walked away, the lie burned.

Murder.

The word chased Tyler across the rolling hills of Lochlain, brown now, parched. The soft light of dawn did nothing to hide the damage of drought, the relentless thirst that not even state-of-the-art irrigation could quench.

Murder.

He took the land hard and fast, letting Midnight Magic run at full gallop. The sun pushed higher, burned hotter, but neither man nor horse slowed. They chased the wind as Tyler had done so often as a boy, wound through the familiar paths of his childhood, crossed dry creek beds that should have flowed with water.

Lochlain had always been a sanctuary. No matter what happened, the land was always there. The land sustained. As a kid, when he'd suffered his first taste of death, a schoolmate who'd drowned in the family swimming pool, it had been the land that had buoyed Tyler, the land that healed him. He'd taken to his horse and torn off as his mother called behind him. His father had gone after him, but Tyler knew the land too well. He knew how to lose himself. How to completely disappear.

By the time he returned late that night, two-thirds of the staff had been out looking for him.

After that, they never looked for him again. A man needed his space, his father had always boomed, but that night David Preston realized that sometimes a boy needed his space, too.

There were other times—the death of his beloved aunt and uncle, his own father's heart attack scare, the morning after losing his virginity when Nikki Rae informed him she just wanted to be friends—that sent him to the land. Sometimes he'd only needed hours. Once, six years before, he'd needed days.

Now murder had come to Lochlain.

Blanking the thought, Tyler urged Midnight Magic west, toward the small town of Pepper Flats.

In slow motion Darci's Pride galloped down the final stretch, the camera work focusing on the strength of her legs, the poetry of her movements. The commentator droned on, but the words were lost on Tyler. He only had eyes for the horse—and the oddly pale woman in the tailored suit standing wordlessly in the owner's suite, holding hands with his mother—and his cousin.

"Bloody hell, Ty, I should have known you'd be here."

The voice jerked him away from the newly installed flat-screen television above the bar to the fuzzy silhouette standing against the late-afternoon sun pouring in through an open door. The man—at least Tyler thought it was a man—bore down on his table at the back of the pub with the wrath of an Aboriginal warrior. "Shaney-boy…that you?"

"Do you have any idea—" his brother started, then

broke off abruptly and slid in across from Tyler, yanking the mug toward him. "How many?"

Tyler leaned back in the sturdy wood chair and grinned. "'Member the first time I brought you here?" They'd been kids—at least, Shane had. The Crooke Scale had been a rite of passage, the rowdy, back-slapping pub where all the grooms and exercise riders killed time at the pool tables. Back then it had been men only. Even now, few women ventured through the double wood doors.

At the time, Tyler's mate had been tending bar and promised to overlook the fact Shane was below the legal drinking age. "How many was it?" Tyler asked now. "Four before you were bent over out back—"

"It was six," Shane corrected, but despite his stern voice, his eyes sparkled. "And you know as well as I do that it was the flu, not the beer."

Tyler shrugged. "You tell your story, I tell mine."

"Then tell me," Shane shot back. "Tell me how many you've had—and just what the hell you're doing at The Crooke Scale when two hundred guests are scheduled to arrive at Lochlain in less than an hour?"

Tyler reached for the mug but Shane yanked it out of reach. "You've had Mom scared half to death," he barked. "And Darci—"

Tyler stilled, refused to look at the television, where he knew he would find her. The sports network was running the same race footage over, and over, and over. They would zoom in on Darci, capture the look on her face as Andrew pulled her into his arms. They just couldn't get enough of her, or her horse.

"You walked out, mate," Shane said. "You just walked out, leaving her to handle everything."

"The way I'm remembering it," Tyler tried to drawl, but knew that he slurred, "you did some walking last night, too."

"But I was there this morning," Shane shot back. "I was at Lochlain when she arrived—we all were. Mom and Dad and Audrey…we were all there when Darci and Andrew arrived—"

"Andrew," Tyler repeated. "They make a nice pair, don't you think?"

Shane kicked him. There beneath the table, Shane's leg swung out and whacked Tyler in the shin. "You're gassed."

Tyler's smile was slow, wicked, but he made no effort to refute his brother's accusation.

"I've been looking—" Shane started, but Tyler cut him off.

"Has Dad?"

Glaring now, Shane leaned over the table. "Yes," he bit out. "Dad has covered every millimeter of Lochlain at least twice."

That got him. That stopped him. Tyler sat back and frowned, tried to stop the rich woods of the pub from spinning.

No. That had been the answer he expected—the answer he wanted. His father knew better than to waste his time looking for Tyler. His father knew his eldest son could take care of himself.

"He's worried just like the rest of us," Shane said.

"Then you're all wasting your time," Tyler growled. "I can take care of—"

"Yourself?" Shane finished before Tyler could. "Is that what you call this?" he asked with a sweep of his arm toward Tyler's dusty clothes. "Sitting in a pub and smelling like a sewer?" Shane shook his head. "What if she was the one who found you, not me? What if she was the one who walked through that door?"

Tyler signaled for another beer. "Then I'd tell her to go away, just like I'm telling you."

Shane swore under his breath. "Why do you do that?" he seethed under his breath. "Why do you sit here and pretend with me of all people? Me, your brother? Don't you think I know? Don't you think I understand?"

Tyler stood. "Have fun at the party—"

His brother moved so fast Tyler had no time to prepare. Shane had him by the collar of his T-shirt and against the wall of the pub before Tyler could blink, much less fend him off.

"Stop," Shane said. "Stop trying so bloody hard to pretend none of this is getting to you. Stop trying to pretend your world isn't spinning. Hell, mate, it's not a crime to be human. Someone torched your barns! Someone damn near killed your horses. As it is they'll never race again."

Tyler stood there so very still, not trusting himself to move.

"A man is dead," Shane went on, more quietly now. "Murdered right there in the barn…and people think you might have been the one to pull the trigger."

And set fire to the barns, his horses.

"Of course you're scared," Shane said. "You wouldn't be human if you weren't. You don't have to hide that. It doesn't make you weak or—"

In one quick move, Tyler twisted free and put his hands to his brother's chest, shoved.

Shane staggered back. "That's right," he bit out. "Push me away…shut me out…just like you do everyone else."

Tyler pulled a few coins from his pocket and tossed them onto the table.

"Your name will be cleared," Shane bit out. "Lochlain will be rebuilt. Darci's Pride will win again…and next year Catch Me If You Can will get his first start. And we'll still be there," he said. "Mom and Dad and me…your family. We'll still be there. But she won't," he added quietly. "Darci won't."

The pub wobbled. Tyler gave it a moment to still, then turned and walked through the double doors into the long shadows of late afternoon.

Lights twinkled from the back patio. String after string surrounded the perimeter and encased the branches of the trees, transforming Lochlain into a picture straight from an enchanted fairy tale.

Barbies smoked. An Australian folk ensemble played "The Pub With No Beer." Rich aromas of pork and beef drifted on the warm breeze of early evening. With the sun setting the solar-powered tiki torches took over, illuminating the paths leading to the drink stations, where waiters in solid white served the wines of Cambria Estates.

"This is fantastic," Andrew said, coming up behind Darci. "I don't know how I'll ever thank you—"

"Don't thank me yet," she said with a strained smile. "Let's wait until after the election for that."

The kiss was quick, over almost before Darci noticed him move. "You're too modest. You promised me Australia, and that's what you've given me."

She'd tried. She'd accepted Andrew's offer of employment almost a month before, drunk on dreams of demonstrating, once and for all, that she was not a child anymore. That she'd grown up. That she was responsible. There'd never been any doubt that she knew how to get what she wanted…it was the consequences that always seemed to get in the way. This time she'd set out to prove that she could design and execute a strategy without getting sidetracked.

That had been her mistake, the fatal flaw in her plan.

"Thank you," she said, forcing a smile as she surveyed the gala in full swing. Over two hundred guests had turned out to support Andrew, owners from every stable in the Valley with the exception of Louisa Fairchild.

"I just really believe—" she started, but broke off when a group of women pointed beyond the paddock, toward the land north of the house.

Darci followed their stares, and through the shadows of dusk, saw him. The big black gelding emerged from the trail at a full run. Loosely holding his reins in one hand, the man leaned forward and urged him on. They ran as one, galloping along the outskirts of the party, slowing only as they neared the paddock.

"Is that him?" the woman nearest Darci whispered.

"I think so," another answered with a horrified little smile. "Doesn't he always wear a hat like that?"

"God, look at him," the first said with a laugh. "Who needs a tux when a man looks like that in jeans?"

"I'll sure take him," her friend agreed as man and horse vanished behind the surviving barn. And something inside Darci twisted.

"Guess he's okay," Andrew deadpanned.

But Darci wasn't. She wasn't okay. She knew Shane had found his brother at The Crooke Scale. She knew he'd been drinking, that he'd gotten into a scuffle with his brother before walking out. She knew all that…but none of it prepared her for the reality of a dirty, roughshod Tyler tearing in from the bush like some kind of irreverent banshee—

"I think the Jamesons just arrived," Darci said, motioning toward a barrel of a man and a slender woman standing with Tyler's parents. "They were hoping to talk with you a little about your thoughts on track safety…"

"Got it." Effortless smile in place, Andrew headed toward one of the Hunter's more prominent families, and Darci took off for the barn.

Peggy caught her first. A local reporter had a few questions. A photographer wanted a picture of her standing in front of the empty spot where the barns had once stood. Darci politely refused.

The caterer had a question. Audrey offered her compliments and wanted to know if she'd seen Daniel or Marnie.

Darci hadn't.

By the time she reached the barn, Midnight Magic stood quietly in his stall while young Zach cooled him down. "Can't say that I know," he said when she asked if he knew where Tyler had gone.

Darci turned and headed back for the house. To get upstairs, Tyler would have to work his way through the guests. He was hot and sweaty, maybe drunk—

Her heart slammed hard. And something dark and ugly boiled inside of her.

Then she saw the single light glowing from the equine medical clinic beyond the small stone office building.

She heard him before she saw him, the warm cadence of a voice still hoarse from too much smoke. It had been ten days. Ten days since fire had swept through Lochlain's barns…ten days since Tyler had run into the smoky darkness…

Ten days since his hopes and dreams and plans went up in flames.

"No worries now, mate," she heard him drawl, and of its own will, her throat tightened. "You didn't miss a thing, that I can promise. I'm knowing what I always told you, that the Classic was *the* race of the season, but it was too hot this year…too dry."

Quietly, Darci slipped through the partially open door leading from the front of the clinic.

"Lots of commotion," he said. "Too many damned reporters."

She neared the first stall, empty now, and forced herself to breathe.

He stood there by his horse, one arm still trapped in a cast, while with his good hand he slid a brush along the horse's side. He had his back to her. His hat still sat low on his head, while his jeans rode low on his hips. His white T-shirt was damp and dusty. There was mud on his jeans just below the knee and on the heels of his boots.

"The only thing you missed…" he went on, his accent soft and rich and hypnotic, even to a fellow native of Oz. For six years it had been the clipped, often formal British accent she'd heard…the British accent even she, herself, had begun to acquire. But here, now, being home, in the barn with Tyler and hearing his Aussie brogue…

She closed her eyes, and for a moment, just listened.

"…was our girl," he said. "You should have seen her, mate. She was really something."

Darci's throat tightened.

"I always knew she was a stunner. I always knew she was destined to make her mark…but yesterday…"

Darci opened her eyes.

"No one's ever stolen my breath like that," he said with a poetry Darci had only heard from him once before, when she'd lain beneath him with her hair fanned out on the pillow and their hands joined… Tyler Hugh Preston was a man of the land. He could charm when he needed to, flash an irreverent smile and distract someone before they got too close. But his words were few. Glimpses inside were unheard of.

"No one else has ever made me bleed like that—"

It happened so fast Darci had no time to prepare. Midnight whinnied and looked up, saw Darci standing in the shadows. His beautiful brown eyes locked onto hers as his ears perked, and Tyler turned. "What is it, mate?"

His eyes met hers, and the moment froze.

"Well, lookee who we have here," Tyler drawled as his hand stilled against the horse's side. "If it's not the belle of the ball herself."

The second she saw his eyes, she knew. Even through the shadows she could see the gleam, not raw and sensual as it had been a few nights before, but wild like lightning.

And instinctively she took a step back.

"Well, hell, mate, did you see that?" he slurred, letting the brush drop to the ground. "Looks like Darci-Anne knows it's not a good idea to sneak up on someone and eavesdrop."

She stood a little straighter. "Tyler—"

He started toward her, his steps slow, measured. "Tell me now, sunshine," he drawled, his voice so dangerously low and quiet Darci could barely make out the words. "You're not afraid of me, are you?"

Chapter Thirteen

Shadows slipped and fell. Silence stretched. Midnight Magic watched. "Of course not," Darci started, but Tyler did not let her finish.

"Liar." The word tore out of him. "I can see it in your eyes." He closed in on her, and even though she knew she should move, get out of the barn, away from this stranger—

"You're drunk," she whispered.

"You think so?" He stopped a breath away, his eyes burning as he lifted a hand to twirl his finger around the tendril of hair she'd let fall from her twist. "That would make it easier, wouldn't it?" he asked. "If I was drunk. You could tell yourself none of this is real."

"No." Her voice scratched on the way out. "You're wrong. I—"

"Maybe I was drunk before," he pushed on, still standing way too close, with the fronts of his legs brushing hers, and the scent of ale and dust and leather swirling around them. "The night of the fire. That was the day you walked back into my life…announced that the only reason you'd stepped foot on my land was because of my cousin."

She tried to take a step back, but the door to the stall prevented her.

"Maybe I started drinking," he said, and the ache kept winding deeper and deeper. "Maybe I didn't stop. Maybe that's why I came outside, spoiling for a fight. Maybe I—"

"Stop it!" With the lash of the words she lashed with her hands, as well, shoving at him, catching him off guard and sending him staggering backward. He made no move to stop himself, just crashed right there on the floor of the treatment room. "That's not what happened and we both know it. You had nothing to do with the fire."

His smile was slow, lazy. "You sure about that, sunshine? Maybe *I'm* the illusionist this time—"

She stepped forward and glared down at him. "You're drunk," she said again. "And frustrated and scared—"

He propped himself up on his elbows. "Anyone ever tell you how gorgeous you look when you get all worked up?" His gaze swept along the short, snug-fitting apricot dress she'd selected for the party. "Does he tell you?"

She stiffened. "What are you talking—"

"He's always seemed a little conservative to me," Tyler rolled on, "but then, after all that time you spent in England, maybe your tastes have changed, too. Maybe you—"

The hurt was swift. "You son of a bitch—"

"There she is," he drawled. "There's the Tara I remember." Deliberately, he rolled to his feet. "All that fire and passion…" His eyes heated. "You should get on out of here now," he said, "before he finds us."

The shaking started, deep, deep inside, but on the outside,

there was only stillness, a frozen shell that defied the slow boil rising through her. She didn't need Tyler to clarify who he was talking about, or what he was implying she did with the man who'd given her the chance she'd been craving for years.

"I was wrong," she said against the rawness in her throat. "Wrong to come back here." To try to help.

To care.

"I thought I could make things better," she whispered, lifting a hand to rub along her arm. It was hot outside. She knew that. Even with nightfall, the wind blew warm. In the distance, the red glow of a bushfire painted the horizon.

But inside there was only cold.

"That's what I wanted," she said. "That's why I approached Andrew. Because I knew. I knew what I did to you all those years ago was wrong." And she'd never forgotten, never forgiven herself. "And I wanted to help...to give something back to you," she said, barely recognizing the mechanical rasp to her voice, or the moisture stinging her eyes. "But I was wrong," she said again. "Wrong to think I could just walk back into your life and—"

The line of his jaw tightened. "And what?"

She shook her head. "I don't know you anymore," she said. "I'm not sure I ever did."

"I'm not the one who lied."

"All these years," she whispered. "I built you up in my mind like some kind of fallen hero. All I could think..." Her words trailed off as the memories swarmed. "I never let anyone else close. Never let anyone else near me. Even when they called me frigid—"

Tyler didn't move. That wasn't what stopped her. It was his eyes, the low hard glitter that stopped her breath, and the unnaturally still lines of his body. "Darci—"

She turned before he could finish, lunged for the door before the rasp of his voice could punish any further.

The night came fast and the hot breeze slapped, and as everything started to blur—the festive lights and the jangly folk music, hopes and dreams and memories—all those tears she'd denied for too many years started to fall.

People were everywhere. Trails of tiki torches wound through the grounds in a clever maze. Even the trees dazzled, masses of twinkling lights destroying the distinction between the star-filled sky and the parched land.

Somehow she'd done it. Somehow between the fire and the drugging scandal and the encroaching shadow of murder, Darci had erased the ugly and transformed Lochlain into something straight from the pages of a storybook. And he—

Tyler swore under his breath and resisted the urge to shove against the row of solar torches.

"Tyler, honey," came a warm voice from behind him, and he turned just as his mother closed in on him. Her hair was loose, soft around her face. Her dress was long and flowing, lopping about ten years off her age. "Are you okay?" she asked. "You look…" Her voice trailed off. "We've been worried about you."

"Wasted energy," he said, pulling her to him for a quick kiss to her cheek. "I just needed…" The land. Space. "Have you seen Darci?"

"Not in the past few minutes, no," she said. "But I saw her with Andrew about half an hour ago. She really did a wonderful job, don't you think? You wouldn't believe all the people who've offered to help—with Andrew and with Lochlain."

"Lochlain?"

"Help rebuild," she said. "Everyone here knows you had nothing to do with the fire."

His jaw tightened, but before he could say anything, a blur of apricot had him spinning toward a group of women. She stood there, tall, unusually rigid, her face pale and tight despite the glow of a nearby torch.

"There she is," his mother said, smiling. "Doesn't she look lovely?"

Tyler was already moving toward her.

"How nice of you to join us," Shane drawled as Tyler cut through two of the tiki torches. "But you know, you might want to get showered—"

Tyler swung around and cut him a back-off look, but when he turned again toward the table of hors d'oeuvres, Darci was gone.

"Saw you coming," Shane said, providing unwanted play-by-play. "Made a beeline away from her friends before you could embarrass her anymore."

Tyler said nothing, just kept cutting his way through the guests milling around the buffet tables. People stopped and stared. The Jamesons turned and watched. Even his father stood stoically beneath a tall eucalyptus, watching.

Tyler was aware of them all, dressed in their crisp, clean clothes, men in khakis and dress shirts, women in flowing sundresses and strappy sandals, knew they all studied him like an uninvited insect at a party. But he didn't let them stop him, didn't let them slow him. He worked his way around the drink station toward the stage where the folk band sent jangly music into the night, until finally he saw her on the far side of the back porch with Julia Nash and Audrey. The other two women had their backs to him, but Darci faced him. Darci watched. And the second he headed her direction, she turned to leave.

"Darci!"

She stiffened but didn't look, kept right on walking.

"Darci!" he called again, this time loud enough for there to be no mistake—loud enough for anyone in the vicinity to hear. "Wait."

Slowly she stopped, and slowly she turned. And when her eyes met his, the glow of silent horror should have stopped him. But didn't. He kept right on toward her, cutting through a group of his parents' friends and striding through a long meandering line leading to a drink station. Around him he was aware of people stepping back, watching, but he didn't stop to look, just kept his eyes on Darci, standing there against the night in her soft apricot dress, with the lights twinkling down on every rigid line of her body.

Stricken. It was the only word he could come up with.

"Tyler—" she started as he closed in on her, but he ignored the warning in her voice—the obvious plea for him to stop—and kept right on walking, not stopping until he stood close enough to touch.

"I hurt you," he said without preamble, and then stunned himself by taking her hand and bringing it to his mouth. Cold. Her skin was so damn cold. "I'm sorry."

He felt her stiffen, saw her wince. "Don't—"

"In the clinic," he clarified. "What I said. I was wrong."

The wind blew against them, sending long blond strands of hair against her face. The effect should have softened the distant lines of her face, but didn't.

"You're drunk," she started, but again he wouldn't let her finish.

"Not really," he said. "At least, not the way you think."

Her gaze darted beyond him, to Audrey and Julia and everyone else trying to pretend they weren't watching, weren't listening. "Not here," she whispered.

"Then where?" He still held her hand, refused to let it go. "Tell me where."

Something flickered in her eyes. "If you'll excuse me," she said to her friends, her voice smooth and polished and refined, that of her English education and not her wild Aussie youth. Posture perfect, she turned and headed for the privacy of the rambling stone house.

He went with her, the length of his stride carrying him in front of her until he was practically dragging her. He forced himself to slow down, forced all those hard combustible edges to soften as he slipped into his role as host and greeted several of his parents' friends, including the owner of Warrego Downs.

"That's some girl you got there," Samuel Summers said with a broad smile. "She gave us all quite a thrill."

"That she does." His smile warm, broad, cordial, Tyler squeezed Darci's hand.

But she made no move to reciprocate, just kept her plastic smile in place as they crossed the porch and walked into the brightly lit foyer, straight into another throng of guests.

Darci stilled, looked around, but Tyler took over, kept her hand in his as he led her toward the wide staircase. When he felt her hesitate, he detoured, swerving through the dining room to the kitchen, where a few servers lingered. From there he opened the door concealing the back stairs and gestured toward the second floor.

"No one will know," he said quietly. "No one will see."

Her expression remained unreadable, but at last she moved, slowly heading up the stairs.

Tyler followed.

At the hallway that cut through the upstairs, he took her hand, leading her past the master suite he reserved for his parents when they were at the stud, toward the smaller room at the far end of the hall. Once the walls had been blue, the shelves lined with riding trophies, the bed a bunk. Now the walls were brown, the shelves filled with books, the bed a big king that dominated the small space.

"Tyler—" Darci said, and in her voice he heard her discomfort with entering his bedroom. She'd been in it before. They'd made love right there in the bed. "Just leave it alone," she whispered.

Maybe once he would have. Maybe only a few days before, he would have. But in the clinic he'd seen something in her eyes, something dark and broken and lost, and it drove him.

Slayed him.

"I can't." He closed the door and then they were alone, the two of them in his bedroom, him raw from the land, her dressed in a soft apricot dress that dipped at her chest and flowed around her legs.

"I tried," he said, and when he stepped deeper into the room, she stepped back, not toward the bed, but the window, where instead of darkness, light glowed from the party below. "I tried to pretend it didn't matter. From the moment you turned around in my office, all chic and stylish in your little suit, all refined and elegant and grown-up, more stranger than woman, I tried to pretend it didn't matter. That you being here didn't matter. That you could have your little party and then be on your way, walk away again, walk back out of my life and everything would just go back to the way it was."

The blue of her eyes darkened, glowed. "That was my intent," she said, and though he knew the words to be true, they stabbed all the same, and the scent of roses and baby powder damn near destroyed him.

"But everywhere I looked, there you were. The night of

the fire," he said, and when her expression changed, softened, something hot and volatile fired through him. "I saw you," he said. "Long before I knew it was you. I saw you with the horses, the men. I saw you dirty. I saw you fall."

Her eyes flared, and he realized he'd just disclosed something she hadn't known.

"I saw you get back up, too," he told her. One of the volunteer firefighters had reached for her, but she'd shrugged off his help and gone right back to what she was doing. "It was you, wasn't it?" he asked. "It was you who sent Hastings in after me."

Her lips parted, but she said nothing, didn't need to. He knew. They both did.

"And you were there when I came out. You made sure I got help."

Standing against the twinkle of lights from below, she squeezed her eyes closed, and damn near slugged Tyler in the gut.

He wasn't sure how he did it, how he stayed at the foot of the bed, a good five steps from where she stood, when all he wanted—

"That should have been the end," he told her. "That should have been where we said goodbye." Without a party, there'd been no need for her to stay.

She opened her eyes and pushed at the hair falling into her face. "That would have been easier."

"But we've never been about easy," he pointed out, and for a long moment the words just hung there among the faint strains of music from below. "When I went to Whittleson Stud…" Christ, she'd pulled open the door in that big oversize T-shirt, without a shred of makeup, and still, something inside him had stirred. "I'm not sure you've ever looked more beautiful."

Her smile was soft, fleeting. "Then you need glasses."

"No." He stepped toward her, but when she stiffened, he made himself stop. "That's not what I need."

Their eyes met and held, broken only by a burst of laughter from below.

"Do you have any idea," he gritted out, "any idea at all what it did to me when I heard there'd been an intruder at Whittleson Stud? That you'd been there alone, that you were scared…maybe in danger." Again he took another step toward her. *"Because of me."*

She shook her head, sending blond hair around her face. "Not because of you."

"Because of me," he said again. "Because, instead of keeping your distance, you'd waded right in and sold me majority ownership of your horse."

Her smile was slow, mesmerizing. "Who are you?" she asked. "And what have you done with Tyler Preston?"

He couldn't help it, couldn't stop it. The laugh rumbled right out of him, and brought a dangerous spark to her eyes. "You mean that arsehole from the clinic?"

Her laughter was soft, surprisingly husky. "No, I mean the bloke who rarely says more than two sentences at a time."

He felt his own mouth curve. "All an act."

"Which? The silent game or—" She broke off, hesitated. "Or this?"

Only two more steps separated them. He eliminated both, stopping so close he could feel her breath. There he lifted his good hand, and touched. "I'll let you be the judge," he said as his fingers drifted across her face.

She watched him, eyes wide, no longer stricken.

"I tried not to think about you," he said. "Not to notice." Or watch. "Not to care."

Her hand found his. "That charm school training," she

said with that endearing little crooked smile of hers, the one he'd seen far too little of for the past ten days.

Bloody hell. The past six years.

"I needed to concentrate," he told her. "I needed to focus."

"Ah," she said. "There he is. The real Tyler Preston—"

He moved so fast she had no time to twist away. He slid his hand behind her head and lowered his face, wasted no time on teasing or tasting. He took her mouth with his and kissed her long and deep and hard, holding her as she stiffened, moving his mouth as she went languid and pushed up into him.

"Do you have any idea," he murmured against the softness of her lips, "any idea at all how long I've wanted to do that?"

She pulled back, revealing eyes drenched with a wanting that had haunted his dreams. "Since the night before the race?" she asked as she lifted a hand to toy with the whiskers at his jaw. "When you tried to pretend I wasn't there?"

His blood heated. He had tried to pretend. As the hours had moved deeper into the night, as they'd waited for the phone to ring with more information about the attempt against Darci's Pride, he'd taken to the balcony, staring out over Sydney instead of turning to see Darci sprawled out on his bed. She'd kicked off her shoes and untwisted her hair, had shoved the pillows into a big bunch before leaning back and turning on the telly. Some mindless show had blared at them, but he hadn't trusted himself to go back into that room.

"Longer," he said now, as her fingers drifted from his jaw to his lower lip.

"That night at Sam's?" she asked, with her eyes so dark and bottomless and steady. "When you refused to leave?"

He pulled her finger into his mouth, sucked quickly before answering. "You mean when you refused to go to your room?"

She laughed. Just like that, right there in his arms, only an hour after he'd shredded her with his callousness, Darci laughed. "Is that what you wanted?" she asked with the dare both in her eyes and her voice, the same dare from all those years before. "For me to go to my room and lock the door?"

He pressed against her, let the hard lines of his body answer for him. "No."

Her smile widened. "I didn't think so."

"But that's not when," he murmured against the side of her face. "That's not when I first wanted to taste you."

She pulled back, tracing her fingers along the stubble at his jaw. "Then when?"

The answer humbled him. "I never stopped," he told her, and now he kissed her again, this time longer and deeper, his mouth taking hers with the hunger he'd tried to abolish. "Never," he muttered, backing her against the wall. His free hand found her hair and fisted it, destroyed the prim, proper twist and let the strands fall like a curtain around her face, as they had so long ago.

"You were like a drug," he told her between kisses. "Something I couldn't stop wanting even though—"

She stiffened. That's what stopped him. There in his arms, sandwiched between his body and the wall, Darci went completely still, all except her heart. He could feel it slamming against his chest.

"Even though I almost destroyed you," she finished for him, and in her eyes, he saw the same pain that laced her voice. "Even though my lies—"

He didn't let her finish. He slid his hand from her hair to her mouth, pressed two fingers. "Don't."

"But I have to," she whispered. "That's why I'm here, Tyler. That's why I came back." She closed her eyes, opened them a heartbeat later. "For you."

The quiet words rocked him. "You mean for Andrew—"

"For you," she said. "By having the party here, I thought I could somehow undo the damage—"

Again he didn't let her finish. But this time he used his mouth to silence, his kiss to quiet.

"The past," he murmured. "It's time to let it go."

She pulled back and looked at him, lifted a hand to feather her fingers against the side of his cheek. "I never stopped," she whispered, and then her hands were sliding down his face to his shoulders. "Never stopped remembering…" Her fingers were spread, her touch soft, achingly tentative. "Wanting," she added as her thumbs slid along the outline of his flat nipples.

And then he couldn't do it any longer, couldn't just stand there and not touch.

Take.

Chapter Fourteen

Everything fell away. All the hurt and the regret, the sting of words spoken in anger and frustration, the plans and the determination, the memories of all the long, cold nights that separated them, it all slipped into nothingness, leaving only Darci and Tyler and a truth she no longer wanted to deny.

"This," she murmured against the sweet wash of discovery. "You." Him. She'd never stopped wanting. Never stopped dreaming. Even when she'd tried. Even when she'd lied. She'd told herself Tyler Preston was part of her past. A foolish mistake. A wild crush she'd taken too far. There'd been regret. She'd never tried to deny that. Because of her, Tyler had suffered. Because she'd led him on, because she'd been dishonest, he'd paid a steep price. He'd almost lost Lochlain.

He should hate her. That's what she'd told herself all these years. Tyler Preston hated her. Blamed her. But the way he looked at her now...

It was not hate glowing in the dark green of his eyes.

And it was not hate that whispered through his touch. "I never imagined—" she started, but he didn't let her finish.

"I did." His voice was brutally quiet. "I imagined," he said, and the melting came harder, faster. "You," he added as his hands slid down her back. "I imagined you, here, like this."

Her breath caught. "Tell me," she whispered, but he only smiled slowly, wickedly.

"I'd rather show you." With the lazy words he again took her mouth, kissing her with the hypnotic heat of the dreams she'd tried to banish from the long hours of the night. He kissed her slowly at first, long and deep and thorough as she melted into him. She could feel him, all of him, so warm and hard against her, and all she could think was more. She wanted more.

Needed more than that.

"Tyler," she whispered against his open mouth, loving the feel of his whiskers scraping her jaw. She could still see him as he'd been only a short time before, when he'd cut through the night and urged his big black gelding toward the barn. Wordlessly she'd watched, telling herself it was horror she felt. Anger that he'd put on such an inappropriate display when he should have been showered and dressed and greeting guests in his capacity as host.

But the thrill had been there, secret, forbidden, winding through her like a mesmerizing drug. She'd wanted—

She'd wanted. In the end, it was as simple as that. Despite all that stood between them, she'd never stopped wanting him. It was that want that had her hands running along the soft cotton of his T-shirt, toward the waistband of his jeans. There she tugged.

The shirt slipped free and then there was only the heat of man and greed as her palms flattened against his abdomen and slid upward. His skin was hot, his chest hard and solid. For a moment she allowed herself only to feel, to savor—but then she wanted more and her hands were moving again, this time to the hem of his shirt. She dragged it upward, ripped her mouth from his long enough to pull the cotton over his head and let it drop to the floor.

And then it was all she could do to breathe. He stood there in the glow of the lone bedside lamp, his shoulders and chest bronze from over thirty years of working the ranch. Tyler Preston was not a man who needed a gym to form his body. He was not a man who needed weights or Nautilus equipment to build his strength. The definition of his chest came from hard physical labor. The plane of his stomach came from a lifetime working with the horses. Lower—

A trail of dark hair teased down to the fly of his jeans. For a moment she stared, remembered. Then she lifted her gaze to his, and reached her hands behind her neck.

His eyes darkened as she eased the zipper toward the curve of her back. Cool air stirred by the ceiling fan swirled against her flesh as her dress fell open. She started to shrug out of it, but he moved faster, pulling her into his arms and slanting his mouth against hers, walking her backward.

There wasn't far to go. With only a few steps the backs of her legs slipped up against the big bed where she'd made love for the second time in her life. The first had been in a Sydney hotel room. In the years since their affair had ended, there'd been only dreams.

Now dreams flirted with reality. His hands moved along her body, big and warm and seeking, possessive but somehow tender. "So soft," he murmured, and the swell inside grew heavier, more demanding. She tugged him toward the big bed, and as he eased her down and hovered over her, she realized that somewhere along the line, her dress had fallen away, leaving only the simple white bra and panties she'd selected that morning. All those years before, she'd lingered at the lingerie shop, choosing black lace to go along with the provocative image she'd tried to create.

The lie.

"I was wrong," he said, and for a cruel moment her heart slowed. "This isn't what I imagined."

The freezing started deep inside as the rich brown walls collapsed around her, but then he propped himself over her and lowered his free hand to her chest. There the tips of his fingers feathered the outline of the plain white bra. "This is better," he murmured. "This is real."

It was. It was real. It was Tyler and it was her—Darci not Tara, white cotton not black lace, woman not girl. Truth not lies.

"I tried to forget," she whispered as her hands found the smooth warmth of his abdomen. She slid upward, toyed with the swirls of dark hair. "I tried not to remember, to imagine…"

As she explored, he hovered there and watched, his body tensing and flexing, his eyes glowing through the shadows.

"But I couldn't do anything about the dreams." She flicked her thumb against one wide flat nipple. "You'd come to me then," she admitted, shifting so that he settled between her legs. Then, eyes locked on his, she slid her hands back down, to the fly of his jeans. There she fumbled, freeing the button then lowering the zipper, until she could feel him, the hard warmth straining against his shorts. "And love me," she whispered, feeling him. Cupping him.

Loving him.

They moved together, her sliding, him shoving, working the jeans down his legs. The shorts went, too. And then the boots, leaving only him, big and naked and stretched out alongside her. She rolled into him and reached for him, found him.

"Like this," she whispered, holding him, squeezing, emboldened by the rough sound that broke from his throat.

"Darci..." And then his mouth was on hers again and they rolled deeper into the bed.

"Your arm—" she started, but he repositioned himself and shook off her concern, sliding his free hand from her face along her neck, to her chest. His mouth followed, trailing little kisses to her breasts. He kissed gently, almost in greeting before taking her in his mouth and shattering the gossamer-fine veil between dreams and reality.

Sensation flooded her. Warmth pooled between her legs. She twisted against him, heard the little mewls that slipped from her throat as he sucked deeper, harder, using his tongue to drive her into oblivion. She wasn't sure when his hand slipped lower, just knew that when he tugged against her panties she lifted her hips and then they were gone, leaving his hand to return to her, and his fingers to slip inside.

Sensation streaked like lightning, and her mind blanked. She moved against him, arched into him.

"So tight," he murmured just as he had all those years before. And just like all those years ago, her body quickened in dark, blinding need.

"Tyler," she whispered, reaching for him. *"Please..."*

He eased back and looked down at her, the glow of the lamp casting his face in a bone-melting play of shadows and light.

"So beautiful," he murmured, and then he was there, nudging against her, pushing inside, and everything else just dissolved. *Shattered.* She welcomed him, took him, curled her legs around his and held on as he went deep, lingered there, his mouth returning to hers as he eased back and pushed in once again.

All those dreams, all those late-night longings she'd tried to destroy. They crashed in on her, drove her as Tyler rocked against her. She arched into him and took him in, felt the sting of moisture against the backs of her eyes. Never had she imagined. Never had she allowed herself to think she and Tyler would be like this again. That they could be. Too much stood—

But there was nothing between them now. Nothing separating them. Wordlessly his hand found hers and his fingers twined, and together like that, she cried out as reality carried her into a place far more exquisite than dreams.

He didn't want to move. He didn't trust himself to. If he moved she might wake, and if she woke—

Tyler didn't let the thought go any further. Waking wouldn't matter this time, because he wasn't asleep. The woman sprawled on top of him wasn't a cruel specter, there to love him in the darkness, only to leave him with the light. She wasn't a dream and this wasn't a lie. She was…

Darci. She was Darci.

Through the soft glow of moonlight, he looked at her face resting against his chest, the blond hair spilling down to his abdomen. Earlier she'd propped herself over him and teased him with that hair, let it dance across his face, then his chest, then lower.

Now she slept.

So did Lochlain. Somewhere along the line the strains of music had quit drifting through the night, and the twinkle of lights had gone dark, leaving only the moon and the stars to light the sky. Vaguely he'd been aware of footsteps from the hallway beyond, but now, like Darci, the house slept.

For so bloody long he'd pushed himself through day after day, determined to let nothing or no one intrude upon the goals he'd set for himself, the starkly delineated dreams he'd fashioned as a child. He'd been a boy then, with a boy's passions and a boy's wants. He'd had no way to know what it would be to become a man, the new needs that would drive him. The new wants. Then Tara had—

Not Tara. *Darci.*

Then Darci had come into his life and for the first time his tunnel vision had wavered. For the first time he'd wanted something even more than he'd wanted to grow his father's dynasty. He'd been ill-prepared, reckless, and he'd gone after Darci despite all the warnings blaring at him. He'd known something wasn't right...but he hadn't bloody cared. He'd just...wanted.

And in the process, he'd damn near ruined them both.

She'd suffered. She blamed herself for the lie, but she hadn't breezed on with her life unscathed. She'd been exiled from the land of her childhood, the land of her mother, shuffled half a world away, where her father could mold her into the daughter he'd imagined.

But Darci had survived. With the same grit and determination that had transformed Australia from a land of exile to a land of opportunity, Darci had survived, and she'd come back. She'd come home to Australia.

To him.

The thought did odd things to his chest. So did the memory of how tight she'd been. She'd been like that before, the first time. But then she'd been a virgin. Six years had passed since then. Surely there'd been other—

I never let anyone else close. Never let anyone else near me. Even when they called me frigid—

The burn of memory started low and wound around

fast, pulling hard, until he damn near couldn't breathe. Lifting a hand, he touched, slid the hair from her face.

Her lips curved in reflex, and his body hardened. They'd made love—he'd stopped counting at four. They'd taken and given, drunk and claimed and possessed, and now even as he told himself not to wake her, she stirred against him, her mouth moving against his nipple, her hand reaching lower.

"Sleep," he murmured as his body came fully awake. Darci slid over him and buried her face in his neck, kissing her way up to his jaw, his mouth.

"Tyler," she whispered against his bottom lip, and within seconds sleep was the last thing on his mind.

She didn't want to wake up. Tyler was there. He'd come to her again, loved her. And this time he'd stayed. She could feel him beneath her, the hard naked warmth, the play of his hand in her hair. If she opened her eyes…

She knew what would happen if she opened her eyes, what always happened. He would slip back into that dark place he'd learned to wall off during the long hours of sunshine.

She didn't want that. She wasn't ready for him to slip away, didn't want the rhythmic beat of his heart beneath her ear to quiet. She kept her eyes closed and stretched, slid her hand along his chest as the pounding grew louder—

"Tyler!"

The urgent voice broke through the dream and kicked Darci's heart into a sobering rhythm.

"I need you to open the door, son."

She jerked back and opened her eyes as the solid warmth slid from beneath her. Sunshine cut in, blinded, made her blink. Squinting, she scrambled up as Tyler rolled from bed and strode toward his father's voice. Tall. Naked.

"For God's sake, Dad," he started, yanking at the door. But just as quickly he went very still. "My God, what's wrong?"

"Get some clothes on," David Preston said. "Hastings is downstairs—"

No more words were needed. Tyler pivoted and grabbed the jeans he'd discarded the night before, stepped into them as he strode out the door with his father. Then...silence.

And Darci started to shake. Everything came crashing back, all the horror they'd managed to block out during the long, heated hours of the night. Something had happened. Something was wrong. Through the crack in the door, she'd seen the somber look in David Preston's eyes. She'd heard the hard edge to his voice, and she knew.

Heart slamming, she bolted from bed and snatched up her dress from the night before, stepped into it as she ran for the door. From the hallway she could hear voices.

At the top of the stairs, one name stopped her cold.

"Sam?"

She closed her eyes, felt the corridor start to spin.

"But he's in Africa," she heard through some distorted tunnel of space and time. Tyler's voice. That was Tyler's voice. But it was off, somehow. Strained. "On safari."

"I'm afraid not," a different voice said, and somehow Darci managed to open her eyes and blink, bring the small crowd of men gathered below into focus. Dylan. Dylan Hastings was there. It was his voice. "He never made the trip."

"What the—" Tyler broke in, but Dylan didn't let him finish.

"Daniel's wife recognized the opal ring—and now forensics has positively identified the body."

Darci felt her knees try to go out from beneath her. She reached for the banister, curled her fingers around the smooth polished wood. "No…"

Maybe she whispered. Maybe she spoke louder. But through the haze came a hand, warm, solid, steady to her shoulder, and wobbly, she turned. Saw him.

Saw Andrew.

He stood there clean and shaved and dressed to the nines in a three-piece suit, as if he was ready to…

Ready to give a speech.

Because he was.

It was the day after the gala. She'd booked him at a luncheon in Sydney.

"Darci?" His voice was low, confused. "Are you okay?"

She blinked up at him, felt something simultaneously hot and cold flush through her. Because no. She was not okay. Sam was not okay….

"Sam's dead," she whispered, and Andrew frowned.

"I know, I heard. I'm sorry—I know you two were close."

She blinked, tried to bring it all into focus, but the pieces, sharp, jagged, kept slipping through her fingers. Her lifelong family friend was dead—and here she stood, barefoot and bare legged, with her strappy dress from the night before hanging from her shoulders, not even zipped, her hair hanging in her face, her skin flushed from a night of lovemaking, looking into the knowing eyes of the man who'd given her the once-in-a-lifetime opportunity she'd spent years trying to create. There was a stark knowing in his eyes…

She'd walked out on him. She'd walked out on the gala. She'd compromised everything she'd been building.

To spend the night in Tyler Preston's bed.

Again…

"Look," Andrew said. "Don't worry about Sydney, okay? I can handle this one—"

"No," she said, cutting him off. "I'll be ready—"

His grip on her shoulders tightened. "I think it's best if you stay here."

"No," she said again, this time stronger than before. And then somehow she shook off her shock and straightened her shoulders, lifted her chin. "I made a promise to you," she said, finding the smooth, polished voice she'd perfected in England, the voice of the woman, not the child. The voice of confidence—not the recklessness of the night before. "And I intend to keep it."

Dead.

Sam Whittleson was dead.

Tyler kept himself very still, stood at the heavily draped window of the elegant living room his mom had taken great pleasure in decorating, and great pride in sharing. It was where she'd received guests, where she'd put their carefully decorated Christmas tree, where, as children, Tyler and Shane would tear down the stairs, ready to rip into their presents. It was where she'd sit quietly in the afternoons, lost in a thick historical romance.

Where she'd come for quiet, peace.

Where Tyler could still see Sam Whittleson as a young man, shaking hands with Tyler's father while his son, Daniel, stood close to his side. They'd been leaving, saying goodbye. Sam had been full of plans about fame and fortune to be made, a bigger life to be led. Daniel had stood quietly, his eyes somber, and though he hadn't said a word, Tyler had known. Tyler had known Daniel hadn't wanted to leave Australia…but he hadn't wanted to infringe upon his father's dream, either.

Now that father was dead.

Tyler glanced at his own father, felt his chest tighten. They'd had a few scares. David Preston's heart had acted up a few times, but he was a strong man, and he'd rallied. In his late fifties, there was much living left to be done.

"So that was the last time you saw him," Hastings said. "At the auction when you bought the mares."

"Told him I'd sell them back to him, too," Tyler said as the water running through the upstairs pipes shut off. His mother was already dressed and in the kitchen. Darci was the only one who'd yet to come downstairs. "Whenever he got the funds."

"If he was so strapped, then what was he doing going off to Africa? Last I knew safaris weren't cheap."

"A gift." Frustration pushed through Tyler. He knew what picture they were trying to paint.

He also knew it was categorically not true. "From his son."

They'd been at it over thirty minutes. Question after question had been fired at him, some multiple times, from multiple directions.

Tyler's answers never changed. He stood there as patiently as he could, answering methodically, thoughtfully, acutely aware that Darci remained upstairs.

He'd wanted to go upstairs and talk to her, tell her. Promise her everything would be okay. He didn't know why Sam had been at Lochlain. To see Daniel was the obvious answer, but Sam's son had already refuted that possibility. The last Daniel had seen of his father had been at the Sydney airport the day before the fire. Daniel had driven him there, left him there.

He'd had no idea why his father had circled back to Lochlain.

"As you can see, Sam Whittleson and the Prestons were on fine terms," Walter Cummings put in. A tall, thin man with a full head of snow-white hair, the distinguished Sydney attorney had been one of the first friends David

Preston made upon arriving in Australia. They'd both been young then, full of dreams and ambition.

Now they'd realized both.

"If there are no further questions…" Walter said, letting the words dangle.

Dylan frowned. "For now. But the investigation is still wide open. Mr. Preston needs to keep himself available."

They considered him a suspect. They thought it possible that Tyler had found Sam in the barn. That they'd argued. That Tyler had shot his friend with a yet-to-be-found gun. Maybe on accident. Maybe by purpose. That the fire had been set to cover the crime.

Tyler had surrendered Lochlain's firearms for testing.

The ugliness of it twisted through Tyler as the detectives left, as he finally took the stairs and pushed into his bedroom, headed toward the hum of the hair dryer coming from the adjoining bathroom.

He found her there, dressed in a crisp tailored suit much like the afternoon before the fire, when she'd strolled into his office to discuss plans for the fund-raiser. Then her hair and makeup had been fashion-magazine perfect. Now her hair was damp, stringy as she worked it over with the hair dryer, and there was little color to her face.

He wasn't sure he'd ever wanted to hold her more. "Hey."

She flinched. Through the foggy antique mirror, he saw her recoil, saw her jump away from him.

"Just me," he said, going in for a quick kiss to the curve of her neck, but as his mouth brushed her flesh, her mouth didn't curve into one of those slow drugging smiles as it had the night before. She stiffened, lowering the hair dryer as she looked at him through sober eyes.

"Don't."

The single word came at him through a hazy tunnel of

time and space. He stilled, held himself like that, without moving, while everything else tilted. "Darci—"

She shook her head, flicking off the hair dryer as she dropped it to the counter. "Please don't," she said, and in her eyes he saw the twist of grief and horror, the stabbing vulnerability that registered on some dark, almost primitive level.

"I know this is hard," he said, trying to keep his voice easy, gentle. "But you're not alone, okay? You don't have to go through this—"

Almost violently she scooted away from him, reminding him of the injured, half-starved wallaby he'd come across while riding as a young boy. Jerkily she crammed the lipstick and mascara she'd yet to use back into her toiletry bag.

"Tyler, please," she said, and with the words her voice broke. "I have to go."

"Go where?"

"To Sydney. There's a luncheon."

"For Andrew."

"Yes," she said politely, packing up her shampoo and conditioner and lotion, jamming it all into the little suitcase he'd retrieved from one of the guest suites so she could dress in private.

"And then?" The question came out cold, purposefully quiet.

"We're going to Perth. I've scheduled a few meetings for him."

"Perth." Away. That was what she was really saying. "Damn it, Darci." He reached for her even as instinct and pride told him to turn away, walk away. "Don't do this."

She winced as his hands closed around her upper arms, looked down at where his fingers curled against the fine lines of her suit.

"I know you're scared," he said against the roar inside of him. "But running away isn't the answer."

He saw her chest rise and fall, heard the frustration in her breath. "This was a mistake," she said, and with the words it all came back, all that bloody perfect poise and diction sliding between them like a sheet of ice. "I..." She hesitated. "This isn't what I want."

The sound that broke from his throat was hard, distorted. They'd both been there the night before. They'd both heard her say please. They'd both heard her cry out.

They both knew excruciatingly well what she'd wanted.

But he didn't say that, wasn't about to beg, just let the silence speak for itself.

Darci pressed her lips together, glanced down, away, anywhere but into his eyes.

"Look at me," he said.

Her jaw tightened as she reached for the hair dryer and yanked the cord from the wall.

"Look at me," he said again.

She worked the hair dryer into her bag.

"You can't, can you?" He heard the challenge in his voice, didn't try to soften it.

Slowly, she lifted her eyes. And slowly he saw. Not the warm glow from the night before. Not even the shock and grief from a few minutes before. But...nothing. He saw absolutely nothing.

"There," she said quietly. "Is that what you want?"

And something inside him snapped.

Chapter Fifteen

Instinct told her to back away. Instinct told her to slip around him and grab for her suitcase, make for the door. Instinct told her to get away, far away before—

She blocked the thought, refused to let it form. Breathe, she told herself, but the way Tyler dominated the spacious bathroom made that impossible. He'd yanked on an old pair of jeans and a faded white T-shirt before going downstairs, but not his boots.

It didn't matter. Tyler Preston did not need boots to make a statement, or send everything she'd taught herself about survival into a dizzying meltdown.

The hard look in his eyes froze her. She'd seen it before, twice—six years before when her father had told Tyler who she really was and how old she wasn't, and the morning after the fire when he'd stood beneath the scorched branches of an old gum tree, staring at the remains of his barns.

It was the same way her father had stared at her mother's coffin.

The urge to go to him—God, she'd wanted to go to Tyler. Reach out to him, hold him. Just hold him.

Somehow she'd walked away. Because even then she'd known. It was one thing to skirt the periphery of Tyler Preston's life, helping him restore Lochlain's tarnished image from a safe distance. But the second she slipped under his radar screen...

She never should have gone into the clinic that evening. She never should have checked on Lightning Chaser. Because it was there that he'd found her, there that he'd first touched her.

There that the collision course had been set in motion.

She'd tried. She'd tried to stay away. She'd tried to stay focused. She had a job to do, a future to build. She wasn't the same girl she'd been six years before, when she'd let an out-of-control crush derail her. She had focus now, discipline. She could—

He moved so fast there was no time to twist away. Through the haze of confusion she saw him reach for her, felt his mouth come down on hers. But for a moment she couldn't move, think, couldn't do anything but hang there in that fragile, broken moment, and drown.

He kissed her with an urgency that shredded her defenses. His mouth was soft but demanding, slanting against hers with a possessiveness that had not been there the night before. His whiskers scraped. His tongue demanded. She told herself to pull away, but in doing so only opened to him more.

He tasted of need and passion and black tea—and a desperation she didn't come close to understanding. Against her back his hands roamed, moved, held.

And deep inside, Darci cried.

"No," she whispered with a hard twist, and then she was out of his arms and backing away, grabbing her bag from the counter.

"Last night was a mistake," she said against the hard rush of her heart. She had to stop this, now. While she could. "I didn't come back to Australia to... Things just got out of control."

"Does that make you feel better?" His voice was unbearably quiet. "Does that make it easier for you to walk away?"

She stiffened, but the question stabbed. That's what she'd done the night before. She'd walked away. From everything. From the party she'd spent weeks planning, from the volunteers she'd recruited to help, from the guests she'd invited, the responsibilities. From her boss...

She'd just walked away. To Tyler. She'd gone in search of him, first in the barn, and then, after his harsh words had driven her back into the night, she'd stood there like a love-struck teenage girl as he'd come after her, as he'd taken her by the hand and led her into the house, up the stairs.

She'd abandoned everything, walked away from everything she'd been working so hard to build.

Just as she had walked away from him before.

"I'm sorry," she whispered. "It was foolish to think we could work together without all those loose ends getting in the way."

The green of his eyes glittered. "Loose ends."

She wasn't sure how she moved, not when her heart quietly shattered. It shouldn't have been possible. But she removed herself from all that, removed herself from the hurt and the want, the awareness that once she walked away, she could never walk back, not this time. She reached for her suitcase, turned from him, walked away. Out the door. Down the hall, the stairs. Into the haze of midmorning.

Away from the blinding need, the reckless stranger who'd stared back at her from the bathroom mirror…the same reckless stranger she'd been trying to destroy for the past six years.

The horse moved slowly, uncertain at first. He'd been kept inside for over a week. He'd been in a sterile stall, fed regularly, brushed and groomed, but always monitored. Always restrained. There'd been no sunshine on his back, no warm breeze at his face.

For an athlete in his prime, it was like being locked in a straitjacket and put in a small white cell.

For three years Lightning Chaser had trained. For three years he'd greeted first Marcus, then Daniel, with the sunrise, ready for the saddle on his back. There'd never been any coaxing needed.

Lightning Chaser could have bloody well trained himself.

"Easy now," Tyler said, loosely holding on to the leather lead he'd snapped onto a new halter—almost all tack had been lost in the fire.

Sunshine lured them toward the door. Despite his convalescence, Lightning moved eagerly, giving Tyler a glimpse of the raw strength that had promised to catapult the Thoroughbred to the top of his sport. He and Darci's Pride would have run a hell of a—

Tyler broke the thought, saw no point in playing could-haves or would-haves. In the end, all that mattered was what was.

Lightning Chaser's life would go on. He would live in

comfort at Lochlain. There would be progeny, a legacy. Requests were already coming in. But he would never race again.

"Nice and slow," Tyler encouraged, but the horse wasn't interested in nice or slow. He never had been. He picked up his pace, practically trotting toward the open door.

Tyler didn't try to stop him.

Outside on the familiar ground of packed dirt and dust, Lightning Chaser stopped and lifted his head, looked around. His ears perked. His tail stilled. And in the rich brown of his eyes, awareness burned. He saw it all, the scorched grass and tree limbs, the big vacant swath of earth where his home had once stood. The demolition remained on hold while the authorities hand-searched the debris for a murder weapon.

"No worries," Tyler told his horse, urging him away from the big equipment toward the back of the office building. That was Peggy's domain, where she planted her wildflowers and hand-watered them every morning. There the debris could not be seen. There, green remained.

"Your mates are all fine," Tyler promised as Windbag and Tulloch raced up to greet them. "You'll see them soon enough."

They would rebuild. Insurance money was frozen, but private donations were arriving daily. Just last night—

He broke that thought, too.

"Feels good, doesn't it?" he asked as the colt finished sniffing the dogs and lifted his head toward the warm breeze. Haze crowded out the blue of the sky, but for the first time since the fire, the stench of smoke did not hang in the air.

"There's nothing a little fresh air won't make better," Tyler promised. His father had told him that, a long time ago. Back then Tyler had been a boy, and he'd believed. Now he was a man, and now he knew the truth. But he also understood the lie. He would tell his own child—

That was another thought he broke.

"I have some more cards," he told Lightning Chaser, pulling a few envelopes from the back pocket of his jeans as he scanned the activity in the pasture beyond. Earlier he'd called Daniel, passed on his condolences. He'd told his trainer to take all the time he needed, had offered whatever help he might need to lay Sam to rest. There would be a small private memorial service. After that Sam would be cremated, and Daniel would take his father to Africa, on safari.

Just as he'd always dreamed.

"This one's from a little girl named Gracie over in Pepper Flats," Tyler said, pulling a hand-drawn card from a pale blue envelope. "She drew a picture of you," he added, showing the crude, stick figure drawing to the horse busily chomping on Peggy's grass. Then he read.

"Dear Lightning Chaser. You are a pretty horse. You are fast, too. I saw you on the telly once. Someday my mom says maybe I can see you in person. Please get well and stay strong. Be brave. My dad says that's the most important of all."

Lightning lifted his head and nuzzled the construction paper, as if somehow he understood. Somehow he knew.

Tyler's throat tightened. Lightning deserved better than this. Goddammit, he deserved better.

"Now this one," he continued as he had every day since the fire, except those spent in Sydney, when Darci had—

He didn't let the thought finish, the memory form. "This

one's from a nice lady all the way in America," he detoured. "Says she's part of a group called Friends of Barbaro, and that they've all been praying for you."

Lightning Chaser lowered his head and went for a patch of Peggy's flowers. Tyler watched him, but for a blurred moment saw another horse, the majestic American Kentucky Derby winner who'd lost his valiant fight against laminitis.

"Tyler."

Recognition bumped against surprise. Turning, Tyler found the border collies escorting a familiar figure around the corner of the office. "Russ." They hadn't spoken since the day before the Classic, when Russ had given Darci's Pride the okay to run. They'd left her stall with no way of knowing that only a few hours later, Russ's son-in-law would return with a hypodermic needle. "How's Kelly?"

Lines of worry crisscrossed the veterinarian's face, aging him by years in the space of days. "Her mother's with her."

"The baby?"

Russ frowned. "She had some spotting, but they did a sonogram, saw the heartbeat."

Tyler let out a rough breath. "She's a sweet girl. She doesn't deserve this."

"Neither did you." Russ stepped forward, lifted a single sheet of paper toward Tyler.

"What's this?"

"My resignation. I can only imagine what you must think."

Tyler took the letter and glanced down at the two typed paragraphs, the words *regret* and *immense sorrow* jumping out at him. Then he crumbled the paper into a tight little ball. "I don't want your resignation."

"Owen is my son-in-law. I'm the reason—"

"I'm well aware of who Owen is and what he did, but it's not your fault, mate. You had no idea what was going on."

"I brought him here. He was my responsibility. I—"

"Take care of your family, Russ," Tyler said as a whistle cut across the breeze. He glanced over, saw Dylan Hastings rushing toward one of the investigators huddled in the rubble. "Take care of your daughter." He made himself continue. "Yourself. And when you're ready, your job will be here waiting."

Russ's smile was tired, resigned. Grateful. "You're a good man," he said, but Tyler couldn't stop watching the two men crouched over something on the ground. Very slowly, very carefully, Hastings pulled out a cloth, picked up what looked to be a gun, and dropped it into a plastic bag.

The murder weapon had just been found.

The breeze was warm. Darci closed her eyes and lifted her face toward it, enjoyed the wash of sunshine. She hung that way for a long moment, letting the warmth whisper over her and around her.

But inside, the cold lingered.

Slowly she opened her eyes and eased off the playful Appaloosa she'd borrowed from a former neighbor, a woman she remembered with vibrant brown eyes and a high blond ponytail. Vivian's eyes had been tired when she'd pulled open the door, the blond ponytail replaced by a conservative bob.

Time had a way of doing that. It had been over ten years since she'd seen Vivian Mason, one of her mother's best friends.

After securing the horse's reins on one of the rails of the old fence, Darci moved toward the small gate and let herself inside the small country cemetery.

They were all here, five generations of Mansfield men and women and children, including the baby sister Darci had never been allowed to meet. She'd been stillborn.

Such a confusing term, she remembered thinking. Still-born. She remembered her mother crying, her father standing quietly at the window. Still. Born. At the time Darci hadn't understood why they wouldn't let her see her sister, she hadn't understood how a baby could die. That was what happened to old people.

But then five years later she'd again stood in the old cemetery, this time burying the most vibrant, alive person she'd ever known.

"Mama," she whispered now, going down on her knees. "I brought you some flowers," she said, laying the small bouquet of handpicked daisies across the earth at the base of a statue of the Virgin Mary, just as she'd done before they'd left for England. She'd made up some excuse about going shopping, had come here instead. Beloved Wife and Mother, the tombstone read, and for the second time that day, Darci wept.

"I miss you." In the end, it was as simple as that. "I'm sorry I haven't been here in a while, but Dad and I were in—"

Through her tears, she smiled. "But you already know that, don't you? Just like you know about Outback's girl. You were there, weren't you? At the race. You were the angel—"

"Of course she was."

The voice froze her. She kneeled there in grass that should have been brown from drought, but somehow remained soft and moist and green, and swallowed hard, didn't want him to see. Tears were for babies, he'd always said. Tears were for the weak.

"She's always there," her father said. "With you, with me."

Darci squeezed her eyes shut, let the wind sweep across her face. "Dad." He'd been trying to call her since the Classic, wanted to get together, to talk.

She'd been deliberately avoiding him. "How did you find me?"

She felt him move beside her, felt him go down on his knee. "Vivian called me."

"She shouldn't have—"

"Yes, she should have," her father said. "She said you'd called, that you wanted to borrow a horse to come here. And she was worried." Against her back came his hand, soft, gentle. "So am I."

She sniffed and twisted toward him, ready for battle. But the grief swimming in the blue eyes he'd shared with his only child stopped her. In his dress pants and pale blue button-down, he was dressed for work, but beyond him stood another of Vivian's horses.

The disconnect rocked her.

"I was wrong to take you away from her," he stunned her by saying, and his voice, that strong booming baritone that dominated her childhood memories, broke. "I thought if I took you away, if I helped you forget—"

Almost violently she shook her head. "I didn't *want* to forget."

His smile was distant, bittersweet. "You're so like her," he said, and deep inside, something stirred. She could still see him, see Tyler, tired and dusty with his bush hat pulled low, standing against the fall of evening in the shadow of Lochlain's surviving barn.

You remind me of her....

"Willful," her father said, but there was no frustration or judgment in the word, only the baffled, too-human love of a parent. "Proud."

It shouldn't have been possible to smile, but something warm streamed from Darci's heart, and the corners of her mouth lifted. "Stubborn."

Her father's smile was wide and, again, baffled, and in that one moment, Darci would have sworn fifteen years—and about a thousand tons of grief—fell away. "Stubborn," he agreed, and Darci's smile widened.

"She would be so proud of you," he added with a wistful shake of his head, and slowly his hand came to rest against the tombstone, the word *Mother.* "She loved you so."

Darci swallowed hard.

"I just don't understand," he started, but shook off the whimsy and kneeled with his head bowed for a long moment. Then he looked up at Darci and lifted a hand to her face, slid a few strands of hair behind her ear. "I'm proud of you, too."

The quiet words rocked her.

Floored her.

"I don't say that enough, do I?" he said, and while the breeze kept slipping around them and the birds kept singing, for Darci, the moment froze. She wasn't sure he'd *ever* said those words.

"I didn't know what to do," her father went on and it shouldn't have been possible but her heart broke a little more, but not for her, not this time. This time for him. Her father. He'd always been bigger than life to her, a strong man who faced life without fear or hesitation. She'd never seen him like this...so human. "For the first time in my life, I didn't know what to do. I didn't know how to raise a daughter. I didn't know how to give you..."

Darci bit back a sob. "Give me what?"

"What she did," he answered quietly. "I didn't know how to fill the void."

This time the sob broke through. For so many years she'd kept it inside, the hurt and the want, the fear. They'd never talked like this. They'd never talked at all.

"I just wanted you to love me," she whispered with an honesty that stabbed into her throat. To notice her. Listen. Understand. "I just wanted you to accept me for who I was."

"And I just wanted you to be okay. That's all I ever wanted…for you to be safe and happy—"

"You were scared to let me fly," she whispered.

Her father's shoulders rose and fell. "Scared to let you fall," he corrected, but she didn't bristle the way she had as a child, when his corrections had slapped like criticism. A new empathy swam through her, an awareness she'd never let herself see, the understanding of what it must have been like for him, a young man suddenly a widower, left to raise a precocious little girl. Grief-stricken, confused, alone, he'd built walls around the child who reminded him of her mother, boxed her into a safe little prison where no one could touch her, hurt her.

Take her from him.

"I held on too tight," he said, "and in the end…chased you away."

"No." The word burst out of her. "You didn't chase me away."

"I hurt you," he said quietly. "I hurt you when all I ever wanted was to protect you."

Her throat worked. Her chest tightened.

"You live life boldly," he said as a few yellowy-brown leaves drifted down around them. Autumn was still a few weeks away, but with the drought, some of the trees had begun to drop a few leaves. "In full color, just like she did. I was never like that. After she died…" He looked away, toward the gently moving branches of a nearby gum tree. The sunlight cut through the foliage, almost seemed to dance.

Darci acted without thinking, reached out and placed her hand over his, squeezed. "What?" she asked quietly. "After Mama died, what?"

The lines of his face softened into a faraway smile. "I used to come here," he said. "Like this. I'd come here and sit with her, talk to her, tell her about you, about the horses…"

Because he'd been alone. Because there'd been no one else. He could have remarried. Lots of widowed and divorced men did. They didn't like being alone, so they found someone else. Someone to fill the emptiness, help them forget.

But Weston Parnell had never done that. To Darci's memory, he'd never even dated. His sole focus had been her.

At the time, she'd resented his iron fist.

Now, her heart bled for the sacrifices he'd made, the pain she'd never even noticed.

"I'm sorry," she whispered. "I never knew…"

His hand turned over, bringing the warmth of his palm to hers, and squeezed. "I didn't want you to."

"But—"

"I wanted you to move forward. I wanted you to be okay. I was afraid that if you knew how completely terrified I was…you'd be scared to."

Once again, moisture filled her eyes. "Dad—"

"But of course now I know I was wrong, that in pretending to be strong, all I did was alienate you."

For the third time that day, tears spilled over, but this time, she made no move to stop them.

"Darci," he murmured, and then he was twisting toward her and his arms were opening, and she did something she had no memory of doing since the day he'd come to tell her something bad had happened to her mother. She lunged for him, dived against his chest and closed her eyes as his arms folded around her, and held. Memories came swimming back, of childhood games and laughter, of book-reading marathons and tickle contests and pillow fights, kissing wars.

How had she ever forgotten?

"Don't cry," he whispered as he had all those years ago, when she'd been a little girl and her mother had still been alive, when a bad dream had awakened her from sleep and both her parents had come to comfort her. "She wouldn't want that."

His words came at her through the shadow of memory, and for a broken moment everything flashed, all the nights she'd cried herself to sleep, wishing he would come, that he would pull her into his arms and hold her, promise her everything would be okay, as he had so many times before. But he'd never come to her, not after her mother had died. Not when she'd cried, not when she'd rebelled. He'd grown more distant, more aloof with every year that passed, every stunt she'd pulled. When he'd burst into the hotel room and found her and Tyler in bed—

Something dark and punishing stabbed through her. There'd been yelling, screaming. He'd gone after Tyler, had shoved him to the wall.

Tyler had made no move to stop him, no move to protect himself. He'd just stood there with that horrible betrayed look on his face.

Darci had run after her father, tried to pull him away. *How could you?* she'd screamed. *How could you do this to me?* For the first time since her mother had died she'd found someone who chased away the shadows, who made her feel safe, warm, loved. In Tyler's arms, she'd found—

Darci blanked the thought, wouldn't let it form. She'd

been furious at her father, but it wasn't until now that she understood why.

"All she wanted was for you to be happy," he said, running his big hands along her back. "For you to live life fully, for you to love like she did."

Passionately.

Blindly.

Darci swallowed against the memory, but out of the whispers of time it grew stronger: her mother sitting cross-legged on the floor, her wedding album open in front of her, telling her daughter about each picture, what it was like to fall in love. *Everything else gets fuzzy,* she'd said.

Nothing else matters…

"I have something for you," her father said, pulling back. "Something I should have given you a long time ago."

Darci rocked back on her heels as her father pulled his billfold from his back pocket and flipped it open, withdrew a small photograph from where he kept his credit cards. "Here," he said, extending the tattered black-and-white image.

Darci took it and stared…and saw her mother smiling back at her. It was a family shot, her mother and father young and carefree with the ocean swelling behind them, in their arms an infant swaddled in a thick blanket, and in their eyes…joy and innocence.

Slowly, Darci looked up. *"Dad…"* she whispered, and through another rush of tears, said three words she hadn't spoken aloud since the day her mother died. Not to anyone. "I love you."

The afternoon blurred. By the time Darci and her father made it back to Vivian's stables, the sun had already begun its descent across the sky. They'd stayed longer than she'd intended, had even gone for a long ride after telling her mother goodbye.

Now she raced toward Sydney, and a full schedule for the evening and coming days. With dignitaries from around the world arriving for the summit, the city was alive with festivities—and protests. She and Andrew had a cocktail party to attend, then the opera. Peggy had called about a reception at Warrego Downs honoring Darci's Pride's victory at the Classic, but Darci had politely declined. Tyler was going to be there....

Tyler.

She tried not to think about him, didn't want to see him as he'd been just that morning, when he'd found her in his bathroom. He'd looked tired, worn, but the warmth had still glowed in his eyes. She'd wanted...

God, she'd wanted. She'd wanted to go to him, hold him. She'd wanted to lift her mouth to his and promise him everything would be okay, feel his arms close around her as they had the night before.

Instead she'd taken an ax and chisel and callously chipped away at him some more.

All she ever wanted was for you to be happy...

Darci pushed the gas pedal harder, accelerated, but her father's words lingered. If she didn't catch traffic, she would make it to the hotel in time for a quick shower before she and Andrew met in the lobby. With luck, she would—

Her mobile phone interrupted the litany. She grabbed it from the pile of folders on the passenger seat and answered, slowed when she heard Marnie Whittleson's voice on the other end.

"Oh, honey," Darci greeted, even though she and Daniel's wife had only known each other a few days. "I've been so worried about you."

"Thank you," Marnie said as the Sydney sky scape emerged from the haze in the distance. "I should have called you back sooner…but things have been intense."

"I understand," Darci said. "How's Daniel?"

Marnie sighed. "Quiet. Trying to stay busy…"

Anything to shut out the pain, to keep himself from thinking about what had just happened—just as Darci's father had. "Just be there for him," she advised, even though she was pretty sure she didn't need to. Marnie had a good head on her shoulders, and a big heart in her chest. She'd be there for Daniel, just as Tyler would….

Her throat tightened. No matter what she did, her thoughts kept circling right back to the same place.

"I think an arrest will help," Marnie said. "Bring some kind of closure. It's just been ripping him up trying to figure out who could have done this to his father. Now that they found the gun—"

Cars zipped around Darci. A convertible honked. "Gun?" The word stuck on the way out. Almost blindly she changed into the right lane. "I didn't realize—"

"They found it today," Marnie said. "Sometime around lunch."

The traffic kept whizzing by, but no matter how hard Darci pushed the accelerator, everything slowed.

"Dylan called Daniel as a courtesy a little while ago to let him know."

Somehow Darci swallowed. "Where? Where did they find it?"

For a long moment Marnie said nothing. When finally she answered, her voice was quiet. "At Lochlain."

Chapter Sixteen

Darci's Pride wouldn't stand still. After days of being cooped up and fussed over, she danced in place, twisting her head back toward the roses draped where a saddle should have sat.

"Easy, girl," Tyler tried, but the restless filly flicked her tail in dismissal and kicked at the dirt.

"Apparently she's a bit camera shy today," Tyler joked as the small group of reporters kept trying for the money shot.

Every time the statuesque Thoroughbred teased them with a perfect champion's pose, just as quickly she turned away. With the sunset bathing the skyline in rich hues of amber, they stood in the winner's circle at Warrego Downs, much as they had moments after she'd taken the Classic. Then she'd reveled in the glory. But now the fabled track was quiet, the majestic grandstands deserted. The hoopla had died down. The crowds had dissipated. The other horses had long since gone home.

Later there would be a reception in Lochlain's honor, but now, only reporters and photographers surrounded them. With the summit about to start, the world media had converged, and the filly who'd beaten the boys made for a nice splash of color.

"Can you tell us what's next for Darci's Pride?" asked a well-known reporter from England. "Any chance she'll be running in Europe?"

"Or America," another reporter called. "I understand you've received several offers from a few of the Kentucky farms."

Tyler stilled. They had received offers, that was true. And Lochlain needed the funds. But the horse who bore Darci's name and owned her heart was not his to sell. Even if she was... "Darci's Pride is not for sale."

"What about racing then?" the British reporter asked. "Will Darci's Pride be returning to England?"

Something hard and dark pounded through Tyler. It was possible. She'd been born there, raised there. That was home, not Australia. Darci herself would be returning at the conclusion of Andrew's campaign. "No plans have been made at this point."

"Is that because of the murder investigation?" another reporter wanted to know. "With the discovery of Sam Whittleson's body, is it true that you've been asked not to leave the country?"

A collective hush rippled through the small crowd. Tyler looked at them all, a few he'd known for years, most of them strangers. Only Julia Nash had the grace to look horrified.

"Sam Whittleson was my friend," Tyler said. "His son is my head trainer." Shortly before leaving for Sydney, Tyler had seen Daniel emerge from the barn atop Razor's Edge, the gelding his father had rescued from slaughter several years before. They'd taken off in a flash, man and animal racing as one.

Tyler had made no move to stop them. He'd understood his friend's need to be alone, to cope in the only way he could.

"I know how much you folks love to sink your teeth into juicy gossip and drama, but I'm afraid you're barking up the wrong tree. Despite the colorful picture the media painted after the Queensland, there was no ill will between me and Sam."

Lisa Loring, one of the young up-and-coming reporters in Jacko Bullock's employ, pushed forward. "Then what was he doing at Lochlain in the middle of the night?"

That was the question. What the hell had Sam been doing at Lochlain? And how in God's name had he ended up with a bullet in his back?

"I'm afraid you'll have to save that question for the authorities," Tyler deferred. "I'm here today to talk about horses, not the senseless death of a man I called a friend."

"Any word on the murder weapon?" Lisa persisted. "Is it true—"

"What about Darci?"

Slowly Tyler turned from Lisa to the far side of the group, where Julia Nash emerged from behind the English reporter. She'd orchestrated the mini press conference, had promised Tyler the focus would be exclusively on the horses. Now she stood there with the oddest sheen of expectation in her eyes.

She'd been at the barbie the night before. She'd seen him all but drag Darci into the house. "What about her?" he asked with the stillness he'd greeted Hastings's questions.

Julia smiled. "My understanding is that Ms. Parnell only sold you partial ownership of Darci's Pride, but with her absence this evening, I'm wondering if something has changed."

The image flashed before he could stop it, of Darci sliding over him, long tangled hair teasing his chest. He'd reached for her, pulled her down... "Nothing has changed."

"So you and Ms. Parnell are still partners," Julia persisted.

This isn't what I want.

She'd crammed her toiletries into her bag and turned from him, walked away from him and back into the life she'd so carefully crafted for herself. The proper life, the one she'd spent years training herself for, full of receptions and cocktail parties, her commitment to Andrew.

"Nothing has changed," Tyler said again, but this time the lie burned. The girl he remembered from so long ago, Tara with her daring smile and teasing touch, her hunger for life and thirst for adventure, the gutsy protocol-be-damned attitude, *was* gone. She'd returned from England a shadow of the girl who'd once made him forget. Everything. For a heartbeat there last night—

Tyler crushed the memory.

"How about Lightning Chaser?" an older American reporter asked. "Any truth to the rumors that upon retirement Darci's Pride will be bred to your champion Thoroughbred?"

Something dark twisted through Tyler. "It's a little premature for that."

"But it is possible," Julia pushed.

"Anything is possible."

Three words. That's all they were. But they settled over the small crowd like a soft blanket drifting down on a newborn. The reporters turned, saw her standing there, not poised and polished and dressed to the nines as she'd been at the Classic or the fund-raiser at Lochlain, at the receptions and cocktail parties and every other event where she'd come in contact with the media. But in faded blue jeans that rode low on her hips, in a simple buttery yellow T-shirt with dirt and grass stains on one sleeve, in a loose ponytail pulled high on her head, with stray wisps falling against her face…the face not of the woman but of the girl she'd been, with sun-kissed cheeks and dry lips. The only difference was her eyes. They weren't refined as they'd been since her return to Australia, nor did they spark with daring as they had all those years before. Now they glowed with a wisdom, a maturity that slugged Tyler like a fist to the chest.

Moving forward, she worked her way through the group as the reporters tossed out questions and the photographers busily snapped her every step.

"Darci," Julia said, smiling, not looking the least bit surprised. "I thought you had other plans…"

"Don't we always?" Darci said, but she didn't glance toward the woman with whom she'd struck up a fast friendship. She kept her eyes straight ahead, on Tyler. "We make our plans," she went on, her voice quiet but strong—stronger than the afternoon she'd first confronted Tyler in his office, stronger than the speeches she'd given on behalf of his cousin.

Stronger than when she'd told him goodbye.

"We work our way down our carefully crafted lists, never allowing ourselves to deviate," she said as Darci's Pride whinnied and turned, took off toward her mistress. "Or improvise."

Tyler made no move to stop her—either of them.

"It's tunnel vision," Darci said, emerging from the small gathering. "We force ourselves to stay focused, never allow ourselves to look left or right, to see what's all around us."

Shadows played against her, the wind coming off the river slapping at the hair slipping from her ponytail. "But I'm looking now," she said quietly as Darci's Pride closed

in on her. She lifted a hand, and revealed a peppermint.
"I'm looking."

Tyler didn't move. He stood on the periphery of the
winner's circle and watched. Peggy had rung him up earlier
to tell him Darci wasn't coming. That she had a cocktail
party to attend…with Andrew.

"Don't you want to know?" she asked, and goddammit she was looking at him again, looking at him with a
fierce glow that tightened like a vise around his chest.
"Don't you want to know what I see?"

The quiet came at him like a shout. The reporters were
still there, he knew that. Photographers still greedily
gobbled up the scene. But in that moment there was only
Darci, and the light in her eyes…the light that fed that dark
place inside of him.

"What?" he asked, and his voice was rough again, raw.
Honest. "What do you see?"

Him.

She saw him, Tyler, as she'd never seen him before.
But that was a lie, and there in the shadows of the vacant
grandstands, with the heat of the day melting into a
spectacular red sunset, the truth almost sent her to her
knees.

She saw him as he'd always been, as she'd always seen
him, but had worked feverishly to deny.

To forget.

She saw him as he'd been the first time she'd seen him,
when she'd been just a star-struck teenager and he'd been
barely a man himself, twenty-eight but still with the
gangly body of youth, and a smile that devastated.

She saw him as he'd been the night they met, when
she'd been dressed in the clothes of someone much older.

He'd been in a black button-down and faded jeans, his shirt open at the throat, his hat pulled low on his head.

She saw him as he'd been the first time they'd kissed, made love, when he'd held her hand and whispered into her heart, told her how special she was…how lucky he was.

When her father had stormed in and dragged them apart, shoved Tyler to the wall… She saw him as he'd just stood there and looked at her with the most scorched-earth eyes she'd ever seen.

She saw him as he'd been in news stories here and there, a magazine article, a newspaper write-up…in her dreams.

As he'd been that day less than two weeks before when he'd strode dusty and dirty and late into his office, and she'd turned to see him standing there…and something inside her had violently come back to life.

The night of the fire, risking his life for his horses—and his men.

When he'd come to her at Whittleson Stud, when he'd touched her, kissed her…

The night before when he'd emerged from the shadows on the back of Midnight Magic, when she'd found him with Lightning Chaser—when he'd found her with Julia.

When he'd taken her upstairs and given her the gift she'd been so long denying him.

Honesty.

"You," she said now, as Darci's Pride nudged her pocket for another peppermint. She handed over the treat then took another step. "I see you," she said slowly, quietly, not giving a damn about the reporters or the photographers eagerly recording every word, every step.

But that was another lie. She did care. She wanted them there. After hanging up with Marnie, she'd tried to stay on plan, to go to Sydney and take a shower, go to a party, but the implications of a gun being found at Lochlain had gnawed at her. Tyler was a suspect, had been all along. Maybe the gun could clear him. But maybe…

She'd called Julia and tipped her friend off about the change of plans, had arranged some of the questions for Julia to ask. She wanted the press to see. She wanted everyone to see, to know she was standing by her man.

Tyler deserved that. He also deserved the truth.

"I see a man of deep integrity and unflinching loyalty," she said, and with the words the ache in her heart tried to choke off her breath. He stood there so unnaturally still. The rim of his hat cast his face in shadow, but she saw the stillness in his eyes. The silent wanting.

The hurt she had put there.

"I see a man who doesn't only believe in dreams, but who has the courage to go after them, to make them come true. I see a man who doesn't let others dictate to him." As she had done. "I see a man who believes," she whispered. "Who gives."

He winced, but before he could speak, she stepped closer and pushed on. "I see you," she said again, and now she touched, she lifted her hands to his and took them, held them. "The only man who's ever made me feel safe. *Alive.* The man I lied to…the man I could never forget."

He stiffened. She felt it, saw it.

"No matter how hard I tried," she added over the thunder of her own heart. Maybe one of the reporters shouted a question—she wasn't sure. Didn't care.

Something in Tyler's eyes changed, a light, a glow that flowed through her like a warm breeze.

"I see the man I walked away from," she said, louder now. "Not once but twice."

His jaw tightened, but again she spoke before he could. "I see the man I love."

This time she heard someone gasp, saw the intrusive flash of lightbulbs. But she didn't turn or acknowledge, just kept her eyes on Tyler, her hands on his.

"You weren't part of the plan," she whispered and tried to smile, but he just kept standing there, looking at her as if she'd taken a knife to his gut. "You weren't supposed to happen. But I stand here now, a woman not a girl, and when I look at you, I see the absolute *best* part of my life."

The lines of his face tightened, but he said nothing, just kept standing there, and for the first time little blades of panic ran along her heart. "Aren't you going to say anything?" she said so quietly only he could hear. "Aren't you going to—"

"Nothing's changed," he said just as he had before, to the reporters, and though her heart kept hammering, something deep inside started to bleed.

"Tyler—"

Against the amber sky, his eyes glowed. "Nothing's changed since the night I found out Tara was just a lie—"

"But she wasn't!" Darci shot back, trying not to let her voice, her heart, break. "She isn't. She's me, she's real—"

"Since this morning," he pushed on, "when the only one who found us was you."

"No," she whispered as he pulled his hand from hers. She wanted to grab it and yank it back, but the hurt held her frozen.

"Nothing you said," he went on in that same oddly quiet voice, "nothing you did changed a thing." And then his hand was back, pressing something small and hard and round into her palm.

Slowly she looked down, and slowly everything else just

stopped, her heart, her breath. There was just Tyler—and the simple gold band in her palm.

"I bought that six years ago," he said against the wash of shock. "I had it with me the night your father found us."

Everything flashed. "But…" Words, thoughts, they crashed, jumbled. "I don't understand…"

"I kept it," he said. "Then when you came back—" his eyes met hers "—I slipped it into my pocket to remind me what you could do to me."

Her heart kicked hard. "And what is that?" she asked on the biggest leap of faith of her life.

"Make me forget," he murmured, stepping closer. "Make me want," he added as his mouth brushed hers in a soft little devastating kiss. "Make me love."

"*Tyler…*" Everything tilted. She swallowed against the emotion in her throat, but before words could form, he pulled her into his arms and his mouth found hers—and everything else fell away.

"Because I do," he whispered hoarsely. "Love you."

Epilogue

They rode hard and fast, side by side, taking the land in an intoxicating rush of speed and homecoming. She'd missed this, the exhilaration and the adventure, the dizzying mix of recklessness and safety that zipped through her every time he looked at her. Touched her.

Loved her.

They rode without destination. They rode without time or obligation, without the shadow of arson and murder that too often she saw in his eyes. They'd talked about it. He'd warned her that he could make no promises about a future he might not have.

But in response she'd only smiled and pulled him closer, lifted her mouth to his.

Tyler Preston was an innocent man. She knew that, his family knew that, his staff, and soon the rest of Australia would know that, too.

Soon she would have to return to Sydney. Andrew had headed off for a quick trip to Melbourne, but they would meet up again in a few days, get back to work. Until then…

They'd brought Darci's Pride back to Lochlain. She'd walked out of the trailer and into the warm sunshine, lifted her head and looked around as if somehow she'd known that this was home.

This was where she belonged. Where *they* belonged.

With the midmorning sun beating down on her and the warm wind whipping at her face, Darci urged the sleek chestnut gelding faster. Tyler's horse followed, picking up the pace and racing a few steps ahead. As always the old tattered bush hat concealed Tyler's eyes, but Darci didn't need to see to know, not anymore.

Happiness tightened her throat. For so long she'd thought to never have this again, to never be here.

With him.

Now the perfection of it swelled through her. She'd missed this, the sunburned land of her childhood, sometimes harsh and unforgiving, but equally full of reward and delight. She'd missed strolling along St. Kilda at sunset and diving the Great Barrier Reef, hiking the Outback and taking in the symphony at the Opera House. She'd missed seeing the colorful hot-air balloons float in the skies above the Hunter. She'd missed the eclectic shopping in Sydney, the way the city practically glittered in the antipodean sunshine.

But most of all she'd missed this, the tangle of freedom and happiness and peace that she'd found only in the arms of Tyler Preston.

In the valley below, Lochlain came into view, the rambling stone house situated among gum trees, the office that remained flooded with get-well wishes and treats, the remains of Barns A and B. But Barn C still stood, and nearby, construction on Barn D had resumed, thanks to the assistance of several neighbors. By the next spring, Lochlain would be back, and Darci's Pride would no longer be the only Thoroughbred racing under the blue and gold banner. The new colts and fillies were coming along nicely, especially a gorgeous little Chestnut fella appropriately named Dare Me.

They must have seen the ute at the same moment. The change was subtle; Tyler only pulled up slightly. But the wall of tension hit Darci like a concrete barrier. Their pace slowed as they approached the barn complex, where Dylan Hastings stood near the exercise track. Sunglasses concealed his eyes, but the rigid stance of his body put him in full cop mode.

"Why don't you go on back to the house," Tyler said as he pulled Midnight Magic to a stop and swung his leg toward the ground. "I'll—"

"No." The word was quiet, forceful. Darci dismounted and joined him, reached for his hand. "This involves me, too."

For a long moment he just looked at her from beneath the rim of his hat. Then his fingers curled with hers and together they walked toward the detective.

"Hastings," Tyler greeted, and the other man gave a quick nod in response.

"Tyler," he said as old Windbag raced up and yapped at his heels. "Darci."

She tried for a smile, but knew the corners of her mouth did not lift. She wanted to say something, to ask Hastings why he'd come to Lochlain without warning.

But instinct kept her quiet.

"There's been a development," Hastings said, ignoring the dog. "I wanted you to hear it from me first."

Darci braced herself, but Tyler didn't move. He just stood there with his hand in hers, and waited.

."We have enough evidence to make an arrest in the murder of Sam Whittleson—and the Lochlain fire."

Against her hand she felt Tyler's fingers tighten, but his face remained locked in granite.

"You're a free man," Dylan added, and though he didn't quite smile, a trace of warmth returned to his voice.

This time the corners of Darci's mouth did curve. Relief and joy burst through her as she twisted toward Tyler and beamed up at him. "Thank God," she whispered, and though the lines of his face remained tight, his arms closed around her like steel bands, and for the first time since the morning after the fire, the tension gripping him lessened.

"Who?" he asked, and with the quiet question Darci glanced back toward Dylan. Tyler was free. Tyler was cleared of all suspicion, just as she'd known he would be. But somebody else was about to fall.

Dylan frowned. "I'm not at liberty to disclose that," he said. "But you'll know when it happens. Everyone will."

The words were ominous, but did nothing to overshadow the incredible gift they'd just been given.

The future.

"Tyler," she whispered, pushing up on her toes. "*It's over...*"

His smile was slow, so perfectly languorous that her bones wanted to melt. And finally, at last, his eyes took on the low, irreverent gleam.

"You must not be paying attention, sweetheart," he drawled in that rich Aussie brogue, the one she'd missed for so many years, the one that had whispered through her during the long dark hours of sleep, when her heart remembered everything she'd foolishly tried to forget. "It's just beginning."

* * * * *

Silhouette Desire kicks off 2009 with
MAN OF THE MONTH, *a yearlong program*
featuring incredible heroes by stellar authors.

When navy SEAL Hunter Cabot returns home for
some much-needed R & R, he discovers he's a
married man. There's just one problem: he's never
met his "bride."

Enjoy this sneak peek at Maureen Child's
AN OFFICER AND A MILLIONAIRE
Available January 2009
from Silhouette Desire

One

Hunter Cabot, Navy SEAL, had a healing bullet wound in his side, thirty days' leave and, apparently, a wife he'd never met.

On the drive into his hometown of Springville, California, he stopped for gas at Charlie Evans's service station. That's where the trouble started.

"Hunter! Man, it's good to see you! Margie didn't tell us you were coming home."

"Margie?" Hunter leaned back against the front fender of his black pickup truck and winced as his side gave a small twinge of pain. Silently then, he watched as the man he'd known since high school filled his tank.

Charlie grinned, shook his head and pumped gas. "Guess your wife was lookin' for a little 'alone' time with you, huh?"

"My—" Hunter couldn't even say the word. *Wife?* He didn't have a wife. "Look, Charlie…"

"Don't blame her, of course," his friend said with a wink as he finished up and put the gas cap back on. "You being gone all the time with the SEALs must be hard on the ol' love life."

He'd never had any complaints, Hunter thought, frowning at the man still talking a mile a minute. "What're you—"

"Bet Margie's anxious to see you. She told us all about that R & R trip you two took to Bali." Charlie's dark brown eyebrows lifted and wiggled.

"Charlie…"

"Hey, it's okay, you don't have to say a thing, man."

What the hell could he say? Hunter shook his head, paid for his gas and as he left, told himself Charlie was just losing it. Maybe the guy had been smelling gas fumes too long.

But as it turned out, it wasn't just Charlie. Stopped at a red light on Main Street, Hunter glanced out his window to smile at Mrs. Harker, his second-grade teacher who was now at least a hundred years old. In the middle of the crosswalk, the old lady stopped and shouted, "Hunter Cabot, you've got yourself a wonderful wife. I hope you appreciate her."

Scowling now, he only nodded at the old woman—the only teacher who'd ever scared the crap out of him. What the hell was going on here? Was everyone but him nuts?

His temper beginning to boil, he put up with a few more comments about his "wife" on the drive through town before finally pulling into the wide, circular drive leading to the Cabot mansion. Hunter didn't have a clue what was going on, but he planned to get to the bottom of it. Fast.

He grabbed his duffel bag, stalked into the house and paid no attention to the housekeeper, who ran at him, fluttering both hands. "Mr. Hunter!"

"Sorry, Sophie," he called out over his shoulder as he took the stairs two at a time. "Need a shower, then we'll talk."

He marched down the long, carpeted hallway to the rooms that were always kept ready for him. In his suite, Hunter tossed the duffel down and stopped dead. The shower in his bathroom was running. His *wife?*

Anger and curiosity boiled in his gut, creating a churning mass that had him moving forward without even thinking about it. He opened the bathroom door to a wall of steam and the sound of a woman singing—off-key. Margie, no doubt.

Well, if she was his wife…Hunter walked across the room, yanked the shower door open and stared in at a curvy, naked, temptingly wet woman.

She whirled to face him, slapping her arms across her naked body while she gave a short, terrified scream.

Hunter smiled. "Hi, honey. I'm home."

* * * * *

Be sure to look for
AN OFFICER AND A MILLIONAIRE
by USA TODAY bestselling author Maureen Child
Available January 2009
from Silhouette Desire

Thoroughbred Legacy

The purse is set and the stakes are high…
Romance, scandal and glamour set in the
exhilarating world of horse-racing!

The Legacy continues with book #9

DARCI'S PRIDE
by Jenna Mills

Six years ago, Tyler Preston was on top of the equestrian world…
until one disastrous night nearly ruined him. Now, after years
of hard work, his beloved Lochlain Racing has reemerged. Then
Darci Parnell—the woman who'd cost Tyler everything—walks
into his office and changes his life forever.

*Look for DARCI'S PRIDE
in December 2008 wherever books are sold.*

Thoroughbred Legacy

The purse is set and the stakes are high...
Romance, scandal and glamour in the
exhilarating world of horse racing!

The Legacy continues with book #10

BREAKING FREE
by Loreth Anne White

Aussie cop Dylan Hastings believes in things that are *real.*
Family. Integrity. Justice. And he knows from bitter experience
that the wrong woman can destroy it all. So when art dealer
Megan Stafford walks into his life, he knows trouble's not far
behind.

**Look for *BREAKING FREE*
in December 2008 wherever books are sold.**

REQUEST YOUR FREE BOOKS!
2 FREE NOVELS PLUS 2 FREE GIFTS!

SPECIAL EDITION®
Life, Love and Family!

YES! Please send me 2 FREE Silhouette Special Edition® novels and my 2 FREE gifts (gifts are worth about $10). After receiving them, if I don't wish to receive any more books, I can return the shipping statement marked "cancel." If I don't cancel, I will receive 6 brand-new novels every month and be billed just $4.24 per book in the U.S. or $4.99 per book in Canada, plus 25¢ shipping and handling per book and applicable taxes, if any*. That's a savings of at least 15% off the cover price! I understand that accepting the 2 free books and gifts places me under no obligation to buy anything. I can always return a shipment and cancel at any time. Even if I never buy another book from Silhouette, the two free books and gifts are mine to keep forever.

235 SDN EEYU 335 SDN EEY6

Name	(PLEASE PRINT)	
Address		Apt. #
City	State/Prov.	Zip/Postal Code

Signature (if under 18, a parent or guardian must sign)

Mail to the Silhouette Reader Service:
IN U.S.A.: P.O. Box 1867, Buffalo, NY 14240-1867
IN CANADA: P.O. Box 609, Fort Erie, Ontario L2A 5X3

Not valid to current subscribers of Silhouette Special Edition books.

Want to try two free books from another line?
Call 1-800-873-8635 or visit www.morefreebooks.com.

* Terms and prices subject to change without notice. N.Y. residents add applicable sales tax. Canadian residents will be charged applicable provincial taxes and GST. Offer not valid in Quebec. This offer is limited to one order per household. All orders subject to approval. Credit or debit balances in a customer's account(s) may be offset by any other outstanding balance owed by or to the customer. Please allow 4 to 6 weeks for delivery. Offer available while quantities last.

Your Privacy: Silhouette is committed to protecting your privacy. Our Privacy Policy is available online at www.eHarlequin.com or upon request from the Reader Service. From time to time we make our lists of customers available to reputable third parties who may have a product or service of interest to you. If you would prefer we not share your name and address, please check here. ☐

SSE08R

Thoroughbred Legacy

The purse is set and the stakes are high…
Romance, scandal and glamour in the
exhilarating world of horse racing!

The Legacy comes to an end with book #12

THE SECRET HEIRESS
by *Bethany Campbell*

When Marie Lafayette's mother's dying confession reveals an
astonishing truth, Marie walks away from her career to find
answers at Fairchild Acres…where she might be the heiress to
the Fairchild family fortune! She falls for racing-world royalty,
Andrew Preston—he's wealthy, handsome…and completely wrong
for her. Men like Andrew don't fall for women like her….

Look for THE SECRET HEIRESS
in December 2008 wherever books are sold.

Thoroughbred Legacy
The stakes are high.

Scandal has hit the Australian branch
of the Preston family. Find out what it will take
to return this horse-racing dynasty to the winner's circle!

Available December 2008

#9 *Darci's Pride* by Jenna Mills
Six years ago, Tyler Preston's passion nearly cost him everything.
Now he's rebuilt his stables *and* his reputation, only to find the
woman he once loved walking back into his life.

#10 *Breaking Free* by Loreth Anne White
Aussie cop Dylan Hastings believes in things that are *real*.
Family. Integrity. Justice. In his experience, the wrong woman
can destroy it all. So when Megan Stafford comes to town,
he knows trouble's not far behind.

#11 *An Indecent Proposal* by Margot Early
Widowed, penniless and desperate,
Bronwyn Davies came to Fairchild Acres looking for work—and
to confront her son's real father. This time she'll show her lover
exactly what she's made of…and what he's been missing!

#12 *The Secret Heiress* by Bethany Campbell
After her mother's dying confession,
Marie walks away from her life and her career…only to
find herself next door to racing-world royalty. Wealthy
Andrew Preston may make Marie feel like Cinderella, but
she knows men like Andrew don't fall for women like her.…

Dear Reader,

On May 6, 2006, I watched a young Thoroughbred race into history. Two weeks later, I sat horrified as that same horse shattered his leg.

I don't know what it was about that valiant horse, but his fight to survive touched me deeply. For months I checked his progress, cheering at every improvement—and feeling my heart break when ultimately he lost his battle.

The horse was Barbaro, and his story was the stuff true page-turners are made of.

During that time, I was contacted about THOROUGHBRED LEGACY, and I immediately knew fate had handed me the opportunity to pay tribute to Barbaro, and the incredible people who loved him.

So sit back and let me take you to Australia, where a man named Tyler will do anything to protect a legacy forged in sweat and tears and dreams. Faced with tragedy, he discovers that second chances sometimes come from the most unexpected places....

Jenna Mills